EARLY AWAKENING

Katrina May

To my family and friends, thank you for believing in me when I didn't quite believe in myself. You gave me courage and for that I will be forever grateful.

Heart You!

CONTENTS

AURAS

"EMANATION AROUND THE BODY OF A LIVING BEING."

RED-ROOT OR BASE CHAKRA - Red symbolizes an enthusiasm for life. A being with red in their aura is emotionally and physically grounded. Red is associated with passion and sexual desires. These beings dislike denying themselves the simple pleasures in life. They are strong, courageous, and self-confident.

+ **DULL RED**-Someone who harbors a great deal of anger.

ORANGE-SACRAL CHAKRA - Orange auras signify happiness with friends, family, and environment. Someone who has a lot of orange in their aura is quick to make and keep friends. They are adventurous, thoughtful, and considerate.

+ **DULL ORANGE**–Someone who is restless and lacks commitment.

YELLOW–SOLAR PLEXUS CHAKRA – Yellow shows inner happiness and balance within one's self. It can indicate a playful spirit, high self-esteem, high intellect, and a hunger for greatness. They are creative, relaxed, and friendly.

+ **LEMON YELLOW**–Accompanies someone with a fear of loss (family, career, love).

GREEN–HEART CHAKRA – Green is the color of self-love. Love and kindness towards animals, plants, friends, family and life accompany a green aura.

+ **LIGHT GREEN**–Healers have this color aura.
  + **DULL FOREST GREEN**–This shade of green shows someone who is jealous and resentful. They believe they are never wrong.

BLUE–THROAT CHAKRA – This is the color of communication. A blue aura reveals someone who enjoys meditation, a calm state, and who stands to protect the ones they care about. These beings are a support system for friends and family. Intuitive and a freethinker.

+ **ROYAL BLUE**–Adventurous or deeply spiritual.

INDIGO–THIRD EYE CHAKRA – Beings with an indigo aura can see into the energies of others. This is someone who is in tune with their inner self. They have the ability to see past deceit and find the truth. They are curious, connected, and gentle.

PURPLE–CROWN CHAKRA – These beings can view the larger picture and love to guide others to their highest potential. They are wise, intellectual, artistic and independent.

PINK – Pink is on the same frequency as green. However, a pink aura shows someone who is happy and in harmony with those around them. They are caring towards others and themselves.

SILVER – This is the color of abundance and wealth.

BROWN – Take caution when brown is present. It signifies greediness and a being who is self-absorbed.

BLACK – Black auras tend to indicate a large amount of anger and grief built up inside. These beings are unable to forgive and holding on to pain. It may also symbolize ill health.

GRAY – Gray exposes low self-esteem, low energy levels, and depression. It also may show doubt.

WHITE – White is the color of protection. It means the being is concerned with spiritual matters and not so much with material things. It may also symbolize health or purity.

PLAYLIST

BY CHAPTER

CHAPTER ONE

THE STORM

~ALAYAH~

Clouds block out the light from the moon just as a bright flash sends shadows dancing across the soft gray paint of my bedroom walls. I gasp and inch the blankets closer to my chin. A loud boom causes the plaster on the walls to shake and the tap, tap, tapping against the window beside me sends a shiver through my body. I focus my attention, eyes darting to the window, my ears picking up on the cry of wolves beyond the walls that surround me.

Another flicker, another moving shadow. Sweat beads on my brow and I wiggle further under the covers. Moisture wells in my eyes, threatening to overflow as memories of my past flood my thoughts.

Another boom and my heart stops for a moment. As liquid leaks through my fingertips, I realize I have them pressed tight to my eyelids, holding back a dam that will inevitably break. A valiant effort for sure, but only moments pass before they coat my cheeks in wetness. A whimper escapes my lips and I relive my childhood.

"Daddy, I'm sorry. Please stop!" A small voice chokes out between sobs right before the last of his blows causes a scream to escape. The roughness of the dingy blue carpet scrapes against my side. The smell of smoke tickles my nose from the burnt cookies and the smoke alarm blares in the distance.

My eyelids spring open, the smoke alarm still blaring and the smell of smoke no longer a memory. My tongue slides across my top lip and I can taste the char in the air. Springing out of bed on shaky legs, I cross the room. Five steps to the door, thirteen down the hallway, twenty-six steps to the first floor. I have it all counted out, in case he comes back for me and I have to run.

I press my hand to the door, feeling for heat, my fingers shaking. My head tilts and I listen before turning the knob. The storm is raging outside. Aside from the blaring smoke alarm, only the creaking of my old farmhouse as it shifts with the wind catches my attention.

"Breathe, Alayah," I coax myself, swinging the door wide. Peering down the empty hall, I let out the breath I'd been holding. Smoke is filtering up the stairs in puffs swirling over the old floral wallpaper. One foot in front of the other, I tiptoe towards the danger, floorboards creaking with each step.

My nightgown sticks to my skin, drenched with sweat even as my teeth chatter. Oh, how I love the cold. It numbs the pain inside of me, the terror that he left deep down in my bones.

Lightning flashes as I reach for the light switch at the top of the stairs. CLICK! The sound echoes down the hallway, bouncing back. Darkness surrounds me, and I flick the switch once more. Nothing.

My ears strain again to listen as I tip my head to the side. Every little noise - an intruder trying to get in, every movement in the shadows - someone waiting to pounce. I force myself to move, crying out as my pinky toe catches on a loose floorboard at the bottom of the stairs.

I must be quite the sight, hopping around on one foot. Yep, I wish I would have called someone to fix that the last time I stubbed my toe. I continue to look for the source of the smoke, hobbling in the dark. Another memory hits me like a sledgehammer.

"What is wrong with those children? They are demon spawn and you; you are to blame for their destructive behavior." His finger inches from my mother's face as he wails, his loud voice causing my gut to twist. Jake and I sit huddled together on the steps, peering through the spindles. My brother's arm is wrapped tightly around my shoulders, filling me with warmth as my small frame shakes uncontrollably.

"John, they are just silly children. They didn't realize they could start a fire with a magnifying glass." She takes a step

back, putting more distance between them. "Heck, I didn't realize you could do that."

I can still hear the slap of his hand against my mother's cheek. I can see the handprint he left on her beautiful alabaster skin, and I can feel the tension like a vice gripping my throat. My gut churns. I remember how the light seemed to fade a little from her eyes that night. I gasp in a few shallow breaths to ease the tightening in my chest over the memory.

Running my fingers along the wall, I find my way to the mechanical room at the back of the house and startle at the amount of smoke billowing from under the door. Internally, I pat myself on the back for grabbing a fire extinguisher as I passed the laundry room.

With white knuckles gripping the fire extinguisher, I press my other hand to the door slowly, pulling it back with a yelp. The door creaks as it swings inward, the view beyond catching me by surprise. An orange glow dances through the room, and flames reach towards me from the fuse box on the wall. Like fingers trying to grab me, they reach closer and closer until I am forced to take a step back. I cough hard and pull my nightgown over my nose.

Holding the fire extinguisher in front of me, I pull the pin, but it won't budge. No click, no whoosh, nothing. Turning my head to the side, I inhale through the fabric and let it fall from my face. I know I need to get this fire out before it does any more damage.

Gripping the extinguisher in my right hand, I pull the pin hard with my left. To my surprise, only seconds pass before white foam is covering the room and it has snuffed the flames.

Exhaustion hits me full force and I have to grab the door frame to keep from losing my balance. Wobbling, my knees try to buckle, and a loud clunk reverberates through the house as the metal extinguisher meets with the old hardwood floor. My breathing comes in brief gasps and I try to calm my nerves, counting backwards from ten. I can feel the nausea creeping up my throat, but it recedes as I get to one.

I take inventory of the damage. The door for the fuse box is stuck in the wall across the room and the box itself, mangled. My guess, lightning struck the transformer in my yard. This mess is going to take hours to clean. My nose wrinkles at the thought. Or maybe it's the awful smell of burnt plastic? Yuck!

Using the wall as a crutch, I limp towards the kitchen and drop into my favorite chair, worn with years of use. I take a moment to collect myself as a shiver runs through my body.

"A nice cup of tea should calm my nerves." I feel the strain of my muscles as I push myself up, using the table for leverage. My hands guide me through the dark, running along the countertop until I reach the opening to the pantry. I drop to my knees, reach under the bottom shelf and feel around for the small gas generator I keep there.

It isn't big, but it's heavy, and it takes a few tries for me to wiggle it out from under the shelf. My arms ache by the time I drag it into the kitchen. The red button sticks as I push it, but with a bit of force the machine rumbles to life. I plug in my electric teapot to boil the water.

"Now what?" I ask, looking around the dark room.

Does talking to myself make me crazy? Since moving into this old farmhouse, I have done it more and more.

"With no one else to talk to, what is a girl supposed to do?" I say. It only takes a few minutes before I am steeping the tea bag into hot water and I retreat to my favorite chair again.

Peace surrounds me as I sip on the steaming chamomile tea that is warming my palms. The smell reminds me of cozy nights by the fire with my mom and brother. Nights when John was absent, and it was just the three of us cuddled up with blankets and books.

I shake the memories away and creep back to my room, senses still on alert. But not as focused as they were when I ventured downstairs to tackle the fury of the fire. A sigh escapes me as I think about the mess again.

Blankets rustle when I crawl into bed, pulling my old, tattered teddy bear to my chest. The fur, bare in so many places, lightly scratches my face. I don't mind the feeling; it comforts me in a way only a child could understand. I tighten each muscle in my body and slowly release the tension as I try to relax.

My grip tightens on the teddy bear, and a memory tickles my mind. A memory of my mother spinning a tale of a lost princess. In the story, they left the princess in the care of another family in a world different from their own to keep her safe from her enemies. Funny enough, her only possession was a teddy bear given to her by her father. I wonder if the fairytale my mom told might have had a ring of truth to it.

My mother never spoke of my real father. She resented the very thought of him. The few times I brought him up, her brows would pinch together and that rosy color would work its way into her cheeks. I cringe. You do not want to be on the receiving end of a redhead's temper. I couldn't see steam rising from her ears, but the feeling was the same either way. She did not want to talk about my father.

I often wonder if it was because she loved him, and he left her. My chest tightens with pain at the thought. Resentment has a way of growing like a pesky weed if it's left to its own devices.

Thoughts of my mother and biological father bring back painful memories. My cheeks dampen with loss. *Why couldn't he have stuck around? Why couldn't she?*

I have always hated nights like these - nights where the storms roll in, covering up the shrill screams of a pain I can never forget. The pain of loss and abuse and knowing that somewhere out there I have a father, a real father who just hadn't wanted me. The pain of knowing that no one can hear my cries for help.

CHAPTER TWO

DARKNESS

~JAKE~

Beep. Beep. Beep... Beep. Beep. Beep.

The big green numbers shining from the nightstand scream WAKE UP. *Four o'clock already. This new job is really wearing me down.*

I grip my head with both hands, putting pressure on my temples. The throbbing reduces to a constant ache. Another late night working with clients and another early morning back in the office.

After graduating from college with a degree in Business Communications, I found myself bartending. I was barely making ends meet working nights at an Applebee's.

One Saturday evening, as I was flipping bottles and pouring drinks, Bob Crawford slid onto a stool at the end of the bar. Bob owns a major marketing firm close to where I live. I didn't know it then, but he was scouting for new talent that evening.

A few weeks later, I get a phone call from the man himself, offering me a position. I couldn't resist the opportunity. Turns out he saw potential in me. Now I'm working a "real job" and putting in over 50 hours a week.

The crucial difference between the two career paths isn't the hours, though, it's the people I'm entertaining. I'm schmoozing business men instead of college students. And I'm getting paid better.

A sigh breaks the silence as I slip out from under my cool silk sheets. While sitting on the edge of the bed with my face in my hands, I realize the stress of adulting hasn't changed, only where the stress is coming from.

I run my hands through my hair and down the back of my neck trying to release some of the tension. A click from the kitchen catches my attention and, in minutes, I can smell the nutty aroma of my favorite coffee.

"Thank God for small miracles and technology!" The edge of my mouth tilts up in the corner as I push myself off the bed. The tile floor feels cold under my feet as I head towards the kitchen.

Dishes cover the counter. I shudder thinking about how I have let this place go over the last few days. My skin prickles with the anxiety of it all. My chest tightens and I let my eyes slide to the clock on the wall. I have a few minutes to tidy up before I need to jump in the shower.

A smile creeps across my face. *How did I ever survive living in a frat house with a bunch of slobs?*

Cleaning soothes me, and it isn't long before I am humming. I save my Yeti cup for last, taking special care to clean the lid before filling it with steaming black coffee. As I bring the cup to my lips, I can smell the delicious aroma and feel the warmth against my cheeks.

"Shit!" I say as molten hot liquid spews from my mouth into the sink. My tongue is hanging out and I'm panting. The pain makes me wince. I reach for the faucet, sticking my entire face under the cold water and watch as the brown coffee mixes with the clear water swirling down the drain.

Surely, Mikal would be rolling on the floor right now. And Cade would be so appalled at my display that he would walk straight out of the front door, shutting it carefully behind him. I can't fathom how those two are friends, but I suppose money and family ties connect them.

I can just see the contempt on Cade's face, the way his nose scrunches up and the flippant wave of his hand any time someone does something he deems inappropriate.

Mikal handles it in stride, though, with a cocky grin and a shrug. His go with the flow attitude and sense of humor makes him someone you want to be around. An addiction that draws you in and doesn't let you go.

Because of these two, when I have time off, I have a free pass to get into one of the most notorious and upscale clubs in the city, Persuasion. We'll head there tonight after I close a deal with a client I've been working on for the last few weeks.

A soft glow from the window reminds me, if I don't get moving, I am going to be late for work. Swiftly, I head to the bathroom. A few inches past the threshold, my foot slips out from under me, my arms windmill, and time seems to slow as I fall unable to catch myself. I hit the floor with a thud.

Wheezing, I'm laying on my back half in and half out of the bathroom, my hands now resting on my chest to catch my breath. My eyes roll to the back of my head and I groan at the way my day is starting.

"Seriously," an angry yell passes my lips as I drop my head back down on the tile floor. Not my most graceful move, that's for sure. The throbbing returns and I can't help but wonder if I should just call in sick today.

A few deep breaths, "This will not be a good day." The words spark a memory. My eyes lose focus, and I can remember the way my mother's voice sounded so soft when she told me how each day is still good until at least three things go wrong.

Well, two down, one to go! I chuckle to myself.

After some interesting maneuvering, I pull myself to my feet and flip on the bathroom light. My hand slides over the faux granite countertop and the sparkle of the stone draws my eyes. It looks nice, but it's cheap. That works for now, but someday I'll have the real deal.

On the shower curtain, a wolf howls at the moon and stars dance in the night sky. A frown returns to my face as I notice the pile of clothes sitting on the floor next to the linen closet. My usually spotless apartment tinged with mess.

The knob in the shower sticks as I turn it and a hiss breaks the silence before water sputters out of the shower head. I make a mental note to check with my landlord. There must be some air in the lines.

Moist steam fills the bathroom like a warm cocoon wrapping around me and I sigh in relief, taking a few moments to enjoy the tranquility. Running my hands through my hair, I can feel the tickle of the bubbles as they flow down my body and into the drain.

The door to the bedroom squeaks when I open it and a rush of cold air caresses my skin, sending tingles and goosebumps across my arms. The hairs on the back of my neck stand up and I quickly pull on the clothes laid out on my bed, turning back to the mirror.

My red hair stands out against my smooth, light skin. The natural highlights give it a glow that women constantly comment on. For a redhead, I'm actually not a bad-looking dude.

The cool granite feels nice against my warm skin as I peer into the mirror, thoughts still on my hair and the person I inherited it from, my mother. My hair, my full lips and my high cheekbones all come from my mother. She was a beautiful woman, whose beauty carried through into my smooth features.

My stomach tightens and moisture beads in my eyes. Even after all these years, it still hurts to think about her. She had her demons, but she tried so hard for my sister and me. It's been almost eight years since she passed away. At thirteen, I didn't understand what had happened. Just that one moment, my mother was tucking me in my bed and the next I was being told that she was no longer with us. The doctor said she died of a heart attack, but I know the true reason she died. Fear and heartache.

With a quick glance at my phone, I realize time is running out. No time to dwell on memories from the past. I need to focus on the future right now.

I bolt through the living area to the kitchen. It only takes a few quick steps to move between rooms. My apartment is not much bigger than a trailer house, really. It's not the castle I envisioned living in as a child. For right now, it works. The low cost makes it possible to put money in the bank for the future. I want a family and I want to take care of them in a way that was never possible for me.

I grab a banana and loop my keys around my finger, then search for the right key to my Intrepid. The car runs great, which is a plus, and I am trying to save money and make excellent investments. Responsible and all that, right?

I shimmy into the driver's seat, feeling my phone vibrate in the pocket of my suit coat. There is only one person who would call me this early in the morning and my heart sinks. Before I can say hello, I can hear the trembling in my sister's voice. "There was another storm last night. I couldn't sleep."

"Oh, Ali." The sorrow is clear in my voice, but I try to keep it under wraps. It pains me that our childhood memories still plague my sister.

"A farmhouse in the middle of nowhere is not the place for a single young woman." I have always wondered what the appeal is to her. Everything scares my poor little sister, and honestly, who can blame her after such a tormented past?

"I know, Jake, but where do I have to go? And honestly, I really do like this place with all its character. I mean, the arched doorways and the extra-large baseboards are beautiful. Not to mention the built-ins. But it's lonely and the noises this old house makes get under my skin. They cause my mind to play tricks on me," Alayah sighs, pauses for a second and then says, "Is that 'Sound of Silence' by Disturbed in the background?"

"It is," I smile to myself.

That smile turns to a frown when Alayah says in a small voice, barely audible, "Well, I guess it's fitting, considering my current circumstances."

"Oh Ali, you know you're always welcome to stay with me in Minneapolis," I say, although my voice is unsure.

"Jake, you live in a one-bedroom apartment above a bakery. There's no room for your bratty little sister." I can picture the faint smile she wears on her face and my lips twitch up just a little.

I know my sister. She's made of pure strength and determination. Even if she can't see it herself. She is such a gentle soul and, underneath the kicked dog mentality, hides the courage and fighting spirit of a wild horse.

I've seen her put on a brave face but, until she confronts her issues, her true character will remain hidden. She's spent so much time trying to project to others what she already has buried deep down inside.

"Ali, why don't you come stay with me over the weekend? It's Friday and you don't have to work again until Tuesday," I say, finally pulling into the parking lot at the office. I need to move this conversation along, so I don't lose my job.

"Well..." I can hear the hesitation, her stubbornness shining through.

"I won't take no for an answer. Pack up some things, get in your car and drive. I will be home around five o'clock tonight and I want you waiting on my doorstep when I pull up. To avoid being late to work, I really must go." I try to put a little determination in my voice.

Alayah's voice turns to fear, "You know, Dad gets out next week." Her not giving me an answer doesn't fall on deaf ears.

"Ali, that man is not our dad. He is the jackass our mom found to take care of her when our real father disappeared and she was pregnant with you." Irritation is clear in my voice and my knuckles turn white from the pressure of gripping the steering wheel. The hate I feel for that man burns with intensity inside of me and I bite my lip.

"That doesn't change the fact that he is getting out of jail in a few days, and I'm terrified that he will come looking for me. I'm the one that got him thrown in there," Alayah says with a little exasperation of her own.

"If I had my way, he'd be in prison. But you have a restraining order. If he comes after you, that's where he'll end up. So, don't worry so much, your older brother has your back and you know it!" A small chuckle escapes my lips and the moment it is out, I know I've made a dire mistake.

Sobbing, my sister says, "You know what he did to me, the horrible things he put me through. Not just that, but a few years after mom died, you ran off and left me to withstand all the abuse with nowhere to turn." The venom dripping from the last comment makes me cringe. And with that, I hear the click and silence as the line goes dead.

The words sting. She'll regret letting them escape because that is who she is, a pleaser and an empath. But she shouldn't have to regret them. The words are true, horrifyingly true.

My shoulders sag. I know deep down in my soul that I failed her. I wasn't there for her when she needed me the most. Our mother was gone and I couldn't stand to watch my sister's demise by the hand of that jackal. The thought sits heavily on my heart.

I was young. It was out of sight, out of mind, but I know I will spend the rest of my life trying to make it up to her. I also know that it will never be enough.

The steering wheel feels cold against my forehead, keeping me grounded as I will my muscles to stop shaking. Guilt and the shame are demons I carry with me, demons that haunt me in my sleep and make me rethink almost every decision I make to this day.

CHAPTER THREE

BEST FRIENDS

~ALAYAH~

My stomach is tangled in knots, and I can feel the wobble in my hands. I glance around my bedroom. "Lean on Me" plays softly in the background and dim light shines through the window as the sun breaks the horizon. My lips pinch together, thinking about the conversation I just had with my brother. I hurt him; my words were like a knife slicing through his chest. But I can't deal with that right now. I realize it is not Jake's fault. He had recently turned sixteen when he left and I hate making him out to be the bad guy.

My arms tighten across my stomach, trying to stop the shaking that I know all too well can turn into a panic attack. I take a couple of deep breaths. The scent of fresh rain and wet grass wafts through the now open window. My weakness grates on me. Because I hate living in fear, but most of all, I hate the man who made this nightmare a reality for me.

After pacing around my bedroom for over an hour, I pick up my phone, running my fingers over the smooth screen and text Jake an apology.

Sorry, shouldn't have blown up.

On the way. Bringing a surprise.

~A

Not even ten seconds pass and my phone dings with a response. My stomach drops, afraid to look at his reply.

Deserved it. Tara?

Another ding.

She is so amazing!

Relief hits me, and I bite my lip. Since I'm unsure if I can keep my promise, I leave Jake in suspense and call someone else I trust to answer early in the morning.

"Hello?" Tara answers with a yawn.

"Hey there. Were you sleeping?" Of course, I know the answer. A blush creeps up my neck. But what do you say when you call someone at this early hour?

"I was, but that's okay. Is something wrong?" Another yawn which causes me to yawn, too. Contagious little things. I pause for a beat too long and Tara continues before I can force any words from my lips.

"If this is an emergency, you get me in my pj's." The mood hovering over me lightens, and I giggle. My eyes light up as I picture Tara coming to rescue me, donning her bright pink Piglet pajamas and a baseball bat. Her infatuation with Piglet is a long running joke between the two of us.

One little pair of Piglet slippers from a crush in third grade was all it took. Her crush, like most, didn't stick around long. But Piglet, much to my dismay, was not a fleeting obsession. I'm more of a *Lady and the Tramp* kind of girl. To each their own, I guess.

"Thanks for the offer, but I think a little chat should calm my nerves. Actually, it's already working... I had another awful night," I say, trying not to let nervousness tinge my voice.

Tara sighs, "I figured you would with the storm and all. You realize, no one in their right mind or not would travel six miles off the beaten path to come invade that old house you live in." Her scolding tone is comforting to me. She's like the mom I no longer have. "They would most likely be too terrified to take your creepy ass driveway, let alone enter a house so old, real live witches could have built it back in the 1690s."

I hold back a smile, trying to keep a straight face and say in mock distaste, "First, you know I don't believe in witches. I don't believe in fairytales or supernatural beings. Second, you could be a little nicer to your best friend." I love the ease of our conversations and how we joke around without offending each other. The bond we share is stronger than blood.

"Anyway, do you want to go to the cities with me later today? Jake invited me to stay with him for a few nights and I want to go, considering 'you know who' gets out next week." My voice shakes. "But driving alone for three hours doesn't sound like fun. So, what do ya say, wanna go on a little excursion?"

Tara responds with yet another yawn, "Well, if you let me get back to sleep so I can function at work, I'll get my stuff together. Meet me in front of my aunt's apartment around noon."

Twitching with excitement, I say, "I'll be ready and waiting."

"Ugh...do you have to sound so excited this early in the morning?" I can just picture her smashing a pillow over her face.

"You know me, terrified one minute and jumping for joy the next. I'll see you later." I hang up the phone, tossing it onto the nightstand with a loud thunk and crawl back under the covers, still a little spooked. Lucky for me, my best friend can make anyone calm even under the worst circumstances. She just has a soothing aura about her.

The idea of sleeping seems far-fetched. The excitement to get away and recharge, an itch under my skin. But after a sleepless night and fighting a fire, the exhaustion is closing in on my consciousness. *I suppose I can close my eyes for a little while* I think to myself, excitement still vibrating through my body... or is it fear?

Hours later, I wake. I have my head smashed against the headboard and my neck is bent at a ninety-degree angle. I blink a few times. My brain is groggy and the pain of a splitting headache has me pinching my eyelids together again.

Slowly, I sit up, stretching out my muscles. I reach my arm over my head and pull it gently to the side. The muscles pull tight for a few seconds and the pain is soothing. I revel in it. Then I move to do the other side. After turning my head, I spot my phone and my eyes widen. "You have got to be kidding me. After eleven thirty already!"

The covers fly off me and I shoot to my bathroom, shedding clothes like they're on fire. My emotions are going wild; anxiety, excitement, joy, but the strongest one is fear. I fear my stepfather getting out of jail; I fear not having anywhere to feel safe, but most of all, I fear I may leave my old farmhouse in the woods and never want to come back.

My nose crinkles as I look at the shower, waiting for the water to warm up. I slip my fingers under the rain head and jump at the icy cold sliding over my hand. Slapping myself in the forehead, I remember I don't have electricity in the house and the mess in the mechanical room still needs to be dealt with. It's going to wait. I'll call someone once I get on the road.

Showers are the bane of my existence, for the mere fact there is so much time to think. Today, though, I don't have time to stand under the water. I need to move my ass. And even if I did, I wouldn't be able to stand the cold for long.

Shivers are wracking my body after less than a minute making it hard to grab the bottles of soap. The shampoo bottle slips through my fingers and I decide not to wash my hair. I grab the body wash instead, leaving the shampoo to sit at the bottom of the tub.

Four and a half minutes and I'm dripping water on the carpet of my closet. I run my fingers along the clothes hanging in front of me. Fabrics of all different textures brush my skin. *What should I wear today?*

I opt for a cute pair of skinny jeans and a beaded tank that flows perfectly over my petite figure. The only attribute I received from my mother.

In the mirror on the far wall, a beautiful woman stares back at me, not the little girl I am inside. No, this woman looks confident and strong. Her wavy and unruly white-blonde hair wrapping around her face and down her shoulders. The piercing ice-blue eyes alight with adventure and determination.

A smile pulls at my lips, and I concentrate on fueling that confidence. Pushing my shoulders back, I raise my chin and straighten my spine. I'm empowered and a giddy satisfaction runs through me. Now if I can just hold onto it for more than a few moments.

As a child, I never felt like I fit in at home.

"What is this, Alayah?" John says as he waves my English paper frantically through the air.

All I can do is stare at him with tears flowing down my face.

"How could you get a 'C' in English?" His anger prominent as his face turns red. The veins in his neck are more defined than usual. "Answer me!"

I tuck my hands behind my back to hide the shaking, my eyes on my feet. "It's just one paper. I'm getting an 'A' in the class."

"Worthless," he mutters and rips the paper in half. The sound of his footfalls reverberating through my chest as he storms out of the room.

The constant insults and painful lessons tore away any confidence or self-respect I might have had. I wasn't good enough for my stepfather, my mother was a shell of herself, and my brother was too young to understand the burning hate I harbored. The self-loathing grew while I was in between those walls, but at school, it was different.

At school I had Tara and no matter what the other kids did or said, she was there for me. She didn't just tell me how amazing she thought I was; she showed me. Tara stood by my side through everything and for that, she will always be my best friend, my sister by choice, not blood.

The woman staring back at me in the mirror is exactly who I want to be. The problem is, I don't know how to let go of the pain. I cringe, wrapping my arms around my stomach and watch as the confident reflection dissipates, leaving in its wake a helpless child.

No, I can't let the woman in me disappear. I won't. My hands move to my hips, back straight, standing tall again. The carpet is damp beneath my feet. It reminds me to stay present as I wiggle my toes. The beige color is so different from the blue carpet of my childhood bedroom. The soft fluffy fibers beneath my toes, a far cry from the ragged, thin layer I grew up with. I have come so far. Today I am going to let go of an ounce of that scared child and grab the glimmer of confidence I saw in the reflection.

Head held high, even if I'm faking it a little, I grab the concealer off my dresser and paint my face, adding a little more color. A quick dab of blush, the brush tickling my cheeks and a little mascara to bring definition to my eyes is all it takes before I am packing it all back into a bag.

To complete the look, I grab a pair of studded heals. Turning back to the mirror, I gasp and run a hand down my body, straightening my shirt. The woman is back and more pronounced. *I can do this,* I think with a slight nod. I can harness this powerful feeling.

"I am strong, I am confident, and I can do anything I set my mind to." The bravado is there, and my smile widens. Warmth creeps up my spine and there is a lightness I haven't had in a long time.

"This look is complete!" I say, my smile growing wider by the minute.

On to packing. One of the many tasks I must complete before I can head to Tara's and get this party started. I slide my hand down to the handle on the dresser and pull. The drawer sticks and I groan, pulling harder. On the third try, the drawer opens and I grind my teeth a little with irritation. These old dressers have their kinks, but at least I have a dresser, I guess.

After glancing at the clock on my phone, I realize my time is dwindling. Oops, I need to get going. I grab a handful of underwear and socks and dash into the closet, stuffing them into my dark gray duffle bag. The rough fabric rubs against my knuckles and I wince.

I pull clothes off hangers and stuff them in the bag, too. Not paying too much attention to what I'm grabbing, my actions like a convict during a heist. The jitters, fumbling in my hurry to get out. It would be nice if I was filling the bag with wads of cash instead of clothes, but I don't think I'd make a very good criminal. I am much better at following the rules than breaking them.

After turning off the water to the house and locking all the doors, I throw my bags into my baby, a 1969 Ford

Mustang. This beauty has an engine that purrs and the vibrations excite the living shit out of me. The rumble under the hood, tires squealing on the pavement, giving me that little taste of freedom I am so desperately searching for. The leather is cold on my exposed skin and the stick in my hand is hard and powerful as I shift it into gear.

This car is the one thing I can say that I actually appreciate about the asshole who is my stepdad. The black exterior with chrome detailing so sleek against the country backdrop, and with a Cobra jet engine, it seems to glide over the highway. I love this car!

My stepdad gave it to me for my sixteenth birthday with a note stating, "This should help make up for the past."

I wince when I think about that note and its implications. Nothing could make up for what he put me through. The gift, more a tool to use against me than an apology because the abuse didn't stop. It was still my dream car, and I accepted it for what it was. A car.

Before releasing the brake and moving my foot to the gas pedal, I double check, making sure I have my money, ID, and cell phone. Yep, it's all here. Wouldn't that be great, get all the way to the cities and realize I left the important stuff at home?

I snicker at the thought because it isn't too far-fetched. I have a tendency to forget things. And misplace things. Really, I just put them in a safe place, so safe in fact that

I can't remember where. A snort escapes as I think about all the time I've spent looking for those things I stashed away in a "safe place."

Just as I pull out of my driveway, my phone rings. The phone blaring Saweetie's "Best Friend" confirms Tara is calling. Our ringers are the same for each other. Because, why not?

"I'm on my way, ended up falling asleep, and didn't wake up on time. Sorry. Sorry. Sorry." Bouncing in my seat as I say the words, one hand on the wheel and the other pressing the phone to my ear.

"Alayah, chill, I just wanted to make sure you were okay." Tara's voice rings out with an irritated undertone.

"Is there something wrong, Tara? You sound a wee bit snappy, which I would like to point out is not your usual style," I say, trying not to come off too brazen. Tara rarely gets defensive, but I have been around way too many people who do.

"They fired me! Me. Fired. Today. Can you believe that? I don't get why I even care. They barely paid me enough to afford rent at my aunt's house, but I did like working with the clients. Helping people is what I'm good at, you know. It gives me a purpose." Tara inhales deeply, catching her breath. For a moment, I can't help but be relieved she skipped my 'snappy' comment and got right to the point.

Once her words sink in though, I'm taken aback and end up stammering a response. "Ah, I ... I don't know what to say. Sorry, I know you enjoyed your job, but you are an amazing worker and an even better person. Maybe it's a sign, a time for bigger and better things is ahead."

"One can hope. We can talk more on the drive. Just get here safe. You know you're not supposed to talk on your phone while driving. It's dangerous," Tara scolds, acting like a mother, which happens more often than not lately.

"Yes, Ma'am. I'll see you in a few." With that, I hang up and focus on the road.

CHAPTER FOUR

EYES ON ME

~ALAYAH~

I t only takes fifteen minutes to reach Tara's apartment. The drive on a normal day would take twenty-five. Today, though, the wind whipping through my hair rejuvenates me. I push the pedal harder to the floor as I speed down the highway in my super charged Black Beauty.

Even if I weren't so darn late, I would do it. The windows down, music cranked, wind whipping through my hair. Keeping the feeling of freedom alive that I rarely get to experience.

When I pull up to the curb, Tara is standing there, bags packed and ready to go. The look on her face just screams-SCREW THE WORLD, I'm ready to party! A wicked smile creeps across my face. Exactly the demeanor we need to adhere to.

Popping the trunk to my Mustang with a click, I help Tara load everything but the kitchen sink and maybe the bathtub into it in silence. The leather handle of her suitcase grinds into the palm of my hand, but I'm not saying a word. I am so not going to risk getting snapped at, so I think I'll just wait until she makes conversation.

In most cases, my skills of observation are lacking. But I notice she has traded her normal attire of sweats for a dazzling shimmery silver mini skirt, black lace up wedges, and a halter top that would make girls with boob jobs jealous.

Tara usually keeps her amazing figure hidden, but I'm not complaining. 'Mother Hen Tara' has gone underground and 'Party Girl Tara' has taken her place. My body vibrates with excitement at what lays ahead.

Tara plops down into the passenger side, slamming the door and crossing her arms. I don't think I have ever seen her so disgruntled in my life, her normal demeanor so level you could balance a cue ball on it.

She glances at me, eyes rolling to the back of her head when she sees my jaw clench. She knows slamming the door to my car is one of my biggest pet peeves. You do not use excessive force on Black Beauty.

"Sorry!" Her voice is a little snarky.

I nod in acknowledgement. I decide to hold my tongue and let her steer the conversation.

"Did you even notice my new look?" Her jaw tenses as she addresses me.

"How could I miss it? Your boobs are practically falling out of that shirt!" I motion towards her chest.

"You know you're just jealous," she replies, the back of her hand brushing against my arm as she slaps me.

"I know." My bottom lip pushes out in a pout, which causes us both to laugh. "You look amazing. If I would have known all it would take to get you out from under those hoodies into the world of fashion was getting you fired, I would have done it long ago."

"Oh," her eyebrows raising, "and how do you think you could have got them to fire me?"

"I don't know, but I would have found a way." My muscles relax as the tension dissipates. I notice we are both smiling like a couple of cougars in a room full of college boys.

"So, Tara, why exactly did you bring your entire apartment with you?" I keep my tone casual, but I am interested to know what this girl has rolling around in that head of hers. Because I have some things rolling around in mine, too.

"Well, earlier you mentioned losing my job might be a sign. I started thinking..." she says, her teeth white against the rose color of her lipstick as she bites her lip, "I don't want to come back here. I told my aunt I was moving, packed up my belongings and decided I was going to move in with you, or..."

"Or what?" I say, frowning. "Don't tell me you are moving off to the Amazon or some crazy thing like that. I couldn't stand you being that far away." My mouth gapes and a little shiver runs through me. A vivid image of me running through the jungle with an abnormally large, hairy black spider hot on my tail flits through my thoughts. "Nope, not for me."

The quizzical look she gives me has me ready to describe that last thought, but I give a little shake of my head and she continues.

"Oh no, nothing like that. I mean, we could...maybe..." I can tell she's nervous, tripping over her words and all, but I really just want her to get to the point. Eyebrows up, lips in a thin line, I give her a questioning look. I can see the change in her features and the determination in the way her eyes become hard and the muscles in her jaw tighten. "We could move to the cities and get an apartment together."

She holds up a hand and my mouth snaps shut as she continues, "It's not like you truly enjoy the old house you're in, and opportunities are abundant in the city. Oh, and there are more people, which would make it harder for the step-monster to find you."

A hint of a smile graces my face at both the step-monster part and the part about moving. I had been thinking about getting out of here, washing my hands of all the lonely nights and starting over before I picked her up.

"You could even take some classes and open your own automotive shop." Her positivity is contagious and my smile widens.

"That sounds nice," I say. I've dreamed of having a shop of my own.

"What do you think, Ali? Should we just start over?" The awe on her face warms my heart. There isn't anyone in this world I would rather have by my side.

"Maybe it would be better to start over." My fear of change spikes, and I add, "But let's get there first and see if we like the city scene enough to live there."

Clapping her hands like a giddy little girl, she practically jumps across the car and hugs me. "I know we will. This will be good for us. Just wait you'll see."

I'm not sure if that is her weird, though extremely accurate, intuition talking or if she is just excited. But I can feel a surge of energy run through me and realize her excitement is rubbing off on me. I have a good feeling about this weekend and the future.

Just then, our favorite song by Walk the Moon comes on the radio and I know it has to be a good sign. The knob on the radio feels rough on my hand as I crank the volume up. We belt out "Shut up and Dance," along with every other song that comes on the radio for the next two and a half hours.

Dancing in a car isn't easy, but we manage that also, with the grace of a couple of baboons. I am not joking. Every car we pass stares, wide eyes, mouths agape like we are crazy, but what do we care? It's so much fun.

"Tara, can you grab the directions?" I say, pointing at the glove box.

"Are you telling me you don't know how to get to your brother's apartment?" Tara raises her eyebrows at me.

"Of course I don't remember how to get there. This girl prefers dirt roads to city streets!" I say a little defensively, "I've only been there a couple times and those are the only times I have ever driven in the cities, against my better judgment."

Sure, I can do it, but driving in the cities terrifies me. The last time I came to visit my brother, I accidentally ran a red light and just missed being squashed like a bug by a semi. Yikes, talk about life and death experiences.

"Keep your pants on." Trying not to smile, Tara flicks her wrist at me and starts digging through the glove box. "Did you ever think that using the GPS on your phone and joining the 21st century might be a good idea?"

"What can I say? I live a sheltered life. Plus, it only gives me the fastest routes. I wanted back roads once we got closer, so I mapped it out myself on Google." She lifts an eyebrow at me and I shrug my shoulders.

The "step-monster," as Tara and I call him, had a pretty short leash on me. He forced me to spend so much time at home that I lost quite a few friends. I got a job when I was fourteen at an auto parts store just to have an excuse to spend a few extra hours away from home each week. A few extra hours where I didn't have to worry about his drinking, his temper, and most of all, his fists.

"Get over, get over. Our exit is coming up." Tara's voice snaps me back to the here and now. Swerving to get into the right lane, I almost smash into a teal Fiat. Tires screech from behind and Tara clutches the doorframe. "Alayah, are you trying to kill us?"

"Sorry." *Who drives those things, anyway?*

With a dozen more turns, we make it to Jake's. In one piece, I might add.

"That wasn't so bad," I say with a small sigh of relief.

"Yeah, I suppose if you don't value your life at all, that was like a smooth Sunday drive through the country-side," Tara states sarcastically. She's still gripping the doorframe. The white of her knuckles is vivid against the black interior of the car. Her breath comes in quick gasps.

I smile to myself. Tara doesn't get riled easy, but my driving gets her every time. "Relax, hun, we made it. So, what are we going to do for the next hour and a half? I don't think either of us wants me to try driving again..." This time it's me lifting an eyebrow in her direction.

"That's for sure." My phone interrupts her shrill voice as it rings. "Karma" blares through the car and I know it's Jake calling. Gotta love technology. Tara and I exchange amused looks. Jake despises Taylor Swift. Especially this song. Which makes it the perfect ringtone for him.

"Hey what's up, J?" I say with a smirk still lingering on my face.

"Where are you?" he asks.

"Just pulled into your parking lot." My eyes dart to the back of the bakery he lives above and I rub my neck. It's going to be cramped, but we will make do for a little while, I suppose.

"Oh great, I'm getting off work early, so I should be home in fifteen minutes. My big deal closed today and I am ready to unwind!" The tension from this morning forgotten. My heart warms knowing that Jake cares about me.

"Congrats, J. That's amazing!" If I remember right, he has been working on this merger for a while and the stress of it was wearing on him. Hopefully, he can unwind for a few days.

"It is! Thank you! Just wait in the parking lot. I have a couple of friends meeting us and then I thought we could go out to eat, maybe go dancing. Sound good?" Jake sure sounds excited.

Most likely, it's more about hoping Tara is here than it is about seeing me or even that he closed a deal today. He has been crushing on her for years. Not sure why they haven't hooked up, other than Tara's "I don't date my friend's brother" rule. I know she likes him. She has since we decided boys were cute and touching them wouldn't give us cooties.

"That sounds great. My surprise and I are dressed to impress. We're ready for a good time," I say, dropping a little bread crumb for him to follow.

"Hell yeah! See you soon." The phone goes silent, and I venture a look over at Tara, who is now scowling at me.

"Your surprise?" Her eyes narrow on me. "I hope you don't mean that I am a surprise for your brother. Because even though he is extremely attractive, and I mean EX-TREME-LY, I do not date my friends' brothers."

And there it is… Why she is so literally putting her foot down, I will never understand. It doesn't tamp down my hope that someday they will get together because I just know they would be perfect for each other. I try not to put too much into hoping for things since I know from experience hope can be a fickle bitch. In this case, I just feel it'll work out.

"It's just a little joke." The corner of my lip turns up in a smirk. "You really think he's hot?" I add, egging her on with a wiggle of my eyebrows.

"I said attractive, hot sounds so childish, and yes, I do." Shaking her head, "Don't get any ideas though." Tara knows those words mean nothing, since she can already see the wheels turning behind my ice-blue eyes.

"You know you two would…" I don't get a chance to finish that sentence, attention momentarily caught as a car pulls into the parking lot with the two most magnificent looking men I have ever seen inside. It's one of those moments you see in the movies, where everything slows down. I am staring, eyes wide and mouth open, as I catch the gaze of a god.

The driver smiles at me with a lopsided grin and my heart stops. His dark eyes burning into me. A sleeve of tattoos covers the caramel skin on his left arm, and I salivate. He has the most perfectly chiseled biceps I have ever seen.

I pull my eyes away from him and over to the passenger of the vehicle. Shock grips me, mouth gaping. In the passenger seat is a male version of me. White-blonde hair, angular face, and if I had to guess, I bet he has the same piercing ice-blue eyes.

The glowing tan of his skin has me in awe. I could spend a year on the beach, sand between my toes, drink in my hand and never get a tan so beautiful. Jealousy washes over me and my eyes narrow. As quickly as I feel it, the jealousy is gone and my focus is back to his hair.

Never have I seen hair so similar to mine. As the sun shines through the window, I can see how it glistens, reflecting the light, causing a rainbow effect. *Does my hair look like that in the sun?*

"Hey, earth to Alayah," Tara says as she slugs me in the shoulder, breaking my concentration on the hotties a few parking spaces over. "What has gotten into you? You aren't even listening to me."

All I can do is tilt my head toward the newcomers, rubbing the spot she punched. That's gonna bruise! I haven't quite found my voice yet. As she looks over, I can see the amazement registering on her face and I know what I must have looked like. There, showing on her face, is the dreamy feeling I was experiencing just a minute ago. Tara looks at me and mouths the word "HOT!" In return, I nod like a giddy schoolgirl recalling her comment about HOT being a childish word. Oh, how the mighty have fallen.

Tara whispers, still a little dazed by the sight before us, "Can you believe what we're seeing? I think you should pinch me now."

The driver gets out of the car, which I am now realizing is a Dodge Challenger SRT Hellcat, midnight blue with everything else blacked out. This just proves how hot these guys are. I rarely overlook a car so magnificent.

Wow. Imagine being behind the wheel and feeling the horses powering that machine. Where my car is classic, this beauty is all power and brute force.

There is a swagger to his steps as he closes in on my driver side door. I fumble to roll down the window, fingers twitching.

"You like her?" His voice is deep, smooth, and rhythmic. Flutters trail through my stomach at the sound. Glancing up, my eyes meet his and tingles work their way over my skin. Metaphorical drool dripping down my chin.

"You know, we could trade for the day. I wouldn't mind getting behind the wheel of a '69 Mustang." I can tell by the way he's looking at me, he has added some bullshit comment in his head like "and in some hot little blonde's pants." Men always thinking with their... well, you know.

"I may have to take you up on that sometime," my words coming out smoother than I would have expected. My gaze shifting to his lips, those strong, full, kissable lips.

"You shouldn't let her drive your car unless you have really good insurance!" Tara quips, pulling me out of a trance.

You can hear the smack as my hand connects with her leg. Harder than intended, but I laugh as Mr. Hotter-Than-Hot extends his hand. "I made sure to get coverage for stunning female car enthusiasts when I bought my policy. I'm Mikal, by the way."

His smirk is a mix of sexy and predatory. With his index finger, he reaches in and lifts my chin. My eyes meeting his again. I can feel the heat working its way up my neck and into my cheeks, not to mention the heat working its way down between my thighs. Those dark eyes have me trapped, like the deepest depths of the ocean, little flecks of green prominent around his pupils.

Gorgeous!

"Why thank you! It isn't often someone tells me to my face." His grin grows and I cringe, realizing I said that out loud. Face meet palm!

Taking his warm meaty hand in mine, I decide my best line of defense is to just forget it happened. "Alayah, and this is Tara."

With a slow grace, he brings my hand to his lips, not sparing a glance for Tara, and gives my knuckles a gentle kiss, just a soft brush. "Pleasure to meet you."

A throat clears from outside the vehicle. I startle, pulling my hand back into my lap as the male version of me interrupts the moment. "Apologies for interrupting this tête-à-tête, but allow me to introduce myself as Cade. It is an absolute pleasure to make your acquaintance." The words emphasized with a stern look in Mikal's direction, a silent conversation being shared.

His formal speech catches me by surprise and it takes my brain a second to catch up.

Returning his attention to me, Cade adds, "Based on the description Jake gave us, I would surmise you are his esteemed sibling. He has regaled us with a wealth of information pertaining to you."

Um… regaled? I'm guessing he means Jake's talked a lot about me, so I just go with that.

"Only the good things, I hope." A mischievous grin returns to my face.

"Indeed," Cade says, his smile not quite reaching his eyes.

Returning his not so generous smile, I wonder, *what is his problem?* Fortunately, I don't have too much time to ponder that because a green Intrepid pulls into the parking lot, tires squealing.

My door opens, Mikal sweeping his hand, gesturing for me to get out. Quite the gentleman. Tara gives a little *humph* and I think *that was odd,* as Mikal gently shuts the door behind me and walks off without another word.

"Don't suppose anyone could have had the manners to open the door for me." The cynical tone of her voice catches me off guard. Her heels click against the tar as she walks to my side.

Slipping my arm through hers, I feel the warmth of her skin against mine. I whisper, "Don't worry, had Jake been closer, he would have jumped over the hood trying to get to that door before you opened it yourself."

Tara mumbles back, "I don't think I can go out with these guys. I'll be a sloppy puddle on the floor, and they're going to think that I'm a total idiot."

Disdain tints her voice, and I wonder why. The scowl on her face and the twitch of her eye tell me something is bothering her. It can't be about the door thing. I'm almost positive she was over that the moment the comment left her lips. That's just her way; never holding a grudge, down to earth, and easy to get along with.

"Tara, you are so amazing with fitting in that I don't see a problem for you tonight. It's me we have to worry about. Sloppy puddle, here I come. Can you believe Mikal kissed my hand? So hot, right!?" Rocking from my left foot to my right, I just can't get my nerves under control.

"Ugh... yes, that was dreamy, or it would have been if it was my hand he was kissing. We get to look at that all night. I'm thinking moving here might not be the worst idea we've ever had." Frown turning into a smirk, I see some of the tension leave her face.

"I agree," I say, a little louder than I mean to, and all three guys look back at us. A little quieter, I add, "Wonder what they have in store for us tonight?"

"Your guess is as good as mine, but I bet it'll be entertaining." Which is a statement I wholeheartedly agree with.

CHAPTER FIVE

BAD BOYS

~ALAYAH~

Jake is waiting, arms open. He pulls me into the tightest bear hug I have had since I was a kid. The pressure of his arms wrapping around me soothes my soul, along with his woodsy scent. A reminder of home, not the home I grew up in, but he is my home; my family, and my heart swells with love.

"I missed you, little sis!" he says as he pushes me back to arms-length, looking me over. "I think you've matured since I saw you last."

"Really, Jake, it's only been a couple months." I grind my teeth at the way he is embarrassing me in front of the other guys.

His arms wrap around me once more and he whispers in my ear, "You can calm down. You will all get along just fine."

Muscles tensing, I move to step away, but he stops me, "I can practically see you trembling and I can definitely feel it."

With a sly wink and a huge smile, Jake releases me to greet Tara. As he moves into my peripheral vision, I find myself staring into a pair of dark eyes. My breath hitches with the intensity in Mikal's gaze.

"Oh, hi!" Smooth Alayah, really smooth.

The corner of his mouth inches up in a lopsided grin. "So, where have you been all my life?"

Cade chooses that moment to cut in, saving me from laughing in Mikal's face. I hide a smirk behind my hand as he says, "Your utter lack of class astounds me, Mikal."

With a sigh, Cade turns back to me, dress shoes grinding the sand beneath them as he moves, "Allow me to beseech your forgiveness on behalf of his misguided conduct. Regrettably, he is accustomed to engaging with inebriated women at bars, and lacks the ability to recognize a proper lady when presented with one."

"Really, Cade, do you have to be so proper and uptight? I was just trying to lighten the mood. Alayah looked a little tense," Mikal says with a knowing look and a shrug in my direction.

I wonder if he heard what my brother had said to me, but there wasn't any way that he could have. Jake said it so low I barely heard him and Mikal was a good ten feet away.

I chalk it up to a coincidence and address the guys, hand on my hip, "Thanks Cade, but I can handle my own in the presence of men and their cheesy pickup lines."

The sweet sound of laughter fills the parking lot and I give Mikal my sexiest smile.

Cade extends his hand and replies, "It is a pleasure to make your acquaintance." As soon as I touch his hand, I get the oddest feeling. It isn't a spark, like we are meant to be together. No, it's more a feeling of recognition, like we have known each other our whole lives.

My gaze moves from our hands to meet Cade's eyes and in that instant I think I see the color of his pupils change and swirl. It's so brief that I can't tell if I imagined it, but they seemed to go from an icy blue like I expected earlier to dark violet in the blink of an eye.

I pull my hand away and give my head a little shake to clear it. Maybe it's just the heat. I wipe the back of my hand against my forehead. For Minnesota, we've been having some extremely high temperatures. I must not be used to it yet.

Or more likely just my imagination. I have been under a lot of stress lately. I won't let that creep me out, not on my weekend away from my past and the scared little girl I am trying so hard to leave back home.

Jake's voice snaps me back into the conversation. "So, why don't we all go up to the apartment? I'll get changed and we can go grab a bite to eat."

"Sounds good," Mikal says, placing a hand on my lower back in an effort to guide me towards the apartment. Even through the material of my shirt I can feel tingles where his fingers caress me. "Afterwards, we are going to take you girls out to this elite club, Persuasion. We'll get there early, but the real party doesn't start 'til midnight. I hope you ladies aren't afraid of staying out late."

"What's there to be afraid of when we have you three to look out for us?" Tara chimes in. Everyone smiles at that except me.

A shiver runs up my body again, not because of the warm hand pressing against my back. No, it's the way Mikal said the last few words, like he might know something we don't. Not wanting to ruin their excitement, I decide to keep my mouth shut, an extremely hard task for me, and follow them up to my brother's apartment.

Dinner goes surprisingly well, the shrimp alfredo only a memory as I use the garlic bread to soak up the last of the sauce from the bowl. With my stomach full, I wonder if my suspicions might be due more to the fact that my crazy stepfather is getting released and less to do with Mikal and Cade.

Three hours talking, drinking, and laughing until our sides hurt pass quickly and I'm glad the night isn't over yet. Jake was right. We all get along great and being around this easy-going crowd has really calmed my nerves.

Tara seems to be having a great time and is getting pretty comfortable with Jake. I'm a little surprised that she is giving in this easy on her rule to not date my brother, but not too surprised. I know my brother can be charming when he has the motivation.

I've been watching their body language throughout dinner. The way they turn their bodies towards each other, how they're almost always touching, and the way they don't seem to mind eating off each other's plates.

This could turn into a promising relationship, and I couldn't be happier for them. Or at least I want to be, but the slight tightening in my chest and the burning inside my mouth from where my teeth pinch the skin screams worry. Will this new found relationship infringe on my friendship with Tara?

I don't want to lose my best friend.

I won't.

Tara's loyal and she loves me – she won't push me away. It will be fine. I'm fine. I take a breath in through my nose and let it out through my mouth releasing my cheek from the vice grip of my teeth. It really will be fine.

Moving on. I also notice the way Mikal almost always watches me and the way Cade is constantly staring at him. Whenever I catch Mikal looking, he just gives me that sexy half smile and joins in on the conversation again. On each account, goosebumps find their way to my arms and my face heats a few hundred degrees.

The tab arrives, delivered by our waitress, a cute brunette with long dark lashes which she is currently batting in Mikal's direction. A different type of heat works its way under my skin, and I have to take a deep breath. Jealous, much?

Mikal, not sparing her a second glance, reaches into his pocket and pulls out a wad of hundred-dollar bills. Crisp hundred-dollar bills to be exact and pays the entire tab. My breath catches for a moment. *How can he just throw money around like that?* Our food and drinks had to be well over five hundred dollars. I was worried about covering just my share. He must have a well-paying career.

I didn't realize how much that idea turns me on until this moment, and that realization makes me a tad uncomfortable. I am not a gold digger by any means, but with money comes power and power equals control. If there is one feeling I want to rid from my life, it's not being in control.

"Well, now that we are all fueled up, are you guys ready for a night on the town?" Mikal says opening the door to the parking lot for us.

"I am so ready to party the night away. Did I tell you guys that I got fired from my job today? What a load of crap that was! I worked my ass off at that place and they just fire me…" Tara speaks up. She is getting into her rambling stage, which is one step away from her slurring stage. With that comes the tumbling stage and I am not in a position to keep her from falling on her face.

She must have downed at least three of Jake's Morgan Cokes during dinner. I was mentally chastising her; I don't want the night to end before it's barely begun. Considering the girl hardly ever drinks, a drunk Tara has the overwhelming possibility of doing just that. I decide not to dwell on the feeling in favor of letting go and having fun. Jake can handle Tara. She doesn't need me worrying and ruining her night.

Cade's deep voice cuts Tara off, speaking as reserved as always, "That appears to be egregiously inappropriate. Our encounter has been brief, yet I have already discerned that your work ethic and character surpass the ordinary standards of excellence." This gets him another look from Mikal, who is also shaking his head, a little disappointed in his friend for his choice of words, or at least that's my guess.

I shimmy up beside my brother and ask in a low voice, "Do you think Tara will get into the club?"

"She'll be fine. Mikal's dad owns the club, so we all get wrist bands. Cade drinks there all the time." The nonchalant way he replies is a surprise.

"Wait a sec, Cade isn't twenty-one?" I gasp. I guess I just assumed they were all over twenty-one since they ordered drinks in the restaurant.

"No, he's twenty and Mikal is the oldest of our little trio. He turned twenty-three last weekend. That was one hell of a party! Too bad you didn't come up a week earlier." A smile crosses his face. I can tell he is remembering something that happened at the party.

I'm about to ask, but we reach the vehicle and I decide it can wait. There will surely be a chance to grill him about last weekend before this weekend is up.

Mikal's already holding the seat forward so Tara can jump in the back. And as I wait for my turn, Mikal runs the back of his hand down my arm, causing those pesky goosebumps to pop up again, "You can sit up front with me if you'd like."

This gets him a "humph" from the passenger side where Cade is letting Jake into the back.

"No, that's fine. Cade can sit in front." I don't really know if I want to sit that close to him and I noticed Cade seems to frown upon any interaction between Mikal and myself. Not wanting to ruffle any feathers, I decide to change the subject as I climb into the back seat, the leather slick against my sweaty palm.

"So, your dad owns this club we're going to?" I couldn't imagine Cade squeezing his muscular body into the back seat with two other people.

Mikal's face goes a little slack and his eyes darken. "Yeah, something like that."

He doesn't elaborate, and I don't ask, as warning bells go off inside my head at the look he gives me. In fact, I think it is the first time since I met him that he has had anything other than a smile or an amused scowl on his face.

Mikal starts the car, and I sink back into the seat. My thoughts about the night and the future swirl around in my head. I zone out, the surrounding conversation a constant hum.

My suspicions about Cade and Mikal return, but I try to suppress them by thinking about dancing and drinking. It's been a long time since I've drunk alcohol and with the excitement of letting loose working its way through my limbs, a smile pulls at the corners of my mouth. I can't help thinking about seeing Mikal with his shirt off, either. The way it clings to his body emphasizes the outline of a six pack. He is sexy, even if he's a little weird. Eye candy is never a bad thing!

As we pull into the parking lot of the club, Tara gives my hand a squeeze. "Are you okay?" she asks in a low voice. "You seem a little distracted."

"Yeah, I was just thinking. Do Mikal and Cade seem off?" I ask in a whisper cupping my hand around her ear. "Like they have something to hide?"

As the words leave my mouth, Mikal's eyes meet mine in the rearview mirror. His gaze holds me in its grasp for a few seconds, the intensity making my stomach tighten. It takes effort to pull my eyes away and my heart beats a little faster at the attention.

"I guess I haven't noticed, but that doesn't really mean anything. I've spent most of the night ogling your brother," she says with a giggle, and I know that she definitely wants more for the two of them than being friends.

"Yeah, so how is that going for you? Planning a wedding yet?"

She pokes me in the side, harder than she intended I'm sure because it stings. I rub my hand over the spot absentmindedly. Her smile is contagious and we both laugh. She's smitten. Pink floods to the tips of her ears and I laugh harder. When our laughter dies down, we notice the guys are all staring at us from outside the car.

"Are you two staying in that car all night?" Jake asks reaching in to help Tara out of the passenger side.

She replies, but I don't quite catch her words as I struggle to get out of the back seat. Mikal's hand reaches in to help. His strength is a little over the top as he pulls me right into his arms. Being so close to him is like inhaling helium in a sauna. Dizziness clouds my thoughts, heat rushes through my body, and I am at a loss for words. The lightheaded feeling is wonderful, and I don't want to let him go.

He bends down, his nose brushing against my ear and whispers, "I really wish it was just the two of us right now, because I would like nothing more than to kiss those beautiful lips of yours." The goose bumps return as he adds, "Just so you know, all our secrets will be revealed soon."

His words make me pause, my muscles tense.

Before pulling away, he runs his nose over the outside of my neck and inhales deeply. That should be weird, but I can feel a dampness between my legs that wasn't there a few minutes ago and I curse my body for betraying me.

He backs away, leaving me to stand on my own two feet, which at this moment, is more of a chore than you would think. I am still reeling from the fact that he wants to kiss me and chilled, knowing that he must have heard the conversation I was having with Tara in the back of the car.

CHAPTER SIX

OUR BUSINESS

~ALAYAH~

The club just screams high class, a hell of a lot higher class than I am used to. Our wardrobe ensures we don't appear out of place, despite our uncertainty about fitting in here. I feel a constant need to adjust my clothing, though, rubbing my hands over the smooth fabric of my shirt.

My heels click as we walk across the white marble floors and the noise grates on my nerves. Are people looking at me? I focus on the surrounding crowd. No one seems to notice the sound as "The Business" by Tiesto blares through the gigantic speakers and the lights flash, reflecting off the pristine marble. I run my hand along one of the dark granite columns that reach from floor to ceiling around the room, letting the cool feel of the stone relax me slightly. I get lost in the feeling and jump when a warm hand touches my arm.

Mikal is standing so close to me, I can smell his musky scent with a hint of fresh cut grass and I'm not sure how much longer I can take this rollercoaster of emotions. The smell reminds me of warm summer days playing in the dirt. It draws me in and I lose myself in the feel of his skin on mine.

He hands me a drink, and I bring it to my lips without questioning the contents. The taste of strawberries rolls over my tongue. I close my eyes, a soft moan escaping my lips. I have never tasted anything so divine.

This is the second time in less than ten minutes he's entered my personal space. Even though his comments sometimes scare me, I'm excited he's near.

I can feel his breath against my ear. "Exquisite, isn't it?"

I nod my head in agreement as I take another drink.

"This should help calm the nervous energy. Try to relax a little."

I open my mouth to answer and he puts his finger to my lips to stop me. "I don't blame you; this is all over the top. You are with friends and family. Let go and have fun."

With his finger still on my lips, I only give him a nod of my head and then, being the classy lady I am, I stick my tongue out to lick the pad of his finger. That sly smile he likes to wield plays on his lips again as he pulls his finger away.

"As long as you stay with us, you should be fine." Contemplating his words, my face goes slack and the quiet laugh that escapes his lips is melodic.

His eyes are boring into mine, telling me he isn't just trying to keep me to himself. There is something he doesn't want to say out loud.

In a little louder voice, making sure everyone else can hear, he says, "Your brother, Cade and I won't let anyone mess with you. Just have fun." As if reading my previous thoughts about the splendor of this place, he adds, "Don't worry about touching anything, just act like you own the place. I do."

How can one man make me want two opposite things so badly at the same time? I want to pull him into a private room, strip him down and explore that gorgeous body while, at the same time, I want to get as far away from him as I can.

And with that thought, I gain my composure. My hand glides against the leather chair as I round the table away from Mikal. Grabbing Cade by the arm, I drag him out onto the dance floor.

I really just need to get info on Tall, Dark, and Scary. Since I can't really dance with my brother and he is off grabbing drinks anyway, Cade is the best option. He's reluctant and stands firm for a moment. I don't really care and tug harder on his arm.

Glancing at Mikal, I wonder if there is a hint of jealousy in his expression, but it is gone in a flash. Interesting.

"This evening has been pleasant. Do you agree?" Cade asks with a nervous smile on his face.

"Yeah, I'm having fun, but what is up with Mikal?" My tone sounds a little more irritated than I would like. I don't want anyone to know that he is getting under my skin. *How could someone go from being so handsome and charming one minute to being creepy and vague the next?*

"I'm uncertain as to the meaning of your statement?" Cade says, tilting his head to the side, an expression I would relate to a curious puppy.

"Well, one minute he acts like he likes me and the next, he's all secretive and, well, kind of creepy," I say, keeping my voice low.

"Oh," he answers with a weary look on his face. His hands twitch a little at my waist. I feel this dance we are sharing is awkward for him.

"Certain matters are beyond your understanding currently. Mikal finds it challenging to withhold this information from you." Looking around nervously, he adds, "Should Mikal appear distant, it is solely due to his efforts to safeguard your interests in the present circumstances."

That brings a billion questions racing to the surface of my mind. "What do you mean, there are things I don't understand? I feel like I'm in some weird Sci-Fi movie."

"Look at me, Alayah, what do you see?" he says, motioning towards himself.

"What do I see? Are you trying to change the subject?" I ask, exasperated.

"I assure you, I do not intend to divert the course of our conversation. Rather, I am seeking an opportune way to respond to your inquiries." Calm and sullen, he adds, "I kindly implore you to answer the question."

I look at him, wondering what he wants me to see. He looks just like me, but that's just silly. He cannot be insinuating that we have any connection. So, I dig deeper, trying to come up with something. But I fail.

"Well, you are male, good looking, tall…"

"Alayah, I know you have contemplated our shared resemblance. I find myself perplexed why you would circumvent the essential facts and instead speak of such trivial details." His tone verging on patronizing.

"Well, I did, I guess, but I kind of wrote it off as a coincidence. There are numerous people who resemble each other in this world," I say.

Moments pass as I study the look on his face. He doesn't add to the conversation, so I continue.

"I've never seen anyone stand out like us, but what are you suggesting? Do you believe there is a possibility we have a relation?" I don't know what to think. This day is getting weirder and weirder.

At that moment, I glance at our table. Mikal's dark eyes are on us with an expression that could suck the soul right out of your body. Those eyes boring into us, hands gripping the table, making the veins on his arms stand out. Yum! Wait, I mean, what the hell is up with him?

"Focus, Alayah. Refrain from concerning yourself with Mikal's emotional state. He is upset I am assisting you in comprehending matters we prohibit him from disclosing to you. What I am suggesting, as you so elegantly put it, is the undeniable existence of a profound connection between us." His irritation is clear in the way he spits the word 'suggesting' at me. As if he's angry that I'm not catching on. "Do you know who fathered you?"

"Do you mean father as in the person who helped to conceive me? Because that would be a no! The other one, the one who raised me, I know him all too well." My words clipped in irritation.

"Your father and my father are interchangeable." He pauses for a moment, taking in the shock written all over my face. "Now let me ask you this - has Jake ever mentioned me to you?"

"Well, no. What do you mean, interchangeable?" I say, not sure where this is going and not wanting to believe that my father is out there somewhere. It evokes emotions of inadequacy. Emotions, I thought, I buried deep down inside myself.

"Jake does not belong to my social circle. We spend time together occasionally. Through those interactions, I realized you existed, but individuals of his nature are not typically granted access to our exclusive group." Looking him in the eyes, I see a quick flash of violet again and realized I hadn't been imagining it earlier. Taken by surprise, I try to put a few more inches of distance between us.

My back bumps into something hard and cool. With the corner of a countertop pressing against my spine, I am forced to step closer to Cade again.

"Let's put further conversation regarding our father off until later. This is not the venue to have that discussion." His eyes glance away and then meet mine again. I can see the stubbornness in them.

"Okay, so no father talk, but our type? What do you mean by our type?" Fear wells up inside me, and I wonder what have I gotten myself into coming here. Could they be involved in a cult?

Maybe they're crazy or is it me? Am I the crazy one? Cade looks just like me. I can feel a trickle of fear working its way into my body again, tightening around my insides like a boa constrictor.

Another quick glance at Mikal, and his predatory stare sends me over the edge. I get chills and the hair on the back of my neck stands up.

I take a breath and focus. When I look at him, his lips pucker like he just ate something sour. I wonder if trying to talk me off the ledge I am currently on leaves an awful taste in his mouth? Like it physically manifests or something.

My muscles are tense, and my mind is running on high alert.

"I advise you to not display signs of fear in this setting," he warns, scanning the room. "Look at me and kindly explain the emotions which arise within you. Do you perceive any intention on my part to inflict harm upon you?"

As I stare at him with disbelief, I try to calm myself and begin reading his body language. His hand is holding my arm, presumably so I won't run away screaming, but his touch is gentle. His relaxed muscles suggest he doesn't intend to harm me.

Though, I think to myself, *an exceptional serial killer might use that tactic in subduing his prey.*

When I look at his face again, more directly into his eyes, I can almost see his soul. His intentions are to help me. There's a desire in his eyes for me to understand. In that instant, I know it's a fact, though I am not sure how.

He will not hurt me.

My shoulders drop and I unclench my hands, letting out a breath I didn't realize I had been holding. "Okay, so we need to talk."

"Regrettably, we cannot pursue this conversation amidst the presence of these beings." Glancing around the room again, he moves me off of the dance floor as I scrunch my face at the word choice.

I stash that away in the part of my mind that I have now labeled "things I need to question later." It's a small dark area in the back of my head, covered with a thin layer of dust.

"Mikal's presence is required for this conversation. We will exclude Jake and Tara. As the less they know, the more secure their safety will be." Cade's tranquil voice doesn't match the tension in his shoulders.

Left. Right. Left. Right. My head moves on its own accord at the mention of Mikal's name. Even though there is unquestionably an attraction there, he's giving me the willies at the moment. "No, that won't work. He scares me."

"You will understand after our explanation. I know our acquaintance is new. You do not have a reason to trust us, but your options are limited. Should my thoughts prove accurate, we never should have brought you to this establishment tonight." I notice his eyes darting around the club instead of focusing on me.

"Then why did you bring us here? If it's dangerous for me, why am I here?" My voice is more high pitched than I had intended. I don't understand what he's talking about, but my subconscious is agreeing with him. I can sense the danger.

His eyes have stopped darting, focusing on something. Tracking his gaze, I spot what looks to be a normal group of people sitting at a corner table.

Upon closer inspection, the intensity of their glares has me on high alert again. Their expressions are murderous, carrying varied levels of intent.

What the hell?

"We need to depart immediately." Cade's steps are steady as he escorts me towards the back door, but his tone is urgent. I notice Mikal has also observed the threat and is making his way, Tara and Jake in tow, to the front exit.

Cade leans down and whispers in my ear, "As soon as we exit, run. Run as fast as you can, don't fret about me. Mikal and the others will await your arrival at the vehicle."

"But…" I protest. He cuts me off with a glare.

"No buts," he says as he opens the door. He gives me a hard shove and yells, "GO!"

I do just that. I run as fast as I can down the alley. Loud clicks echoing around me from my heals hitting the pavement.

Remember, I'm good at following rules, and Cade has just laid out rules to keep me safe. I can do as he says. I can go to the car without letting curiosity get the better of me. Or can I? Before I make it a hundred yards, I hear an ear-piercing shriek and my blood runs cold. I stop dead in my tracks and spin around, eyes wide and heart racing.

Even after how weird this night has been, I'm not ready for the sight before me. The entire night has been unbelievable, but this is mind-boggling.

Brilliant white light shines from the alleyway, causing me to squint for a moment, waiting for my eyes to adjust. I run my hands over the front of my body, making sure I'm not melting.

While I don't feel any heat, my mind connects the sight with the brilliance of the sun. I'm pretty sure standing too close to the sun would cause the flesh to melt from your bones. As I check for damage, I am rewarded knowing my skin is still attached, just the way it should be. The light seems to come from everywhere and nowhere all at once.

As my eyes adjust, I can make out a form in the center of the light. The more I focus, the more details I can decipher. It's Cade. Cade is in the center of the light or, more specifically, the light is emanating from Cade in all directions. My mouth opens and closes a few times. I'm at a loss. It's so beautiful, like an angel coming down to Earth.

I'm stunned at the beauty until movement off to the side catches my eye. I turn my focus in that direction and dread clutches me instead. Dark figures move just outside the light, pressing against it as if trying to snuff it out. The shadows ooze like slime from three figures standing in a triangle surrounding Cade.

Another dark figure lays motionless on the ground not too far from the fray. A scream bubbles up in my throat and I work to suppress it. The figure on the ground, a dark-haired woman who had been sitting with the group in the corner, is missing her head. I know it's her because the head is laying a few feet down the alley, her vacant eyes seeking me out.

Stunned, I'm trapped in a moment of indecision. The whole scene feels surreal. I have only ever seen one person dead and that was my mom. As the scream is about to escape, a hand covers my mouth. I can feel warm breath on my neck as someone whispers, "I wouldn't bring attention to myself like that if I were you."

I twist out of my captor's grip with little resistance, and my eyes fall upon Mikal. His face set somewhere between amusement and rage.

"You need to get to the car like Cade said, and I need to go help him." The tone of his voice doesn't leave a lot of room to argue.

I turn on my heels and start speed walking towards the car. Muscles tight, breath laboring. Upon turning the corner, I glance back. Three dark figures lay on the ground, all missing their heads. The fourth is vanishing down the alley in the opposite direction with his long black trench coat flapping behind him.

I hear Mikal say, "Should we follow him?"

Cade answers in a low tone, "No reason. He will grace us with his presence soon enough. We need to converse with Alayah immediately and gain control of this situation. Her understanding is imperative to our survival. Unfortunately, I believe she may have witnessed enough to frighten her away."

"Or just enough to make her curious," Mikal scoffs. When the guys turn toward me, I round the corner and sprint to the car. I regain composure before opening the car door, concealing my emotions from Jake and Tara, but it exhausts me. I climb into the back seat and collapse.

"Ali, are you okay? What happened back there?" Tara asks, laying a gentle hand on my arm. Her touch eases my body's reaction to what I just experienced.

"I don't know. Cade told me we had to leave and told me to go straight to the car." I let out a long sigh and then add, "Jake, how much do you know about them?"

"What do you mean? We hang out once-in-awhile." He looks at me, confused.

"Are they in a gang or something?" Tara says with fear in her voice. "I mean, those other people were following them and they looked pretty tough. Mikal looks like he's a little rough around the edges with all the tattoos."

"He was acting secretive when he walked us to the car." Jake says.

"Tara, are you stereotyping right now?" I ask.

"Ah, I wasn't trying to, but you have to admit there is more to him than a pretty rich boy acting like a badass. I can feel it," Tara says, a blush working its way to her cheeks.

"I don't think they're in a gang. I mean, I guess we don't hang out that much, but nothing weird has ever happened and definitely nothing this suspicious," Jake's voice wavers. He is unsure. Tara's hand moves to cover Jake's, stopping his nervous fidgeting.

All three of us take a collective deep breath, exhaling at the same time. Our smiles are instantaneous, easing the tension in the car.

"I don't think they're in a gang," I say, trying to smooth things over. I can see Tara, usually the calm one in our group, deflate just a little more and I know she has been holding back her fear for our benefit.

My mind moves back to the alleyway and I can't help but think Mikal was right. The events I witnessed tonight intrigued me as much as they scared me.

Curiosity is clawing at my insides. What had Cade been implying during our conversation?

"Maybe they have history and didn't want us to get involved in an old quarrel." Jake's voice is hesitant, like he doesn't quite believe his own comment.

Tara opens her mouth to speak. Realizing the door is opening, she holds her tongue and her teeth click together. The scent of burnt flesh accosts us. We all recoil, but no one says a word about it.

Cade climbs in the passenger seat with a worried look that is directed straight at me. "I'm sorry for that particular inconvenience."

Lines of tension crease his forehead as he says, "I hope this first impression won't discourage us from the opportunity to get to know each other better."

I don't hear Mikal open the door and jump when his deep, silky voice says, "Where to?"

"I think it's time to call it a night," Tara says, emanating disapproval of how the night has been progressing. All signs that she has been under the influence have vanished.

Without another word, Mikal puts the car in drive and peels out of the parking lot, tires squealing the entire way to the stoplights. My heart skips a beat at the sudden change and a gasp escapes my lips.

CHAPTER SEVEN

EYES CLOSED

~ALAYAH~

Okay, he seems pissed!

Yes, this is the first thought that flits through my head on the way back to the apartment. My eyebrows pinch together and I notice the faint sound of the radio just barely over the screaming of the engine. No sounds come from my companions.

I'm not the only one deep in thought, I suppose. My chest tightens and I wonder about the man in front of me. Sending out calming thoughts, I focus on the back of his head.

My hands move to my chest in a silent plea, and I take a couple of deep breaths. In one, two, three, four, five. Out one, two, three, four, five. The moisture from my hands leaves no marks as I wipe them down on my skinny jeans. Gripping my thighs, I continue in one, two, three, four, five. Out one, two, three, four, five.

As the car flies around a corner, too sharp for the speed we are going, I gasp. Just a small one and my focus breaks. I don't think anyone notices until I lock eyes with Mikal in the mirror. His pupils dilate and the corner of his mouth pulls tight. I feel the car slow and I relax. Mikal's shoulders drop and the tension between us eases.

The faint smell of burnt rubber wafts through the car and Tara's leg tenses beside me. The only sign she is awake. Her eyes closed, head laying against Jake's shoulder. Jake's hands fidget as he stares out the window. The muscles in his jaw are tight, but he doesn't pull his gaze.

How am I going to get away to talk with Cade and Mikal? Do I want to? I sigh, turning to look out the small window beside me. The greens and browns blur as we pass a park on the outskirts of the city.

Maybe, just maybe, they can explain what I just saw and enlighten me on the similarities I share with Cade. The thought has my chest tightening with anxiety again. Will digging for answers comfort me or will the information turn my world upside down? Does it matter? Today has already thrown a wrench into my not so perfect but mostly normal, sheltered life.

I don't understand why no one else has mentioned the fact that Cade and I look so much alike. That might just be the weirdest thing to have happened since Tara and I started this little adventure. The more I think about it, the more it bothers me and questions surface that I need answers to.

Why don't I look anything like my mother and brother? Where is our father? Who is he? Could Cade be his child, too? Are we related or is this just a weird coincidence? These questions continue to swirl through my mind until we reach the parking lot outside Jake's apartment.

The engine quiets as Mikal puts the car in park. The streetlights cast a dim haze over the other cars and I can see black flashes soaring overhead. Shadows against the night sky. A little shiver runs through me and I scrunch up my nose. Bats!

Hands clammy, I fidget with the uncertainty of what's coming. It's waring on my nerves. Wiping my hands on my jeans, I take in the scene. Mikal is still gripping the steering wheel, white knuckled. His muscles defined by the tension, and I have to admit, he is super sexy as he works to gain his composure.

Cade is thinking; lost in his own little world, just as I was moments ago. He has that look on his face, like the entire world is offending him.

Whispers draw my attention. Tara and Jake are having a hushed conversation beside me, their hands clasped together. The focus on one another is so intense they don't seem to notice the way I stare at them, taking in their body language. Shoulders tucked close together, whispering, lips inches apart. A smile pulls at the corner of my mouth.

When I pull my gaze away from them, I meet Mikal's dark eyes. The intensity behind them is so overwhelming. I can feel him searching for something, but I'm not sure what. There's more to this man, hidden deep inside, that I desperately want to explore.

I glance away quickly, focusing on the parking lot and all the surrounding cars. Tingles cover my body and my cheeks heat. He hasn't looked away. The sensitive skin on my bottom lip burns as my teeth pinch the flesh. I fight the sensation his attention brings observing the landscape beside us.

A flash of white deep in the trees on the other side of the parking lot has me focusing hard. The intensity of my stare met only with darkness. A minute passes. Then another flash of white. What was that? My eyes dart back and forth. More time passes, but I see nothing. No more flashes of white in the darkness. Just my mind playing tricks on me, I suppose. But I can't shake the awful feeling that someone is watching us. Watching me.

No one makes a move to exit the car and I don't want to be the first. So I stay still.

Steering my mind in a different direction, I strain to bring up an image of my father. Nothing. All I can visualize is a blurry, faceless silhouette. There were no pictures of him, nothing left behind, but the teddy bear on my bed.

Thinking back, I'm not that sure my mother knew who he was. She never talked about him. Jake never talked about him either. If Jake and I are full blood brother and sister, he must have been around for a while. The three-year age gap would indicate that. So, why does it seem like he didn't exist?

As a small child, I had worked up the nerve to ask my mom about him.

My three-year-old mind curious, little hands pulling at the hem of her shirt. Shaking with a nervous energy. "Mommy, where is my real daddy? Why isn't he here to protect us? John is scary. He has mad eyes."

Her voice is tense, almost robotic, as she replies, "Your daddy left us. John is here taking care of us, keeping a roof over our heads. He is the only daddy you need."

In hindsight, I realize had John gotten wind I mentioned my real father, there would have been a very severe beating waiting for both my mother and me.

The click of a door handle draws my attention as Cade turns slightly in his seat. His eyes are soft, almost questioning, as he gazes at me. His lips pulled down in a sullen frown.

I give him a slight nod, letting him know I am coping. His door opens with a barely audible creek. He pulls himself out of the front seat, using the frame for leverage. His movements slow and deliberate as he releases the lever on the seat, causing it to spring forward. I jump with the sudden movement and Tara's hand grasps my leg for a second before sliding out of the car with Jake. The leather interior squeaking as the weight of their bodies moves away.

Still as a statue, Mikal stays put. But as I slide to the passenger side of the car, his hand whips out, grabbing ahold of my arm, startling me a second time. His grip on my arm is feather light but does nothing to calm my racing heart. One too many attacks as a child has my senses on high alert. It's a subconscious reaction at this point.

"Can we talk for a minute?" He looks a little deflated as I draw my arm away and get out of the car.

Turning to Tara and Jake, I ask, "Do you mind if I meet you up there? I want to talk to these two for a minute."

Tara starts to protest but Jake cuts her off, "Are you sure you are okay, to um, walk up alone?"

"Yeah, it's fine. I won't be long." Giving them the best smile I can muster, I shoo them towards the apartment. As they turn to leave, I can see the reluctance to abandon me to Cade and Mikal.

I wave my hand again and broaden my smile. Jake slides his hand into Tara's and pulls her towards the door, sparing one more glance in my direction.

When I turn back to the car, I am surprised to see that Cade has climbed in the back seat and left the passenger seat for me. I get in and shut the door, being extra careful not to close it too hard. Pet peeves, you know.

"I understand fatigue and shock have taken hold of you. We will give you a brief summation and then you may return to your quarters to rest," Cade says in that weird yet intriguing way he talks. I wonder how he was raised because typically people from this era don't speak in such a manner.

"Um, okay." I am not sure how to follow that statement, so I just wait for one of them to explain.

Mikal seems to catch on to the fact that Cade confuses the bejesus out of me and saves me from the awkward silence with a knowing smirk.

"Well, like Cade said," he gives Cade another little head shake, "It has been a long night, so I think the actual explanation should wait for tomorrow. Why don't you just choose three questions that you would like us to answer tonight, and we will cover the rest later?"

"Do you believe that such a method is appropriate, Mikal, without commencing from inception?" Cade asked.

"I think it will give her some answers she seeks without scaring her away." He pauses, "Hopefully." An eyebrow and a challenge raised in my direction.

"Okay, my first question is, why do you and I look so similar to each other and so different from the rest of society?" I figured after all the questions I had asked myself in the car, this would be the best place to start.

"To be concise, we share a common paternal lineage. We originate from a distant community where the citizens, our citizens, bear a striking resemblance to ourselves. Although, you and I are unique in a magnitude of ways. We can discuss the extended version tomorrow if that suits you." I knew that was the only answer I was going to get, but it still shocks me and I feel my mouth hanging open. I close it with a snap.

"You were being honest, I guess. I didn't believe you when you said it in the club," I stammer out.

"I do not deceive unless I have no other choice," Cade states. "During my formative years, I resided alongside our father in the elemental realm. Although I lack precise knowledge of the underlying motives, I have deduced our father left you with your mother because our people were at war. Given your status as the rightful heir to the throne, it was a strategic measure implemented to assure your safety and well-being. There are undoubtably inquiries father will need to address. However, I expect tomorrow I will have the opportunity to provide a more comprehensive explanation."

Slowly my weary mind catches up to the words he spoke and I inhale sharply, choking on the influx of air. I cough hard and my eyes water as I try to catch my breath.

"Did you just say…" another cough, "I'm the heir to the elemental throne?"

"That's right, princess. One day you'll be the leader of the elementals," Mikal taunts. The wolfish grin is back and I kind of want to slap him. Or kiss him? I'm not sure which.

"That's right, you bear responsibility to our people. I apologize for the suddenness of this information and wish to elaborate, but it's growing late. We must bring this conversation to a close shortly," Cade says.

"Fine, I'll let that go until tomorrow. I'm getting tired, anyway," I reply. A yawn escapes, emphasizing my statement. I battle with the weight of my eyelids. It takes more energy than I want to expend.

A princess, though? The leader of an entire race? I'm not ready for that. I just want a mechanic shop of my own and to live under the radar, far away from the step-monster.

Mikal speaks up, "Last question, please."

"I have so many I don't know which to ask next." My brain groggy, I'm straining to come up with something at the moment. "Wait, did you say last question? I still have two."

"No, you asked your second when Cade implied you were the heir to the throne," Mikal challenges and I realize he's right. I don't want to admit it though, so I ignore him.

I must spend too much time in my head because Mikal continues. Thank goodness he doesn't push me on being wrong. I am so not in the mood.

"Just pick one that will help you sleep tonight," Mikal says with a smirk that doesn't quite reach his eyes. I figure he knows I won't be getting much sleep, anyway.

"Well, who or what were those things in the alley?" I'm worried about the one that got away coming after us.

"I got this one," Mikal says, looking at Cade. "Those, my dear, are minor demons." When he sees my disbelief, he adds, "Yes, demons from Hell. When they get the chance to escape, they find a host body. Someone who doesn't have a lot of willpower like a drug addict or someone with a mental illness and they inhabit their body. The only way to send them back to Hell is to cut off the host's head."

"You mean you kill the host?" Hand on my chest, I think I am going to be sick.

"Is that your fourth question?" Mikal asks, amused at how that information has affected me and throwing a knowing jab in at the same time.

"Enough, Mikal. He derives pleasure from causing discomfort, a trait that seems to be ingrained in his genetic makeup," Cade states with authority, which makes me sit a little straighter in my seat. Mikal's smile vanishes and his demeanor mirrors that of a kicked puppy. In that moment, I feel bad for him, not too bad considering his cocky attitude, but a little.

"The host is already dead. The demons kill it and then use the body until the expiration date, or the time that the host would have died had it not been overtaken by the demon," Mikal states.

"You may ask one more question before we conclude our discussion for today. We can reconvene tomorrow," Cade finishes. I don't know if I can handle anymore tonight, but I appreciate Cade giving me the opportunity for another question. I go for something a little less creepy.

"Cade, what was it like being raised by our dad?"

"He is an honest man who cares greatly for the well-being of all races. He is a ruler first and a father second, though in his own way I believe he makes choices based on what he believes is best for us. A great deal of stress accompanies his position. When the time is right, you can meet him. He mentioned he would like to make your acquaintance." His hand moves to my shoulder, and he gives a small reassuring squeeze.

A smile pulls at the corner of my lips, but remember what I said about hope. She can be a fickle bitch. I want so badly to meet my real father, to live the fantasies I had as a child. That little girl was the apple of her father's eye, loved, cared for, and protected.

Passing over the newest question in my head, realm? - a word that has come up a couple times now. I turn and grab the smooth chrome handle, letting myself out of the car. I say my goodbyes and turn to head up to the apartment on my own to face Jake and Tara.

The burden of this information has me feeling a little uneasy in a much different way. I do not lie… hardly ever. I actually totally suck at it and never have I ever lied to either of them.

Right before I shut the door, Cade interrupts my thoughts and I realize he is still in the back seat. "Alayah, remember, you may not disclose this information to Jake or Tara. The danger associated with this information is grave."

Mikal chimes in, "The less they know, the better." With a wink, he reaches over and shuts the car door, leaving Cade to remain in the back seat. With an awkward little wave, I turn and hurry to the apartment building.

Grabbing the door handle, the metal cold against the palm of my hand, I shudder, throwing a quick glance over my shoulder. Mikal and Cade are still sitting in the parking lot having what looks like a very heated and animated conversation. Hands flying around, heads shaking. I don't have the energy to linger.

My legs shake as I climb the stairs to my brother's second-story apartment. Exhaustion is too small a word for what I am feeling at the moment. The adrenaline from the night must be wearing off. Sweat beads on my forehead and my hands shake as I open the apartment door with my spare key.

Two very curious faces block the entrance. Tara reaches out, touching my arms just as my vision blurs. "Are you okay?" is the last thing I hear as everything fades from view. My body hitting the floor hard.

CHAPTER EIGHT

I'M GOOD

~ALAYAH~

I can hear the glass breaking and little feet running through the house. A loud thunk reverberates through the rooms as Jake slips, and a cry of pain bounces from wall to wall. Pulling my teddy bear to my chest with one hand and the blanket over my head with the other, I try to block out the sounds.

It doesn't work. I hear his feet thump-thump-thumping on the stairs as he tries to make his way to his room. A door slams as he enters his bedroom, hoping to avoid the beating he knows is coming.

More pounding footsteps, angry footsteps, coming down the hall. I flinch. My feet hit the dingy carpet as I slide out from under the covers and race to my closet, legs shaking. The hangers squeak as I push the clothes aside. I need to hide; I need to be invisible. Pinching my eyes together, I pray quietly, "Dear lord, please make me invisible."

The toys make noise as I shuffle them around and I hold my breath for a moment. One toy at a time, I make a pyramid to surround myself and tuck myself into the smallest ball possible. Trying not to breathe too heavily, I count slowly backwards from one hundred, my slight frame shaking.

The words of an evil man drift down the hallway, "Jake, you little bastard, you can't hide in your room all night. Open the door or I'll break the damn thing down."

I can't hear a response from my brother, just a small whimper. He knows this is going to be bad, as do I. My limbs will not stop shaking and the tears running down my face burn with the intensity of the situation. Even though John's anger isn't directed towards me, I am scared for my brother.

Mom is no longer here, she died a few months ago, and there is no one to interfere with the beatings anymore. Not that she even tried in the last few years of her life, but at least there was hope that she would try. Now there is nothing but fear.

The door rattles as John tries to get into Jake's room. "Open the fucking door, you little shit. I can't believe you would leave the kitchen in such a mess." More rattling, and then John changes tactics, his voice much smoother and less angry, "Alright Jake, just open the door. If you come down and clean up, I won't be angry anymore."

Don't fall for his lies, Jake, I think to myself. He has used this before, but I hear a click as my trusting older brother unlocks the door and lets the evil into his room.

"Your fucking leg is bleeding all over my carpet, you little shit," John yells as he enters the room. The horrific screaming, why won't it just stop? Shrill, terrified screams fill my ears and they just won't stop.

A gasp rushes out of me as I wake. I can feel myself shaking from another nightmare, only these nightmares are actual memories and I can't get away from them. Strong hands are gripping my arms and the rough calluses against my skin tell me the one holding me, shaking me, is male. The scent of warmth and fresh cut grass surrounds me, calming my nerves.

"Stop!" I try, but cannot get the word out of my mouth. It sounds more like "sop" to my ringing ears.

My eyes, matted with tears, don't want to open. As I force them, I see Mikal with his lips turned down in genuine concern. It only lasts a second before he schools his features. With a lopsided grin, he comments, "Well, glad to see you're back in the world of the living and that ear piercing shrill of yours has stopped." That's when I realize the screaming from my dream that wouldn't stop was me.

A chorus of voices chime in around me, "Shut up, Mikal." The next thing I know, the warm rough skin that was gripping my arms is being pulled away and with it, the comforting scent. I feel a sadness creep through me at the loss of that warmth.

Tara and Jake move into view as a small smile graces my lips. A feeling of relief replaces the emptiness that had filled my chest as I see my brother's face. My arms react without conscious thought as they wind their way around his neck, causing me to sway, a bit dizzy.

"Easy there, A, you've had a long couple of days." Jake's hug tightens and loosens in an instant, but he keeps his hands on my back, steadying me. My eyes take in his appearance. His clothes are rumpled and lines of stress show around his eyes, but I don't notice any bruises or blood from my memory. A long, deep exhale passes through my lips, allowing the tension to leave my body. Once my evaluation is complete, I pause and slowly scan the room, moving from one face to another.

"Wait, what do you mean a long couple of days?" Huh? I focus on remembering what happened. The last memory I have is Tara's face and darkness. I glance past Jake towards the window and realize it's light outside. I must not have woken up all night.

"Ali, you were unconscious for two whole days. We didn't know what to do. I was so worried about you." The air of panic in Tara's voice is soul crushing even though I can tell she is trying hard to cover it up. "We called Cade and Mikal. They explained you were in shock and your body needed to... I think he said..."

"Reboot," Cade chimes in.

"Yes, reboot. It took you longer than my grandma's old computer. And that thing, let's just say it had to be one of the first ones ever made." Tara is rambling again, not only does she do that when she is drunk but also when she is worried.

I scan the room, noticing the pinched eyes and tight muscles. Concern is clear on the faces surrounding me. Everyone except Mikal that is. His nonchalant attitude shows as he pipes in, "Yeah, didn't expect it to take you so long to come to, but we knew it was just a matter of time."

"Mikal, stop acting like you weren't at her side almost every minute of the day since we called you." Oh no, now Tara is scolding him. I have to smirk at that.

"Whatever, I was not. I left plenty of times." Embarrassment is kinda cute on Mikal.

"Yeah, when you had to pee," Jake snarks. Everyone but Mikal laughs at that, including myself, but I can see this conversation is hurting his ego. It's eye-opening to his protective nature towards me. So, there's that. Kind of endearing, if I do say so myself.

Trying to give Mikal a break from the joke at his expense, I change the subject, "Okay, okay, so what happened while I was in la-la land for the past two days?"

"Tara and Jake will update you as Mikal and I have business endeavors to attend to." My heart sinks a little at Cade's words. The corner of Mikal's mouth twitches just slightly. I'm not sure if he's amused that I seem to be saddened by the fact they are leaving or, if he too, is feeling a little disheartened by the idea.

The jingle of Jakes keys breaks the silence, and he says a quick goodbye, letting us know he'll also be leaving. It's Monday, a workday for him.

Holy crap, it's Monday!

My heartbeat speeds up in a moment of panic. I have work tomorrow and there's no way I'll make it back. It'll take a few days to recuperate and frankly, I don't want to go home yet.

Wait, I am pretty much my own boss. I make my own hours. A quick call to the shop and I can reschedule this week's appointments. My heart slows and my muscles relax. Crisis averted.

Tara doesn't have a job to get back to and I don't mind staying here for now, instead of alone in that little old farmhouse.

I school my emotions and focus on spending a little girl time with my bestie. Much needed girl time. My fingers wrap around her wrist and I pull her down to sit beside me on the couch. Her landing isn't graceful and I bite the inside of my cheek to keep from laughing out loud. Lucky for me the guys didn't see that escapade.

A click echos down the hallway as the door closes behind the guys and I don't waste a second before drilling Tara with questions.

"What happened while I was out? Why didn't you take me to the hospital? How's it going with Jake? Is it just me, or is Mikal acting weird again? Why was Cade so quiet?"

"Ali, stop, one at a time. Plus, we have all day to talk. Your voice is scratchy from not being used. Let me get you some water." Tara is in mother hen mode, always looking out for my well-being. I know she won't answer me until she feels comfortable that I'm comfortable. Only then will she deal with the onslaught of questions, my anxiety, and the rest of my mental comfort.

She's not stubborn unless it comes to taking care of me, so in this scenario it's best to agree with her.

"You're right, a drink would be good, but then I want all the dirt." Watching me in a coma-like state for two days was hard for her. I can tell.

The water, cool in my hand, intensifies the sandpaper feeling on my tongue. I take a long drink. The wetness against my lips feels nice, but my stomach churns. Too much too fast. I lower the glass and concentrate on keeping the contents of my stomach down. When I lift the glass back to my lips, I sip the water instead. Jake would not appreciate me puking on his couch.

"First, we didn't bring you to the hospital because Jake called Cade and he told us not to," Tara continues, "They must have been close because they were back within minutes. They both seemed concerned about you, Mikal especially. I wasn't lying when I said he was by your side the whole time. It was a little over the top."

"It could be endearing? Maybe? He's kinda cute, you know," I say, trying to hide the blush that is coloring my cheeks.

"You mean gorgeous!" Tara interjects.

"Well, yeah, there's that," I laugh at her excitement. For the last year, she's been trying and failing to find me a boyfriend. The options in a small town are limited; unless I want to date Old Al at the diner or Rudy the mechanic. Well, I guess there's some potential with Rudy. At least he shares my love for cars. Most of the eligible bachelors my age went off to college. I didn't.

I stayed and worked. Every penny I made by working since I started my first job went into buying the farmhouse. Every penny I made after, went into my secret stash.

In the past, I hadn't had many boyfriends; not because the boys didn't ask. They did, but I had to turn them down because of the step-monster. He wasn't too keen on me having any freedom and I avoided revealing my home life to anyone. It was quite the balancing act, to say the least.

"So, what's going on between you and my brother?" Now it's Tara's turn to blush.

"Well, since you were on the couch and Mikal took up the floor beside you," Tara starts.

"Wait, WHAT?" My eyes shoot up to hers and my head tilts in question.

"Let me finish please," she looks at me with an eyebrow raised, waiting for me to interrupt again. I take my cue to be quiet and zip my lips in an over dramatic gesture.

A smile graces her face as she continues, "Mikal took up permanent residence beside you while you were out, which was odd since we all just met, but whatever, I guess. I stayed in your brother's room... with your brother." Her smile widens as the last words fall from her lips and I can tell she is falling for him.

"So, what's the dirt? Did you guys, you know, do the horizontal tango?" She covers her face and shakes her head as I continue, "Did you fuck like rabbits while I was out cold on the couch?" I give her a little push and smile as she peeks through her fingers.

"We did, and it was awesome. I think I'm in love! He is so gentle and caring in bed and there are times we go at it like rabbits." At that, I cover my ears and now it's Tara's turn to give me a little push. "You're the one that asked!"

"I know, but then I remembered we were talking about my brother and it got weird. It will take some time to adjust." I lean back and sigh, "And did you say times? Like plural? Mikal was here the whole time and I was only out for two days."

She bites her lip and gives me a sly smile. "This relationship is new and exciting. I think we've both been into each other for so long that we are making up for lost time. Plus, we were quiet when we were in the apartment, but his car has been christened, too."

"Oh geez," I say, exasperated, and then I give her a genuine smile, "I am thrilled for you. You're a good match."

"Thanks, Ali. I was worried about what you would think. One more thing and don't get mad. Jake and I talked about moving in together." The creases around her eyes and the way her fingers fidget show her concern at how I'll react.

"Tara, hun, that's awesome! But will you help me find an apartment in the neighborhood?" The smile of relief and the way her eyes light up is picture perfect. I have a moment where my anxiety takes hold. My chest tightens. The internal panic creeps up on me as I think about what I am going to do with my life. I take a deep breath and look at Tara; seeing how happy she is diffuses my anxiety. Everything will work out.

"Of course, I will." Throwing her arms around me, she adds, "I love you!"

"I love you, too. You're the best thing since sliced bread." We both laugh. "Goodness, I'm such a dork."

"Yeah, most of the time." Her teasing is endearing. "You asked about Cade, too. He was weird in the opposite way Mikal was, keeping his distance, coming and going and making a ton of phone calls. He seemed only slightly concerned, like he had knowledge of something we didn't."

She scans my face, looking for what I don't know. "Do you remember what happened the night you fainted? Like whatever happened before that overwhelmed you so much?"

Well, I remember a lot of stuff that I can't tell Tara right now; not until I have time to talk to Cade and Mikal. I have to give her something, though.

"I don't remember everything, but I remember a conversation with Cade before coming up to the apartment. Cade thinks I'm his sister."

A quick look of surprise passes over Tara's face. Then, she seems to contemplate my words and, with a nod, says, "You guys look a lot alike. I guess it could be true."

"He says he knows my real dad, and that I will meet him 'when the time is right'," I say, air quotes and all, trying to sound like Darth Vader.

"Right, so cryptic." Tara is still in thought when a loud BOOM shakes the apartment and interrupts her concentration. The vibration, like driving an old truck down a bumpy dirt road, has me off balance.

. I shield my face and in the same instance the windows shatter, sending pieces of glass flying through the room. Heart racing, I'm paralyzed. It's only for an instant, but in this case, an instant could get me killed. My mind is moving a million miles a minute, but the connection between my brain and my muscles is severed.

Tara grabs the back of my shirt, pulling me to the floor, just in time to miss getting very literally cut to pieces by the shrapnel.

Chapter Nine

Sooo Mature!

~Alayah~

When the glass stops falling, I peek out from under my arms. The same arms that are protecting my head, a very important part of my body, if I say so myself. What I see is a lot of dust in the air. The rays of light from the now shattered window reflect off the particles and draw my attention to how thick the air's become.

The smell of burning grass tickles my nose, followed by the much less pleasant smell of burning plastic. I cringe. A reminder that my farmhouse needs some work.

I draw my eyes to the floor and smile as the shards of glass sparkle like prisms in a window. My eyes follow the light dancing around the room.

Pretty!

Weird thing to be thinking after an explosion. Although a quick thought, it's one that seems a little out of place for the situation.

I gaze over at Tara after what seems like an eternity, but I'm sure is mere seconds. She is taking in the scene in the same childlike awe that I am. Her head bobs up and down like she heard me. I didn't think that to myself after all. The awe of the moment doesn't last long as the door to the apartment comes flying past the living room, hitting the wall at the end of the entry hall.

The apartment shakes from the force. We gasp in unison and Tara clutches my hand. I'm still too stunned to do anything. Tara doesn't get up, but her gaze scans the living room, landing on the spot where a door had been minutes ago. She must be in the same boat as me, stunned.

My eyes grow wide as two exceptionally tall men walk through the now completely open doorway. It seems the attire for this mission is riot gear, all black with helmets and a face shield. I have no clue what we've gotten ourselves into, but I know it has something to do with our mysterious new friends and my past.

"Alayah Rose Rawlings, we summon you. Please accompany us to the Master," one of them says in a robotic tone. His movements are stiff as he raises his arm and points directly at me.

"You busted down our door!" I shriek; so much for staying calm under pressure. I take a breath, gaining control of myself and continue, "I'm also going to assume you set off the explosion outside. The one that shot shards of glass at us at a really high speed. So, I'm going to pass. I don't think it's in my best interest to go with you."

The light from Tara's phone catches my eye and I see she has it behind her back, the screen glowing with a connected call to Cade.

I can feel the heat of a blush surfacing on my cheeks. Did he hear me freak out? Oh well, at least he will know what's happening. Smart girl, Tara.

Trying to get a little more information for him, I continued my conversation with the robotic men in front of me, "So who are you guys and why do I need to go with you?"

They advance and I put my hand up as if to say stop. They stop. Huh?

Their helmets turn in an almost synchronized movement as they face each other. Their eyes hold for a moment before they lock on me again. If I could guess the expressions beneath the tinted visors, I would say confusion. I mean, mainly because that is, in fact, what I am feeling at this moment.

"We are here to take you into custody on behalf of Master Mahoney." They take a step closer; I hold my hand up again. They stop. Soooo weird!

"And if I refuse your escort service?" I quirk my eyebrow in a curious challenge.

"Our instructions are to bring you in unharmed, but if we need to use methods of restraint, our instructions are to do so." He looks at my hand, still in the air, tries to take a step forward, but stays rooted in the same spot. He tilts his head, as perplexed as me. Why can't he move forward?

Weird, but it's working, and I may keep this conversation going long enough to allow Cade or Mikal to get to the apartment. Do I want them here? I don't want them getting hurt, but I also witnessed a glimpse of their abilities the other night. I think they're my best bet for not getting taken to some suspicious Masters' house.

"And again, I ask, who are you?" I hate when people ignore my questions. I wouldn't ask if I didn't want to know the answer.

"That's classified information. This conversation is over. Come with us now." His demand holds little meaning as long as he cannot get any closer to me. With my hand still raised, I cock my head at him in another challenge.

Just as I'm about to stick out my tongue and wiggle my fingers like a child, both men drop to the floor, shaking erratically, blue sparks emanating from their bodies. Tara and I jump, scooting backwards on the floor. Well, more of a crab crawl with our hands. Unlike Tara, I'm too focused on the sparks to look at where I'm putting my hands and end up cutting myself. Instantaneously, all hell breaks loose and I don't get the chance to assess the damage. Dang it, am I going to need stitches or will a bandaid suffice?

Cade, Mikal and another God-like man enter the apartment, each equipped with long cattle prods in their hands. Before Mikal and the new guy can reach down to grab the two men in black, both of them shoot up at lightning speed and tackle my unsuspecting self.

What. The. Fuck.

I thought I was in the clear. Pain shoots through my side, followed by a snap. Pretty sure that's a rib.

Those assholes broke my flippin' rib! They're going to pay for that when I can move because right now they're holding me down, uncomfortably secure. The man on top of me is no longer sporting his helmet, and what lies beneath has my hair standing on end.

Here goes another…what the fuck?

His pale white skin is translucent, with dark red veins pulsing just beneath the surface. There isn't a lick of hair on his head. Instead, black swirls run up his neck from under the collar of his shirt, wrapping around his ears and covering his scalp. In his mouth are four long pointed fangs which are working their way towards my exposed neck. My arms shake with the effort it takes to keep him away.

The worst has got to be his breath. My stomach rolls as the scent of roadkill wraps around me. Whatever he is, it's seriously creepy and I may have just peed myself a little.

Yep, that just happened.

Squirming like a mouse caught in a trap, I try my damnedest to get away from that nasty mouth and those fangs. It all seems to happen in slow motion. I notice the other guy is still wearing his helmet. His face is hidden, but it seems he is trying to avoid watching what's happening right in front of him.

Suddenly, there is a blast of that heavenly white light I have only ever seen once before in the alleyway. Right in front of my eyes, both the men in black disintegrate. Yes, they disintegrate and turn to ash right on top of me. Talk about gross! I think some may have gotten into my mouth.

Remember how I was trying to avoid puking in my brother's apartment? Well, that is an epic fail as I hurl all over the glass covered carpet. I just inhaled or ingested, whatever you want to call it. I just ate dead guy ashes! Who wouldn't puke?

Tara is by my side in a minute, being very cautious with all the glass scattered around us as to not also cut herself. At least one of us has the instinct of preservation.

In a moment she is wrapping my hand in a piece of cloth. I'm not sure where she got it, but I'm more concerned with what the hell just happened in my brother's apartment.

Jake is going to be so pissed. He loves his stuff probably more than he loves me if my childhood memories are accurate. *Focus Alayah!* I have to remind myself sometimes.

Something between a squeal and a laugh falls from my lips.

The new guy sets his sights on me and says, "I think she's in shock."

"No, she just found her inner dialogue amusing," Mikal pipes in with that knowing smirk. Either he can read my thoughts or he's extremely observant of my little quirks. After what I saw today, it wouldn't surprise me if the asshole *could* read my thoughts.

I focus on him as I shout it in my head... *ASSHOLE!* He smiles at me, a sexy wolfish grin that has me a little wet between the thighs (or it could just be because I peed myself). Ah shit, I need to go change clothes.

I wobble as I stand up. Much to my surprise, I find the three men are instantly at my side, trying to steady me.

"I've got this, guys. I'm fine." They seem extra protective today. Please don't let that be the new norm. I can't imagine having these men hovering over me all the time, suffocating me. On one hand, it's stoking my ego, but my independence is way more important.

As I excuse myself to go to the bathroom, I notice Mikal still has a grin on his face. One that I now realize is accentuated by a five o'clock shadow, giving definition to his broad jawline. Could he be any more sexy? Or any more irritating?

What a jerk!

I turn to shut the bathroom door and am stunned to see Cade standing there, about two seconds away from getting his nose smashed in by a very heavy wood slab.

"Shit. Sorry, Cade." Holding my chest I add, "You scared the crap out of me, didn't hear you coming."

"That is not the least bit surprising," Cade says with a grin.

What the hell is that supposed to mean?

"Did you need something?" I ask.

"We need to converse." His eyes hold mine for a long while. The colors swirl, which I have noticed happens when he is serious about something. And, as always, he's cryptic as hell.

"Right this minute, or can I change clothes and freshen up?" I rush to get the words out.

"It is of the utmost importance we learn all we can about the attack, but I can allow you time to freshen up. Please move swiftly. Time is of the essence." He must have seen my face shift to something resembling *are you fucking crazy* because he adds, "I mean, the longer we wait, the fewer clues we will find."

With that, I shut the door in his face and dig through my bag of clothes. What would someone wear to go on a witch hunt, or should I say, vampire hunt? That's what they were, right? I stare at my face in the mirror and it hits me. Those could have been actual vampires. I gasp a few times, hyperventilating, as my anxiety gets the better of me.

Splashing some cold water on my face, I try to steady my breathing. *I got this.* No reason to panic. *Breathe.* A small radio in the windowsill plays "Kill Bill" by SZA and I can't hold back the giggle that bubbles up inside of me. A messed up song to go with the messed up situation I just found myself in.

I pull on a pair of skinny jeans and a baby blue hoodie as I hear a light knock followed by Tara's comforting voice, "Ali, are you almost ready? The guys are getting anxious and Jake just got home. He wants to see that you're alive."

"Yes, I'll be out shortly," I say as I take another deep breath and compose myself.

"Just so you know, your brother is being a bit dramatic. He may be more concerned about the apartment than he is about you right now."

As I open the door meeting Tara's desperate face, I conclude…"It probably is the apartment. He's allergic to messes."

We both laugh, not because it's that funny, more because it's the truth.

I puff out my chest, "I got this."

With a shared smile, we return to the living room to confront the aftermath of what was probably our wildest day ever. I'm guessing it won't be the last one, though, and that both excites and scares the shit out of me.

What happened to my lonely, unimportant, and frankly boring life in my little farmhouse?

What I see when I turn the corner from the hallway to the living room has me back on high alert. Seemingly untouched by glass shards, Jake's face is pushed into the carpet, with a knee in his back.

And who does that knee belong to? None other than the new guy, whose name I haven't been told.

"What the heck is going on?" I walk over to the pair and push Mr. Tall-Dark-and-Extremely-Handsome as hard as I can to get him off my brother. He doesn't budge! Not even an inch and his dark eyes seem to pierce me right to my soul.

"Hey, doll, I'd appreciate if you kept your hands to yourself at least for the moment," he says with a raised eyebrow. A rumble, almost a growl, sounds from behind me. I don't need to turn to know who that came from, but I do and I see Cade with a hand pressed against Mikal's chest, gently holding him back.

"Hey, doll?" I spit back at him, "Who the hell are you and why the hell do you have my brother on the floor?" That arrogant little attitude is cute when coming from Mikal, but from this guy, not so much.

"Well, babe," that earns another dirty look from me and another low growl from behind me, "My name is Dante Divine. I am the fae king, and I'm here to help you become the queen you were born to be. I won't be able to do that if this bothersome little toad injures you because they destroyed his apartment."

Taking in what he just said through the anger I'm feeling is no simple task. Maybe that's why the shock of the statement doesn't really affect me, or maybe it is because I have now decided this guy is batshit.

"Are you f'ing with me?" I reply in a deadpan tone. I turn to Cade and Mikal, "Why did you bring this lunatic with you?"

Cade's eyes widen and his face pales. At the same time, Mikal's smirk grows into a full-on, sexy as hell smile.

Cade responds, "ALAYAH! Please consider your w ords..."

Dante laughs and replies, "I'm not fucking you yet, darling, but I could see how we might end up in that position."

My jaw drops and about two seconds later, in what seems to be slow motion, Mikal slams his fist into Dante's face.

There's a crunch and blood sprays the room. There's a collective gasp and then silence. No one so much as blinks as we wait to see what will happen. I, for one, am cheering internally because this guy just crossed a line. There is nothing I like more than for some douchebag to get put in his place. I still have to wonder why Cade seems so worried?

Dante snaps his head back to stare at Mikal. His teeth, coated in blood, turn into razor sharp daggers before my eyes. The beautiful white smile he flashed at me minutes ago is only a memory, replaced by something fresh out of a horror movie. His ears form points and his face shifts, causing the angles to sharpen. He is still stunning to look at, but his features change enough that I know I would shit myself if I ran into him in a dark alley.

Out of the corner of my eye I see Cade throw his hands up in resignation, hear him mutter something like "here we go again," and watch him walk out the door.

Mikal looks straight at Dante, not backing down an inch. "Don't talk to her like that again! Your Highness." The last two words are spat out with a resentment as thick as molasses.

Even Dante's voice is traumatizing when he says, "You will keep your hands off me or I will rip them from your body." He then turns to me and in an instant his face is back to normal, "I apologize, that was uncalled for, Princess." Mikal seems to relax and I just nod, not knowing what else to do in the moment.

Dante asks Jake if he has calmed down and with Jake's nodded response, he lets him go. Dante's eyes slide to Mikal one last time before he nods to the rest of us and says, "Princess, until we meet again." He gives a slight bow and the sound of his boots hitting the hallway tile is the last thing we hear before he is gone.

I take a step towards Mikal, placing a hand on his chest. His eyes meet mine and a heat consumes me. Flames licking my skin, causing my body to burn. I close my eyes and the heat dissipates as if it had never existed. The hard muscle under my hand tenses and then there is nothing but air. Mikal is gone.

Tara helps Jake off the floor and checks him over, rubbing his cheek where it's red from being pressed against the carpet. Our eyes meet and I realize they both look the way I'm feeling...like, what the fuck just happened? Again!

CHAPTER TEN

UNHOLY DAGGER

~ALAYAH~

"Cade, I don't think I need an escort to get my belongings from the farmhouse," I say with a roll of my eyes. We've been arguing about this for the last few hours.

Things have cooled down a little after the encounter at Jake's apartment two days ago. The apartment is unlivable at the moment, so Jake and Tara got a place together in a nicer neighborhood. With Tara getting a job at a local vet clinic, they can afford a two-bedroom unit.

They want me to stay with them, but Cade insisted I come live at the "Mansion," at least that's what I call it. A ten-bedroom, eleven-bathroom home about ten miles outside of the city on a thousand-acre wooded lot, set back in the woods a few miles, with a hidden driveway. You would have to know where it is to find it.

This place makes my little farmhouse look like a pebble compared to a beautiful mountain. And I'm not so sure I want to move in, but I concede. For now, I will pack up my belongings and stay with Cade, Mikal and the revolving door of guests they mentioned stay here on the regular. It's going to be hell for the girl who's used to living on her own in the middle of nowhere. Tara is the only person I ever invited to my house and now I can kiss walking around naked goodbye.

"Mikal's presence in this matter is essential. His cousins, Eddie and Pablo, will accompany you." Cade's voice is powerful, his shoulders square, and he's standing tall as he speaks. This is an argument I will not win. Aside from sneaking off in the middle of the night, I don't think the opportunity will arise for me to leave without an escort.

"Fine!" I say, stomping my foot like a child throwing a tantrum. Heat works its way up the back of my neck and I grind my teeth. I realize they want to keep me safe, but I dislike being told what to do. Of course, Mikal graces us with his presence at that very moment.

Chuckling, he says, "Well, isn't that becoming of the new little princess?" If he notices the glare I send his way, he doesn't give any outward indication.

"The boys are in the U-Haul and ready to go," Mikal states to Cade. His eyes turn in my direction, "And you, princess, will ride with me in the Jeep."

He extends a hand in my direction, curling his index finger in a come here gesture. I roll my eyes and address Cade.

"Cade, if he's going to act like a condescending asshole, you can find someone else to accompany me!" I say it even though I don't mean it.

I secretly want to spend six plus hours in a vehicle with Mikal. Not only am I into him, I still need answers. I want to know what they've been up to the last couple of days. They've both been busy. Busy avoiding me, at least.

"When you and your companions return, I will escort you to your new accommodations. One room is available. We reserve the two most luxurious rooms for our female guests. Given Cassie is the sole female occupant, you are fortunate. You will have the esteemed privilege of staying in the purple suite," Cade explains as we walk to the Jeep.

"I'm just guessing here, but is the room purple?" I snicker to myself.

"Indeed, but not in the way you may imagine. See for yourself upon your return," Cade replies.

"So who is Cassie?" I ask.

"Cassie, well, she's just Cassie. She is a little eccentric and purple isn't her cup of tea. In fact, whiskey and leather seem to be more in line with her style," Mikal pipes in and I watch Cade's face pull back in a grimace.

Mikal's usual smile turns into a scowl as he talks about her, and I wonder if there is some bad blood there.

"Don't fret, she keeps to herself." I notice the subject change as Cade adds, "You will have your own space. The Purple Suite is capacious."

"It will be perfect." I give Cade a reassuring smile, and make a note to google capacious. I realize Cade is worried I'll flee the first chance I get. But I'm just not sure why. I've taken this all in stride. As I duck into the passenger side of the Jeep, my eyes meet Cade's one more time before I turn my attention to Mikal.

"You ready to roll?" Mikal puts the Jeep in drive, not even waiting for me to buckle up.

"As ready as I'll ever be, I guess." My eyes grow big and I hurry to get my seatbelt on. The squealing tires add urgency to the task. I get thrust back into the leather seat as the Jeep lurches forward and I hope my neck won't be sore in the morning.

"Can we please make it there in one piece?" I gasp and my hands cover my face in an attempt to shield myself. When I peek through my fingers at the side mirror, I see that the U-Haul is right behind us. I guess Mikal isn't the only crazy driver. His cousins must have a death wish, too.

Mikal just smirks and glances at me out of the corner of his eye, "You'll be fine; I'm a skilled driver."

"Famous last words."

A mile out of the cities, I realize an anxiety attack could happen at any moment. As we barrel down I-94, my heart hammers in my chest and a thin layer of perspiration covers my forehead. I focus on inhaling and exhaling to halt the frantic beating. My knuckles are white where my fingers wrap around the "oh shit" handle. I tighten my grip with every lane change Mikal uses to get around "those slow assholes." Mikal's words, not mine.

"So why do we need your cousins with? I really don't have that much stuff that we need the extra help," talking through clenched teeth I reach out and turn the station on the stereo. While the tune is catchy, I don't like the message behind "Unholy."

"Honestly?" Mikal asks. I see his fingers twitch and his jaw clenches. I wonder if anyone has ever had the balls to touch his radio before? "Vampires attacked you, and while I'm an amazing fighter, who knows what they will throw at us now that they are aware of you? Not to mention they now know we are protecting you."

"Do you think they'll come back? I know Cade seems to be cautious, but I didn't think you were the type to worry." I need to get more information, so playing with his ego seems like a sure-fire way to get him to slip up and tell me something useful.

"It's unusual, but I take my job seriously. And as much as I don't want to worry about anyone extra, you've kind of grown on me. I wouldn't want to see you hurt." His expression is serious. "Plus, your brother would cut off my balls if anything happened to you." And there is that playful side of him I'm starting to love.

Wait, love? I meant like.

"What, don't you think you could take Jake down if need be? I thought you were oh so tough." I give him a sideways glance, hoping to rile him. I realize Mikal is talking about Cade, but I push a bit.

"That little runt, ha," he laughs, but covers it with a cough when he sees my face fall. "I meant Cade would make sure my life was hell if anything happened to you."

"So why am I in danger? Because before I met you guys, I felt pretty secure," I say, not really feeling the truth to my words.

"Did you?" he asks, "Because I would say you were a little worried about your stepdad getting out of jail. As you should be."

"Well, yeah, but only because he hates me for putting him there. Now vampires and God knows what else is after me." I still can't get over how creepy those two vampires were.

I see his hands tighten on the steering wheel, veins popping out with the pressure, and I can't say that doesn't make my lady bits tingle just a little. "Your stepdad is no ordinary man, Alayah. He is a demon, a high demon, and he controls those men you saw at the apartment along with the minor demons that were at the club."

"Wait what?" This is news to me. I mean, I knew he was crazy and evil, but a high demon? That sounds bad even though I don't understand for sure what it means.

"My guess is that he knew you were powerful and sought a relationship with your mom to keep tabs on you. Most supernatural races can feel power from others, to one degree or another. His ability would be more pronounced considering his status and your relation to the elemental king," Mikal says with a sigh.

"The elemental king? A high demon?" And the plot thickens...

"I shouldn't be telling you this without Cade here. It's definitely above my pay grade, but Cade chose not to come and you need answers." He runs his hand through his hair.

I wait patiently, making little circles on my thigh with my index finger.

"The elemental king, your father, is like the ruler of all rulers. The top dog that keeps all other supernatural's in line. Demons and vampires exist, which you now know. And, of course, that asshole Dante who is the fae king. But there are other races, too; witches and warlocks, pixies, elves, trolls and shifters like me." He glances at me, waiting for my reaction.

"Wait, you're a shifter? Like a werewolf?" I'm sure I look like a weirdo; my eyes have to be enormous right now.

"There are many kinds of shifters, just so you know werewolves do not exist, but wolf shifters do, and yes, I am one. There are bear shifters and birds, cats and pretty much any animal you can imagine. Along with some creatures that you wouldn't consider animals." He scrunches up his nose at that last comment, which has me wondering what could really disgust mister macho, but I figure that's a question for a different time. This is a lot of information to take in.

"So then, I'm an elemental? What is that?" I ask, wondering if I really want to know.

"Elementals are a lot like witches and warlocks. They can perform magic but also have control over the elements. There are air elementals, water, earth, fire, and spirit. Your family, though, is very special. They do not have an affinity for just one element. They can wield them all to some degree, along with the ability to cast spells." He exhales after that long explanation and waits for my next question which, of course, he knows is coming even after only knowing me for a few days.

"Wouldn't that make me only half elemental, though?" I have to be diluted; my mother was human.

"In theory, but we found out some interesting things while you were out cold. Your mother was part witch." I hold my hand up to stop him.

"Don't you think I would have known if my mother was a witch?" I ask, and my forehead scrunches in contemplation.

"No, because she didn't know. Humans raised her, not witches. She didn't have enough witch blood in her to make her aware that something was different, therefore you wouldn't have known either."

"So, I was right then. I am diluted? And does that make Jake part witch?" I say, my eyes glued to the side of Mikal's face. This conversation is getting good and I can't wait to hear more.

"Well, Jake would be a warlock, but his father was human. Your stepdad killed him from what we gathered and then charmed your mom into being with him. We believe your stepdad made your mom forget Jake's dad completely." There is a brief twitch in his jaw as he grinds his teeth together. Something I wouldn't have noticed if I wasn't so intently watching him. His frustration is obvious, but I'm not sure what part bothers him so much.

"Does Jake know?" I ask with my hand over my mouth. My chest tightens and I feel tears well in my eyes, but I hold them back.

Mikal slides his hand to my leg, just above the knee, and gives it a reassuring squeeze. My heart skips a beat.

"No, and we can't tell him, as the more he knows, the more danger he will be in." The intensity behind his eyes tells me that this is a very serious matter. "What we found out about you is the most intriguing, though."

His hand is still on my leg and I revel in the feeling of his thumb moving back and forth over the fabric of my jeans. It's comforting and thrilling. I try to stay focused on our conversation, but the movement continuously draws my attention.

"And what is that?" I'm not sure how much more I can absorb. I take a deep breath and wait for his reply.

"While you would think that you would be less powerful, the reverse is true. All elementals take on the characteristics and the powers of their father. So if the father is an elemental, even if the mother was human, the child is a full elemental. If the father was human and the mother was elemental, the child would be human as well. In your case, though, that small amount of witch blood could amp up your elemental powers. As the heir to the throne, you might be the most powerful elemental we have seen in thousands of years. Or possibly ever," he pauses so I can get a grasp on what he just said.

Disbelief clouds my mind, "But I don't have any powers."

"That's the thing, though. No one will know until you come of age. Male elementals get their powers at birth, but females do not get them until they turn nineteen. No one knows why that is, and most elementals grow up in our world with two elemental parents, so they train from the moment they are born. For girls, they are prepared for coming of age. In your case, we aren't sure what will happen, as most races do not intermix."

Okay, now I'm speechless. Talk about your world being flipped upside down numerous times in less than a week.

"Well, it seems you know an awful lot about me. What about you, Mikal? What is something that not that many people are privy to with you?" I ask, curious. I want to get to know this man better.

He turns towards me, drinking me in. His eyes trace up and down my body and my throat grows tight. The feel of his hand on my thigh is more pronounced than before, and I wonder if he will answer the question.

His tongue darts out to wet his lips and his adam's apple bobs. I follow the movements with interest and try not to squirm in my seat.

His voice is thick when he speaks, "Not only do I have a deep love for cars, I'm a pilot and own three planes. But I'm guessing you are looking for something deeper, aren't you?"

I nod.

"I am a writer, a poet, if you will." His gaze darts away from me.

Is he embarrassed?

"That's wonderful, Mikal. Can you recite one for me? One of your poems?" I ask as excitement runs through my body.

I wait while he contemplates. *Will he tell me no?* Slowly he begins, his voice a melody.

"Onto the dark shines a beacon, Out of the lonely midnight gloom. Flee creatures of the night, for an angelic power shines through.

Onto the dark shines a beacon. Evil speeds away. Leaving only peace and tranquility for the goddess of the day.

Onto the dark shines a beacon. Strong willed and pure of heart. Saving men from turmoil, capturing the souls that cannot depart.

As the chosen make amends and fulfill their destiny, the circle of life will be complete. The night becomes a long forgotten fantasy."

A tear tickles my cheek as it slips down my face. I turn to Mikal, my voice barely a whisper, "That was beautiful."

He clears his throat and nods, but doesn't say a word. A blush adorns his cheeks and I smile to myself. I doubt many people have heard one of his poems, and I'm elated that he would share something so personal with me.

Glancing up, I realize we are close to the exit that'll take us to my farmhouse. The time tells me it's only been a little under two hours of driving.

I raise an eyebrow at Mikal...

"How did we get here so fast?" I ask, astonished. "This drive should have taken at least another hour, if not more." I've been so involved in the conversation I lost track of the speed, the weaving in and out of traffic, and the near-death experiences that accompany Mikal's driving.

That wolfish grin is back. "Due to my impeccable driving skills, of course."

I shake my head and reply, "Of course!"

The sun shines through the leaves as we make our way down my driveway and I take a moment to enjoy the beauty. Looking in the side mirror, I realize that Mikal's cousins aren't behind us. "Where are Eddie and Pablo?"

Mikal smiles, "They couldn't keep up in the U-Haul. They'll be here shortly, though."

His eyes go to his hand, still on my leg, and he winks at me as he pulls it away. Emptiness creeps into my chest. *Why do I miss the feeling of his hand on me?*

I step out of the car and hear the gravel crunch under my shoes as they slip a little on the loose rocks. I raise my arms above my head and stretch out my muscles, realizing how tight they are from the drive. The country air smells divine. It's fresh, unlike the smog in the city. Even the air at the "Mansion" smells tainted from being so close to the suburbs.

The driver's side door is open and Mikal is still sitting in his seat with one foot on the ground outside the Jeep. He's on his phone, fingers moving at a rapid speed. He must be texting someone. I walk towards my house, but Mikal holds up a hand and says, "Alayah, you need to wait until I check the premises."

"Everything looks fine. Why would anyone be here?" Bewildered, I stop and look in his direction. I can see his eyes scanning the woods around my house.

"You can never be too careful and right now my job is to make sure you stay safe, so please let me do my job." He seems a little irritated with me, but I take another step forward, testing his resolve.

Out of the corner of my eye, I see him move in my direction. He walks right up to me, grabs my waist, and sets me down by the passenger side. He steps towards me, causing me to take an involuntary step backwards. My back presses up against the Jeep and his arms surround me.

With his hands on the Jeep behind my head, I am pinned in place. If I move, we'll be touching.

His voice is low as he says, "From the moment I laid eyes on you, I felt an irresistible urge to protect you. Not because it's my duty, but because you awakened a primal instinct in me."

Butterflies circle my stomach as he peers into my eyes. Our lips are inches apart. *Will he kiss me?* His right hand moves from the car to the back of my neck and he pauses. My breath catches in my throat.

What is he waiting for?

"I need to keep you safe, Alayah. More than I need air to breathe or the moon to run under," Mikal says, his silky words awakening a need in me, a need to taste his lips and feel the power of his wolf.

My gaze trails from his lips back up to his eyes, which must be all the incentive he needs. His mouth is on mine in an instant. His tongue caressing mine as my hands work their way under his shirt and over the hard muscles beneath it. I can feel his V as I run my fingers across the top of his jeans and he shivers, enjoying my touch.

Without warning, he jumps away from me, his head turning to look down the driveway.

"Eddie and Pablo are almost here." He runs a hand down his face and then turns back to me, "We can't let anyone know what just happened.

I take a step closer to him, tilting my head.

"That can't happen again. For both of our sakes. I'm sorry," he says, and it's as though a bucket of ice water gets dumped over my head.

I'm confused and embarrassment tints my cheeks.

I open my mouth to speak, but before I can get any words out, I see the U-Haul coming up the driveway. I want to walk away from Mikal and whatever just happened, but I figure I might as well stay put. I haven't met Eddie or Pablo yet.

The U-Haul pulls to a stop and a young boy gets out of the passenger seat. He couldn't be over sixteen and looks nothing like Mikal. The boy has a goofy grin on his face and, as he approaches with a little skip in his step, I have to smile to myself.

As the driver's door opens, it pulls my attention in that direction. In contrast to the boys' darker skin tone, the driver is Caucasian with blond hair that seems to gray at the edges. Of course it's hard to tell considering the lighter color. He has to be in his late thirties to early forties.

I turn to Mikal with a quizzical look, "Cousins, huh?"

"I'll fill you in later, but not by blood, by bond." He nods to Pablo as the young boy bounds up to us.

"Hi! You must be the princess, Alayah, is it? I'm Pablo. It's really exciting to meet you. Other than Cade, I haven't met any royals yet." He sticks his hand out to shake mine. I smile even bigger, shaking his hand. It's hard not to with all his bubbly energy.

Eddie appears beside Pablo, throws an arm around the boy and says, "Sorry about this one. He has little to no manners." He extends a hand, "Alayah, I'm Eddie and I am proud to make your acquaintance."

I can see Pablo flinch a little at that. "No problem at all, Pablo. Your upbeat attitude is contagious and I love it. Eddie, it is nice to meet you, too." Pablo's smile returns and Eddie nods in acknowledgment.

"Now that introductions are behind us, can we go check the house so Alayah can get in there and start packing?" Mikal is talking directly to Eddie, but before they move, his head swings towards Pablo, "Hey bud, can you stay out here with Alayah until Eddie and I give the all clear?"

Happy with his assignment, Pablo agrees and you can see his excitement as he bounces on the balls of his feet. It was a long car ride, though not long enough in my opinion. I still have things I want to discuss.

Eddie and Mikal head toward the house and I turn to Pablo, "So you and Mikal are cousins, huh?"

His smile drops just a little. "Well, not really. I don't know how much I can tell you," he seems to contemplate,

"I am part of his posse. I guess you could call it. Eddie found me in pretty awful shape about a year ago. A rouge... um man, had roughed me up pretty bad and left me for dead. If it wasn't for Eddie and Mikal, I probably would've been put down." He flinches a little at his words, "I mean, I would have died."

His fingers fidget with the hem of his shirt and he kicks rocks with the toe of his shoe. Not wanting to point out what he just said or spook him anymore, I reply, "Well, I am glad that Eddie found you then."

His eyes meet mine again and he seems to relax a little. "Me, too. He took me in and is teaching and training me. That's why I'm here, to learn what it means to be part of this 'family'." As he says the word family, his fingers lift into air quotes.

So definitely not blood cousins. He must be referring to the pack. I would assume they have a pack if they are wolves like Mikal.

Just as I'm about to ask Pablo another question, I see movement out of the corner of my eye deep in the woods. Nothing seems to be out of place as my attention draws in that direction. I take another few seconds to watch and listen.

Shrugging it off, I bring my focus back to Pablo just as I hear a whizzing past my ear. There is a glint of silver and a thunk as something imbeds itself into Pablo's shoulder.

My eyes widen at the blood oozing from the wounds made by a Raphael style dagger. My heart beats heavy in my chest. I only have milliseconds to think as the air surrounding us fills with a shrill scream of pain.

Chapter Eleven

DEMONS

~Alayah~

Pablo's eyes grow big with shock, looking at the dagger sticking out of his shoulder. I grab him and pull him to the ground just as another one goes flying past my head. Glancing back at the woods, I realize there is no way to make it to the cover of the house without getting skewered.

Between the trees, bodies of all shapes and sizes scurry and I don't have time to catalog the differences. I'm guessing these are demons with the jagged teeth and different colors of skin. By my count, there are over 50 beings and all of them are holding very sharp weapons.

I make a split-second decision and pull Pablo behind the Jeep. The metal bumper is hot against my hand. I peek around the side of the vehicle and shout Mikal's name with urgency. My voice stops the creepy demon things in their tracks. They cover their ears, some of them dropping their weapons.

Good to know. They don't like ear-splitting screams. Alayah - one, Demons - well, I guess they get at least one point, too, considering there is still a dagger sticking out of Pablo.

I'm contemplating whether I should pull it out. Tara could tell me, but she isn't here.

I hear a loud BANG as the door to the farmhouse crashes into the siding, drawing my attention. Two enormous wolves plow through the opening, leaving the screen door to sway back and forth on the one hinge that is still intact.

The larger wolf is a deep brown, the same color as Mikal's hair. The smaller yet still gigantic wolf has a sandy blond coat; that's Eddie. They are exquisite as they collide with the intruders. My eyes widen and my mouth hangs open at the ferocity they show, biting and tearing through demons like candy wrappers at Halloween. In a split second, half the demons are down. The other half retreat, trying to get away, but they fail miserably. I watch the powerful, lean muscle move under Mikal's thick fur. Amazing. The demons don't stand a chance. Mikal and Eddie are quick and precise, not letting a single one get away.

The lyrics to "Demons" by Imagine Dragons pop into my head.

"Those two can handle this," I say out loud. My gaze stays on the majestic wolves a split second longer before turning my head to check on Pablo. A gasp escapes when I see who's standing over him. My body shakes as recognition brings the horrors of my childhood to the front of my mind. I need to move.

I jump to my feet, shuffling backwards, hoping not only to get away from the step-monster, but to lead him away from Pablo. His eyes are closed and his skin is pale, but I can see the rise and fall of his chest. At least he's alive.

Lips pulling up in a creepy ass way, John drawls, "Alayah, dear, did you miss your daddy?"

Trying to keep my shaking to a minimum, I respond by spitting at him, "Stay the fuck away from me!"

"I would, Alayah, but I need you. You're instrumental in my plan to overtake the realms," he says stepping in my direction. I didn't realize he could get any creepier, but one minute he's a human standing about six feet tall and the next his body shifts, growing to over eight feet. Red scales cover his skin. A scorpion tail whips around behind him and he has a whole *Venom* thing going on with his face.

My eyes grow wide. I want to be anywhere but here, with him. The theme song from *Jaws* pops into my head and my heart beats to the tune.

His gaze flicks behind me. "Well, you little shit, it's time to go. It looks like those wolves of yours finished disposing of my distraction."

He reaches out too quick for me to move away and grabs my arm hard. The scales on his palm prickle as they connect with the soft skin on my forearm. A shiver runs down my spine. *This is not good.*

I pull hard against him, but it's no use. He has me and he isn't letting go.

The next thing I know, I'm spinning, surrounded by darkness and I can't tell up from down. I can feel my stomach pitch the way it does right before you lose your breakfast to the porcelain throne the morning after a long night of drinking.

The last thing I hear is the bloodcurdling sound of a wolf howling before I am suddenly standing in a room encased in stone. A musty smell accosts my nose, and the damp air feels chilly against my skin. There are shackles hanging from the wall and I lose my breath as I realize I am in a prison cell from the Middle Ages. *Man in the Iron Mask* style.

Standing in front of me is the step-monster, literally, in all his red scaly monster glory. His giant body fills a good portion of the room.

Still trying to get my bearings, I seethe, "Where did you take me, you scaly prick?" I'm shaking again, but not because I'm scarred. I'm pissed that this asshat is back in my life. Not sure where all my bravado comes from, I stand firm. "You have some nerve thinking you can get away with this shit, you psycho."

"I'd say watch your language and the way you speak to your elders, but I'm a little impressed. The scared kitten I left behind during my stint in jail has found her hiss and some claws," he snaps back at me. "You are in my home. Well, the prison below it, I guess. In the second ring of Hell." He spreads his arms wide and chuckles like it's a pleasant conversation between friends. *I think not.*

I move a few steps away from him, giving myself a better view of the room. The walls are old stone, the gray color blackened by mold. Dirt covers the floor, but stone peeks out in a few areas around the room, dashing my hope of digging a tunnel out of this cell. Behind John stands a metal door with a small window. It's no bigger than my fist.

I glance behind me, keeping most of my attention focused on the monster in front of me. The back of the room has three sets of chains hanging from the wall. I can see the remnants of bloodstains around the room, along with something green that I really don't want to know about. The musty smell is overwhelming and urine taints the air, making me want to gag. I bring my hand up, covering my mouth and nose for a moment. It doesn't help.

There is nothing else in here. Nothing I can use if he leaves me down here to die, that's for sure.

"Why am I here? And what do you mean Hell, like it's an actual place? What do you need me for?" My breath hitches a little. I think some of the adrenaline from earlier is wearing off, and I can't help but think about Pablo. I hope Mikal and Eddie got to him in time and that they are all okay.

His eyes watch me retreat and take in my assessment of the room. "So many questions coming from the little bitch of a child that barely said two words when I was around."

"Maybe that's because you're a fucking demon, both figuratively, and now I guess literally, too. You did everything you could to terrorize me. I never knew if what I was going to say would cause you to beat the ever-living crap out of me or my brother," the words come out in a rush.

"That little wuss is not your brother. You don't have a brother; you don't have a family. I am the only one who ever cared for you and everything I did, I did to make you tough. So you could survive this world long enough to fulfill my plans."

Is he just saying this to get under my skin, or does he not know about Cade? A hint of doubt sneaks into my mind, but I push it aside. I may not understand this world and what's going on, but my instincts tell me that Cade is very much my brother, my family.

"What plans might those be?" I ask, considering he didn't really answer me before.

He sneers at me, "All in good time. Enjoy the accommodations. You're going to be here for a while." Turning his back on me, he walks through the wall and is gone. Not out the door, which is closed, but through the freaking wall.

I run to the wall, hands feeling around for an invisible door, a weak spot, anything that would help me get out of this disgusting hole, but there is nothing. The stone is smooth in this area. I wonder if others have experienced the same. How many would have to rub their hands against the stone to make it smooth?

What the literal fuck!

This is just shit. I pound my fists against the wall. Pain reverberates through my arms with each strike, but I keep going until my hands are numb. I keep going until I numb the pain inside me and then I strike the wall one last time, just because.

Whose life is this? I'm stuck in a dungeon in Hell. Until a couple of weeks ago, there was no excitement in my life. I was a normal girl just living day to day, trying to make the best of the hand life dealt me. And now, I'm completely lost. I don't know who or what I am.

This place is nasty, but my legs are tired. They need to rest. Has it been minutes or hours since John walked out of here through the damn wall?

I still can't believe that happened, even after all I have seen. What a weird world this is.

How am I supposed to get out of here? I doubt anyone knows where I am. My phone is in my back pocket, but to my dismay, there is no service in Hell. No bars at all. I even tried calling 911, but it failed to go through.

Who would have thought? I snicker to myself.

At least, I can still find some humor in my messed up situation. The phone is a waste for now. My heart sinks as I turn it off, watching the colors fade to black. I need to conserve battery in case I get out and find my way back to…Earth? The Mortal Realm? I don't even know!

"Arrrrrrghhh!!!" The frustration spills from my lips.

Just when I am about to bite the bullet and sit on the nasty blood and piss covered floor, the lock on the door turns and it swings open.

I jump to the side quickly. *This may be my chance to get out.*

Before the person comes into view, I hear, "I wouldn't try anything if I were you. This is not your chance to get out of this cell. Even if you did, there isn't anywhere to go." The voice sounds so airy, like a spring breeze.

Wait what? I didn't say that out loud. Shocked into inaction, I stand there dumbfounded as a woman walks into the room. "You can leave through the open door, but you won't get far. Plus, you will not enjoy the punishment."

The only reason I believe this being is female, other than the sound of her voice, is the long purple hair cascading down her back. There are no determining features. She is beautiful. Although, it's a beauty that could also describe a feminine male. Her light blue skin glistens and contrasts with her eggplant-colored hair.

"Who are you?"

She looks me up and down. "I am Natash, and I will look after you while you are in the cells."

"How'd you end up stuck with prison detail, Nat?" I quirk. If I can get on her good side, maybe I'll figure out a way to escape this putrid hole.

Her eyes close until only slits remain. "Natash! I have a unique set of abilities, which makes me a suitable candidate for this job."

As she moves further into the room, I can see through the slit in the side of her romper. I thought it was just pants and a tucked in shirt, but it's one piece. The silver fabric looks out of place in this dingy dungeon. What interests me, though, is the metal glinting inside her pocket.

As I eye the dagger, her tone is icy. "I wouldn't take action on the thoughts swirling around in your mind."

"Can you read my mind?" I ask, a little astonished. But I'm even more astonished when she answers my question, in what seems to be an honest way.

"I can read minds. That is one of my many abilities, but I didn't need to read yours. You were thinking of going for my dagger. It's written all over your face," she tsks at me, "If you want to make it out alive, you need to work on… what do humans call it?" She lifts a slim finger to her lips in thought and then her eyes light up like a lightbulb just turned on. "Oh yes, work on your poker face."

Confused, I ask, "Why would you give me any advice that would help me?"

"Well, at one time I too was a prisoner here, and honestly, I still am. While I take my job seriously, I also understand your situation." A little of the tension recedes from her eyes and I decide to continue digging.

"Still a prisoner?" The longer I keep her talking, the more I can learn.

"Demar forced me into a blood oath." At the curious look on my face she adds, "I think you call him John or step monster." Her lip twitches up in the slightest smile, but as quick as it shows up, it is gone. "The oath keeps me from leaving until I fulfill my debt and I want to fulfill my debt so I can get back home."

Her eyes twitch, and I wonder if she believes her own words.

"Home? So, you're not from here?" My curiosity getting the best of me.

"Of course not. I am too beautiful and, as a royal of the fae court, I do not belong in Hell." She tucks her purple hair behind one ear so I can see the pointed tip. "I was born in Faery with my family. Although I have been here so long, I'm not sure what it will be like when I return."

Feeling she has given me so much, I decide to give her a little information as well. "Do you know Dante?" Her armor cracks a bit more and I smile internally.

"He is my cousin and the first in line to be king. How do you know that name?" Her voice is stony, but her eyes glisten with hope.

"He helped me with a situation, a friend of a friend, I guess you could call him. I've only interacted with him briefly, but he was well." I leave out the disrespectful comments he shot my way and how we didn't see eye to eye. She doesn't need to know about that. I only hope it helps her to know that someone she cares about is alive and well.

"How long have you been here?" I ask and watch as sadness replaces the hope.

"Long enough to know that I better get back upstairs before Demar finds us talking." She turns and grabs something outside the door. As her hands come into view, I see a bucket of soapy water and a tray of food.

Looking around, she must decide the cleanest place to set the tray is on top of the bucket.

She steps out of the door one more time and returns with a blanket and a jumpsuit similar to hers. Not as flashy, though. The drab brown does nothing for my skin tone. My face drops. I realize I'm a prisoner, but anything would be better than this shade of brown.

"Clean yourself up, eat and drink. I don't know when I can bring you anything more than bread and water after today." She schools her features into the stoic look she had when she first arrived. I wait as she exits, closing the door behind her. Just as it is about to latch, I hear the faintest whispered words of, "thank you!"

CHAPTER TWELVE

TALKING TO THE MOON

~MIKAL~

"Fuck!" I shout at the woods and out into the world. This cannot be happening. I watched the demon grab her, and then they were just gone. He used a portal, but it could have taken them anywhere. My guess, though, is he took her to Hell, where he's most powerful.

I run my fingers through my hair, tugging on it. Why did I kiss her? I can't get involved with the Princess. It's a death sentence.

Frustration is clawing at my insides, and I need to get moving before I destroy things.

My eyes find Eddie, where he is tending to Pablo. "Once he heals, I need you to pack up all of Alayah's things and bring them back to the estate."

Eddie's mouth opens, and I hold a hand up to stop him. I'm sure he wants to help search for Alayah, but there is no way I want to come back to this damn farmhouse.

"Eddie, that's an order. I need to get back. But first, I need to call Cade. The clean-up crew is on their way and they should be here within the hour to get rid of the bodies." It would be so much easier if demons just poofed into ash when you killed them, like vampires do.

"Make sure you get everything. Look for secret spaces where she may have hid things," I say, walking to my Jeep.

"Yes, boss, we'll take care of it. Pablo should be ready in about fifteen minutes. He's lost a lot of blood, but he's young, so he heals quickly." He glances over at the boy, who no longer has a dagger sticking out of his shoulder. We moved his unconscious body into the shade of a large oak tree.

Eddie's face remains calm as he checks the wound again. I take a moment to calm my racing heart. I hate giving Eddie orders. He is my family. Well, better than family because he is nothing like my father. He's kind and caring. He has a beautiful wife and two little boys, and he still took Pablo into his home. His heart is good and pure. The thought of that boy suffering tore at his soul.

Outside of our working relationship, he has been a mentor to me, less like cousins, I guess, and more like an uncle. While on the job, though, I'm in charge and I need to be professional. As does he.

"Perfect. When you are back, text me. I might need your help to follow any leads I come across." I nod to him and turn on my heel to leave. This has got to be the shittiest day ever. Cade is going to slaughter me for losing Alayah. I messed up, I seriously messed up!

Alayah's face pops into my head and the terror I saw in her eyes right before they disappeared. If I never see that look again, it will be too soon. That being said, I would give anything to see her again. To see she is safe and to hold her in my arms.

We have a connection, but I recognize it can't go anywhere. I am a sworn protector to the elemental crown, and they forbid us from getting involved with our charges.

She doesn't understand this yet, but when she has her awakening, suitors from all the different realms will come to court her. She will need to choose a husband, a king, to rule beside her.

This is an odd situation. She didn't receive elemental training, but Rorak, the King, had his reasons for it. His wife, Ivy, died in battle when Cade was a child and Rorak never remarried.

The line is strongest when passed down to a daughter, but Rorak didn't have a sister. The crown went to him as the eldest boy in the family. It's the first time this happened in over five thousand years and, while it wasn't unheard of, it wasn't ideal either. The Kingdom almost didn't make it through.

Rorak is smart though. He formed an alliance with the Shifters. My dad, being one of Rorak's most trusted advisors, agreed to tie us to the elementals as their protectors.

I push the thoughts aside as I get in the car and make the phone call I have been dreading. I don't even get time to breathe because Cade picks up on the first ring.

"Mikal, this better be good. You realize I have a meeting with the fae today?" Fuck my life. Cade is not a huge fan of the fae and diplomatic meetings make him edgy. I'm sure that since I punched Dante in the face, he is going to make any negotiations that much more difficult, just to prove a point.

"We ran into a minor problem." I take a deep breath, ready to get it over with.

Cade says, "What sort of minor problem, Mikal?" The way his voice drops low when he says my name is eerie, and I don't want to continue.

"Alayah is gone, Cade. That demon that's after her sent a hoard to this damn farmhouse. As Eddie and I were finishing the last of them, he popped up and sucked her into a portal with him." Wait for it....

"You will return promptly. Then, you will dedicate every waking hour to ensuring Alayah's safe return, or I assure you, I will dismantle you without hesitation, Mikal." And there it is, the threat I was waiting for. A laugh escapes my lips and I cover it with a cough. The more pissed off Cade is, the more normal he speaks. He will not gut me, but he's upset.

"I'm headed back right now, Cade. I sure wish wolves could make portals. It would save a shit-ton of time, but since I have to drive, it will probably take me an hour." I glance at the clock. It's only been twenty minutes since the demon took her, but that's twenty minutes too long.

"Assuming I can successfully negotiate with these arrogant fae, I will meet you at the estate within the hour." Not wasting any time, he hangs up the phone and I hear silence.

I pull up to the estate, the pristine white siding reflecting the light of the sun. It's blinding but beautiful. Beautiful like Alayah's hair.

STOP! I cover my face with my hands and rub roughly. I need to get a grip. I am in charge of her safety, not her heart. *Head in the game.*

Luckily, I made it back in record time, but now the tough shit begins. I lean my head against the steering wheel, needing a moment to compose myself before facing the problems that stand before me.

I slam my fist hard into the dashboard. "Fuck!" I yell to nobody and to the universe. And then I rub the dashboard where there is now a fist sized dent while apologizing to my poor baby. The Jeep didn't deserve that.

I can just see the disapproval written all over Alayah's face. She loves cars more than me. I smile to myself because if that isn't sexy, I don't know what is.

Gathering my courage, I step out of the car and shut the door. The first person I see when I enter the estate is Cassie.

"Hey Cassie," I say, trying to be polite.

"Fuck off, Mikal," she responds while flipping me the bird. Cassie is a badass and if it wasn't for her screw-the-world attitude, she would be pretty good looking. But she hates everyone and everything. She is so over the top negative, and that really is a turnoff. Her blue-gray eyes, black pixy cut hair, black attire and tattoos might do it for some guys, but it's not my type. Not like the pretty blond I want warming my bed at night.

Not to mention Cassie hates me. I never understood why, but I would guess I remind her of someone from her past, and from what I understand, that past is full of pain and betrayal.

"I'll be in the office making phone calls. A demon took Alayah, so if you would like to help, I would appreciate it," I throw the words over my shoulder and keep walking.

"Why on Earth would I help you? And for some chick I have never even met. She means nothing to me." The disdain dripping from her lips disgusts me, and I turn on her.

"I get that you only care about you, but Alayah is a good person, and she doesn't deserve to be at the mercy of a demon; most likely being held and tortured somewhere in the depths of Hell. So, if you can find a little spec of light in that black heart of yours, we can use all the help we can get." My body is shaking as I continue, "Otherwise, go on doing whatever you do all day, like slaughtering puppies or putting the fear of God in little children. I don't care, just stop being such a bitch!"

My breath comes out in quick gasps and I can feel the heat on my face. I'm sure I am red with anger. I'm mad and scared, but I try to calm myself because I don't like to be an ass. That is exactly what I am doing right now.

Cassie looks a little taken aback with her mouth gaping open. Mostly, we just let her be herself and keep a wide berth. She closes her mouth and then astonishes me when she says, "You think they took her to Hell?"

I can't read her. Other than knowing she had a shitty past and needed a place to stay for a while, like most of the supernaturals we offer a haven to, I don't know that much about her. I can smell the fear on her, though. The slight change in her earthy scent that has me thinking I hit a chord.

"Yes, I do," I say.

"I spent most of my childhood as a prisoner there." She looks forlorn as she continues, "Did you see who took her? I might actually be of help."

"It was her stepdad who she calls John, but I don't know what his demon name is. I got to see his demon form before they vanished into a portal. Big red scaly fucker with a mouth full of teeth taking up half his face," I shiver as the memory hits me. My wolf pushes to the surface, ready for a fight and, with how exhausted I am, it's a struggle to keep him at bay.

Cassie's eyes widen a little and her body tenses. She can see my wolf as my eyes change and my fists clench. Little sparks of magic flit across her fingertips. She is preparing to protect herself in case I go full wolf. I take a deep breath and rein in my wolf. Cassie relaxes.

"If he could make a portal, he must be powerful." Her forehead creases and she says, "High demon?"

In unison, I say, "He's a high demon."

That gets a quirk of her lips. "Jinx!" she says, and I pause. Dammit, she got me and even though it's a child's game, I don't speak. Maybe there is more to Cassie than meets the eye. At least for now, I think she might help.

"There is only one high demon who might fit that description. He wasn't around much when I was there, but he worked with Master Mahoney," she says and pauses in thought. "You said her stepdad, right?"

I look at her with my eyebrow raised.

"Oh right, Mikal, you can speak now." And she laughs to herself, not a sound that she lets out often.

"Yes," I say, simply.

"It might just be him if he spent most of his time in this realm. That could explain why I didn't see him in Hell often. His name was Demar, and he was an evil son of a bitch." I can see her twitch as a shiver runs down her body.

"Aren't they all?" I quip.

"Not all but most, yes." Cassie's eyes go a little blank and I can only assume she is reliving a memory from her past.

"Hey Cassie, do you have any way to find out where they might be?" I question.

"I have a few connections, but it will cost you. I don't do shit for free and these aren't beings that I would purposely get back on the radar of without it being worth my while." Her poker face is in place, waiting for my reply.

I agree to make it worth her while. The fact that she is staying here for free doesn't get past my radar, but I keep that to myself.

We expect most of the supernaturals who stay here to contribute in some way, but Cade has a soft spot for Cassie. He hasn't asked a thing of her. I don't know if it's the fact she is a witch (and a powerful one at that), if he fears her, or if he just has a soft spot for the hardships the girl faced. Nonetheless, he has left her to her own devices.

Maybe, just maybe, this will give her motivation to contribute.

"Cassie, can you make a portal if we find out where Alayah is?" I hold my breath, knowing it's a long shot.

Her head gives a little shake. "I am strongest in Offensive Magic. Portals have never been my forte."

"I will have to talk to Cade then. I know he can do it if we can't find anyone else, but it will cause a lot of political problems for him, so I would like to avoid it if I can." This is going to be tough and the longer Alayah is gone, the more damage that can be done. I let out an exasperated sigh.

"I have a friend." My eyebrow lifts. "Yes, Mikal, I know I'm a bitch, but I have friends. Anyway, I have a friend who might get us in under the radar." She grabs for her phone.

"Us?" I question.

"Well, you know I love a good fight. Killing demons sounds like a fun afternoon activity to me." Her smile doesn't quite reach her eyes and I feel it is all bravado, but I let her spin her tale the way she wants.

"Okay, you call your contacts and I will call mine. Let me know what you find out." I turn toward the hall that will take me to the office.

"Mikal, I hope Alayah is okay," Cassie says with what seems to be genuine care.

"Me too, Cassie, me too."

CHAPTER THIRTEEN

BLINDED BY THE LIGHT

~ALAYAH~

Alone again, I eye the bucket of soapy water topped with food. I take Natash's advice and decide to eat first. The sandwich isn't grand, but it is full of meat. It's light in color, like chicken.

Do they have chickens in Hell? A question for another time, I suppose.

The tray contains something that is yellow and prickly, *pineapple*? When I take a bite, it tastes more like a raspberry. The juice is warm as it drips down my chin. It's delicious, but if there is one thing that bothers the hell out of me, pun intended, it's being sticky. As soon as I finish the fruit, I dip my hands into the water and rinse my face.

The last item on the tray is a glass of water. The glass is cool against my lips. I take a few gulps, not realizing how thirsty I am.

Blah, not water. Coughing, I try to spit it out. The thick sweet drink catches me by surprise. As it flows down my throat, I notice my thoughts become more clear and the aches in my muscles recede.

I wonder what this cool liquid might be. Whatever it is, I am thankful for it now, knowing that I am going to need all the energy I can get to survive my capture and to find a way out.

I strip off my sweaty clothes and reach my hand into the bucket. Bubbles tickle my skin and the warmth of the water relaxes me. The washcloth is soothing, and the way the water darkens with each dunk in the bucket satisfies my need to get clean.

A sudden chill runs from the top of my head, all the way to the tips of my toes. I wonder if there are cameras down here. Everything seems so old, but I get a creepy suspicion someone is watching me, which makes the hairs on the back of my neck stand up.

I'm not a modest person per se, but I also don't like the idea of being vulnerable. Being naked with an audience definitely makes me feel vulnerable.

It's like all those dreams I had in elementary school, you know the ones, where you get to school and you realize everyone is pointing and laughing. When you look down, you see you are in your underwear. Consumed with shock and embarrassment, you wake up breathing hard with tears running down your face.

I wash quicker, not giving myself the opportunity to enjoy the warmth of the water running down my skin, and decide to get dressed before washing my hair. Usually, I would wash my hair first. It's a habit, but with only a bucket of water to work with and a nagging feeling that someone is watching me, I decide my body is more important at the moment. If my hair doesn't get washed, I will just have to tie it up in a ponytail and deal with it.

My fingers touch the romper as voices float down the hall, not too far from my cell. Hurrying to get it on, I realize I forgot underwear. There don't seem to be any fresh ones and my old ones are gross from sweat, so I guess I am going commando for the unforeseeable future. I grab my bra and sniff. It will have to do. I race to finish dressing. Just as I get the zipper up, the lock turns on the door again.

I nudge the bucket, tray and my dirty clothes into the corner as faces come into view. First is Natash, her eyes downcast and mouth tilted in a frown.

Next is John, or I guess Demar is what I should refer to him as. Unlike Natash, he has a wide grin, or so it seems, on that enormous mouth of his. He claps his hands like a child at Christmas and his joy sends a chill down my spine. If I learned anything while living with him for all those years, when he is happy, it's just as bad, if not worse, than when he is mad.

"Alayah, Alayah, Alayah, we are going to have some fun!" His glee is traumatizing.

And just like that, I am back in another memory.

"Maryann, I'm home and I picked us up the best supper." Jake and I are sitting at the kitchen table. Jake's working on his first-grade homework and I'm coloring a rainbow for mom as John walks in the front door, his eyes radiating joy.

"Oh John, you're home early. What did you get us? I was going to make spaghetti but I haven't started yet. It's not too late to make the change." I notice the tension in my mother. The way the skin crinkles at the edges of her eyes and mouth, but I can tell she's trying to hide it. A forced smile graces her face as she greets him walking through the kitchen door.

John's smile widens as he pulls the dead, partially squished raccoon from behind his back and watches to see our reaction. The smell wafts in my direction and it's rancid, the fur hanging off in patches. Mother covers her mouth in shock at the same time Jake covers his nose and I gag.

"John, is this some kind of joke? Get that disgusting thing out of here," Mom squeals as she backs away.

This is the first time we really get to see the evil that is John. As his eyes narrow a little, he states, "Maryann, you will cook this raccoon for you and the children or I will shove it raw down your ungrateful throats."

"You can't expect us to eat that. It will make us sick if not kill us," Mom gasps.

John's smile returns, enjoying the worry in my mother's voice, as he says simply, "You will do it and you will enjoy it."

Throwing the disgusting creature on the table in front of us, John grabs a beer out of the fridge and recedes to the garage.

I shiver with fear as mom picks up the dirty raccoon. She walks it outside and through the tiny kitchen window, my brother and I watch her throw in the woods behind the house.

Half an hour later, I twist my fork into the noodles on my plate and take my first bite of spaghetti. As I swallow, I tip my chin to the ceiling and thank the lord for my meal. Then, I plead with him to keep John from coming back into the house.

I realize the lord must not have heard my prayer when John returns from the garage, stumbling, a few hours later. His attention catches on the plates of spaghetti next to the sink, and his anger takes over.

His rage is worse than I have ever seen. Jake and I put ourselves to bed, just to stay out of John's way. Even with our ears covered, we can hear our mother's screams echoing through the house.

My eyes focus again as I am pulled out of the memory and back to the reality of the present moment. I hate the monster staring at me and want nothing more than to end his miserable existence, but I have no misgivings that I'm prepared to take him on.

I decide I am going to do everything in my power to prepare, so one day, sooner rather than later, I can stop him. Stop him from hurting innocent people, from haunting my nightmares, and stop him from breathing...in the most painful way possible.

I can feel that anger welling up inside of me as an almost overwhelming heat builds in my chest. The pain and fear I have felt my whole life adding to the anger and, as he takes a step closer to me, the smile growing wider on his face.

I explode.

As if I willed my urge to stop him into existence, a glowing light flashes from my body, similar to what I saw in the alleyway with Cade, but blue.

Natash's eyes widen with astonishment as I throw her and Demar back into the wall. Looking at my hands raised out in front of me, I gasp, not sure what the hell just happened.

Mesmerized by my skin, which is glowing like someone just lit a lightbulb inside of me, I take a few seconds to regain my composure. And those few seconds are a few seconds too long because John is back on his feet.

The rage I expect to see on his face is non-existent as he lets out a horrendous roar of laughter.

"Alayah, that was impressive. Uncontrolled but impressive nonetheless. I am excited to see what other powers you have." Looking over at Natash, he adds, "The pina fruit and the faery nectar seem to have done the job in starting her awakening before her enlightenment. Fabulous!" He claps his hands together and my head turns toward Natash. As soon as I glance that way, she drops her eyes to the floor.

I want to say she betrayed me, but what do I know of her situation? The ten minutes we spent talking earlier didn't really make us besties. The fact she won't look at me gives me the feeling that she might have regrets or, at the very least, she feels guilty. I can work with that.

"Well, it's a bit of a disappointment that I didn't have to beat it out of you. That would have been way more fun, but for today I will leave you with this," he says and his hand whips out from behind his back. A book the size of a tablet sails through the air to my right. I try to grab it, but it slips through my fingers. Dust plumes as it hits the floor.

My reflexes are slow after all the energy I lost doing whatever it is I just did. Not only that, but I can't help but stare at the two of them, a little perplexed since I'm seeing something I have never seen before. There is a haze around each of them. Colors dancing around them, following their movements.

Black surrounds Natash, and my heart hurts a little. What does it mean? Is black bad? Evil?

My attention shifts to Demar, who's wrapped in forest green. It wafts out from his skin and gradually turns to a dull red at the edges.

What do the colors mean? I don't have time to figure this out right now, so I am going to table it. Another thing to figure out later. I let out a breath I didn't know I was holding and the air whistles as it passes through my lips.

"Yeah, Natash, I don't think we have to worry too much about her being a threat, as she clearly doesn't know what she did or how to fight." Looking at me side eyed he says, "Maybe if you cooperate, we can teach you, but for now you will stay here with the filth." With that, he disappears down the hallway.

Natash steps forward, a mask of indifference back on her face. "He won't teach you anything that will help you. Not until he can fully control you and use you for his plans."

"What plans?" I question.

"World domination, power, control. The usual villain stuff." She looks me up and down. "If you want to fight, I will help you, but in return, you will get me out of here. I'm ready to go back to my people."

I open my mouth to speak, but she cuts me off. "It will not be an effortless task. Demar has bound me by a blood oath, and it is difficult to break. Kill him to free me."

"It will be my pleasure, Nat. I have been longing for that for many years." I'm sure she can hear the hate in my voice as I say the words.

"You and so many others, Laya." She smiles.

I notice the nickname and the corners of my lips turn up.

"Read the book he gave you. It won't be all that helpful since he wants to keep you in the dark for now, but there may be a few scraps of information you can use." She starts towards the door, "I will do my best to get you more information and sneak down here to train you. It will be difficult and we will need to be careful. We are only alive because of our worth to his cause. If the benefits don't outweigh the hassles, he will end us."

I nod in understanding.

"Nat, what did you see when that burst of power came out of me?" I ask, trying to make sense of what is happening to me.

"What do you mean? I saw nothing other than you lifting your hands and the look of determination on your face." Her lips pull to the side and her eyebrows pinch together.

"No burst of light or anything like that? Does my skin look different to you?" I question, looking down at the glow I can still see.

"No," she states, shaking her head briefly, "Why? Did you see something?"

There's a nagging feeling in the pit of my stomach that's telling me to keep this to myself. That, coupled with not knowing if I can truly trust Nat, I decide to play it off for the time being. "No, it just felt so powerful and I certainly feel like electricity is prickling over my skin. I just wanted to make sure nothing else was going on."

"Ah, well, that was a large burst of power that you are feeling for the first time, so I'm sure it has some lingering effects," she says as she takes another step away from me. "One more thing, Alayah, he knows you are powerful, but he doesn't know you are from the royal line. A princess no less and the future ruler of the throne. It is in everyone's best interest that he doesn't find out."

Quick as a flash, she pulls the dagger from her pocket and it goes flying past my head. I can feel a dribble of warmth run down my ear and as I pull my hand away, I see the blood adorning my fingertips.

My head swings back and forth between her and the wall behind my head. The dagger is stuck in the wall run through a massive cockroach. It's the size of my fist. I give a girly little squeal as I shake the disgusting feeling away.

Just as I step towards the wall to grab the dagger, it disappears and I hear a crunch as the cockroach hits the stone floor.

Nat sends a wink and a "You're Welcome" at me as she exits.

I pull the blanket out and sit down. The rough fabric scratches at my exposed skin, but it's better than the floor, I suppose. I miss the cozy blankets I have at home, especially the black and gray leopard print blanket that sits in my favorite reading chair. A sigh works its way from my lips and I swallow the lump in my throat. My hand wraps around the book Demar left, but I can't look at it yet. I have to catch my bearings. I tilt my head back against the cool stone wall. How am I supposed to get any sleep after seeing that mammoth cockroach? My cheek brushes against my shoulder as I try to shrug off the heebie-jeebies.

Chapter Fourteen

SHE'S GONE

~Alayah~

I am pulled from a deep sleep by scraping outside my cell. As I open my eyes, I realize it is dark, darker than usual. The only light is a sliver coming from the small window of the cell door and a slight glow from my skin that it seems only I can see.

I sit up, wiping drool from the corner of my mouth and down my neck. Unsure where that came from because my mouth is as dry as the desert in a drought. I move to stretch as the light from the door vanishes and a rough gravelly voice says, "I realize I'm a looker, but the drool might be overkill!"

As the door creaks open, a ray of light illuminates a creature no taller than two feet. It's just a silhouette against the dim light from the hall. Shadows cover its face, but I can make out deep wrinkles between flaps of skin, almost like a Shar-Pei. Its arms are long and clawed hands drag against the floor. The sound is like nails on a chalkboard, making me shudder. And similar to Nat and Demar, it has a haze around it, but the haze is yellow. I blink my eyes a few times, wondering if it is some sort of reflection of light from behind the creature, but when the creature moves, the haze moves with it.

The creature isn't exactly ugly, or maybe it's so ugly it's almost cute. I push myself up and scoot back until my shoulders press tight against the wall.

"Who are you?" I ask.

"Oh lovely, lonely girl, I am Gruffandorf," he says, tilting his head to the side. "My friends call me Gruff and my foes, well they don't live long enough to call me much of anything."

I snicker at his words, but the look he sends my way when he asks me, "*Are you friend or foe?*" has me reeling a bit. He looks dead serious. There's not a tick or a quirk of his mouth to show that it was a joke.

"If those are my options, I will definitely go with friend. But I should ask you the same thing. Are you friend to me or foe, Gruff?" His name seems funny falling from my lips and I say it again under my breath, just to test it out.

Gruff springs up and grabs the top of the door with one of his long arms. He hums, a deep gravelly sound and it takes me a minute to catch the tune. He twirls through the light. I see how his gray skin shimmers like a granite countertop when the sun hits it just right, and I am in awe of the beauty. There is a beauty in everything if you pay attention. The yellow haze around him doesn't seem to change as he moves, though.

"Ain't No Sunshine," I say tapping my lips.

He nods his head and keeps humming.

Speaking of the sun, I miss it. I miss the warmth on my skin as I sunbathe on my deck with my favorite book. My shoulders fall and I realize that won't be happening again for a while, considering the circumstances.

"Poor radiant, relevant child, I am a friend. At least as close to a friend as you will find in this realm." My eyes snap to his black orbs. He continues doing a one armed pull-up as he talks, "Natash sent me. The high demon does not know I am here. He is busy in the mortal realm right now, looking for a warlock. A special warlock who knows not of his linage. Similar to your situation, I assume. Since that ghastly demon cannot sense me, we should have some time to train you."

Demar is gone for now. *Do I trust Gruff?* I stare at him as I question myself. I realize I ponder his words too long when he raises his voice and berates me.

"Stand child, you will not be much use sitting on the floor." He drops from the door frame and moves closer.

I rise, stepping back a few inches. I'm not sure how close I want to be to him just yet.

"Aren't you a demon? I thought Demar could sense all the demons in this ring of Hell?" I ask.

"Shhh! You crazy, curious child, we do not speak that name in my presence. I am not a foul demon. I am a noble troll," he exclaims, puffing up his chest like a proud peacock.

I snort, "Um, you're tiny. I thought trolls were supposed to be gigantic creatures living under bridges and eating children." As his face falls, I do my best to hold in another laugh and cover my mouth with my hand.

"Well, you thought wrong, my dear, ill-mannered, impolite lass. You do not seem to understand all that much about this world," he says, crossing his long boney arms.

"I'm sorry Gruff, I didn't mean to offend you. You're right, I have no clue about any of this!" Guilt churns my stomach. "Will you please forgive me and help me learn?"

"First lesson," he says, holding out one clawed finger, "Do not insult those who can kill you quicker than you can say *I'm sorry!*"

And out of nowhere, something shiny flies past my head and hits the wall right beside me. Astonished, I look at the wall. The glint of a dagger catches my eye and I throw my hands up in the air.

"What is with everyone I meet here throwing daggers at my head?" I shout.

"Well, girl, now I know we will have to work hard to hone your reflexes. You seem to have none." Gruff doesn't look impressed.

"What?" I ask, a little put out.

"None, nada, zero, zilch. You have no reflexes!" he shouts, arms flailing around.

"Well, to my defense, I wasn't expecting you to throw a godforsaken dagger at me within ten minutes of meeting you, FRIEND!" I exaggerated the word on purpose.

"Second lesson for today: always be on alert and expect the unexpected," he says with his hands resting on his hips like an old nursemaid. The position looks weird, considering his arms are almost as long as his body. "Now grab the dagger and throw it at me!"

Under my breath I say, "Well, you asked for it."

The dagger is stuck in the wall pretty darn good. I grip the leather wrapped hilt and pull. My hand slides off. I try again, pulling harder than I intended, making my movements sloppy. Further proving Gruff's point about my reflexes I'm sure.

I turn and, out of the corner of my eye, catch his position. The weirdest thing happens as I complete my turn to throw the dagger. Time slows. I can see Gruff's muscles flex from the angle he is standing. I just know he is going to move to the right and mid throw, I adjust. He moves to the right just as I expected and, as the dagger is about to pierce his heart, he grabs it out of the air.

"My fragile, fumbling child, it seems you have some tricks up your sleeve after all," he says. The sound of clapping echoes through the small space and I smile. Gruff does a little jig, hopping from one foot to the other.

Again, I laugh at him. He just looks so whimsical with his skin rolls flapping up and down. I think he smiles back before he quits hopping and asks, "So how did you know I was going to move to the right?"

"I'm not sure. As I went to throw the dagger, time slowed and I could see you were readying yourself to move out of the way. I adjusted accordingly," the words spill from my lips and I shrug.

"So, you do indeed have some skill hidden under all the damsel in distress vibes you're putting off," he says as his eyes trail from the top of my head to my feet. He circles around me and his eyes meet mine again. His head bobs once in acknowledgement, almost as if I might impress him.

And then I open my mouth, "I'm not sure how that happened."

His approving look dissipates, "I'm sure we can work with whatever that was."

Gruff tosses the dagger back at me hilt first and I catch it, barely bobbling it at all. I smile to myself. I'm already making improvements.

What seems like hours of training later, my arms are like jelly as Gruff tells me for the millionth time to throw the dagger. As it hits the wall and falls to the floor, also for the millionth time, I stomp my foot like an irritated toddler. I've been doing that a lot lately. Am I going to need therapy after this?

Gruff slaps the palm of his clawed hand over his forehead just as Natash peeks her head in the door.

She takes in the scene, eyes moving from my face to Gruff's. Gruff is rigid, not the bouncing, swinging troll he was when he entered my cell. My jaw aches from hours spent grinding my teeth and I know Nat can see this isn't going well.

"Gruff, it's time to leave. I need a minute to talk with Laya before Demar returns," she says. Her voice is peaceful, and I let some of the tension in my shoulders dissipate.

"Today is hopeless anyway. I will be back soon and we will try again," he says as he storms out of the room.

"So, training hasn't gone well, it seems," she says. Her eyes follow Gruff's retreating form.

"So it seems," I say. "I just don't understand. The first time I threw the dagger, it was like everything slowed. I could anticipate his moves. But I'm thinking that was a one and done sort of ability."

"Laya, you don't mind if I call you that, do you?" I give a little shake of my head and she continues, "What were you thinking or feeling when you gained that ability?"

"Irritation! Because he, like you, had thrown a dagger at me and just missed my head. I really like my head!"

I say, waiting for her to elaborate. My voice is whiny. I don't like the sound, but I also don't have the energy to hold it together.

"Irritated? Or angry?" she asks with a smirk.

"I was angry," I say. "Being thrown into a world that I know nothing about has left me feeling helpless and angry. Angry that I am weak, that I am lacking knowledge, and angry that I do not know who to trust. It all sort of bubbled up to the surface." I let out a long exhale and let my muscles relax. It feels good to say that out loud. "I am tired of being helpless and in the dark."

"Good. Anger can be an excellent motivator as long as you harness it and use it in the correct manner," she says. "Now you just need to focus on that feeling. Pick up the dagger and throw it at me, but this time think of all the hurt and confusion, the anger and the pain."

I do as she says; I think of the pain that John put me through, losing my mom, being thrown into this confusing new world and not knowing how to make a place for myself anywhere. How am I supposed to move forward? How am I supposed to be the person, or elemental, that I was born to be? I don't even know what that means.

This time when I throw the dagger, a tingling flits across my skin and everything stops except me and the dagger.

Nat seems frozen in time. At the very last millisecond, I realize I have the dagger aimed directly at her heart. Not wanting to kill Nat, who is fast becoming a friend and ally, I move just a tic. And release the dagger.

Time speeds up and Nat grabs for her shoulder, the blood trickling through her fingers.

"That was unexpected," she says as she pulls the dagger out, letting it fall to the floor. "Had your aim been an inch over, you would have hit me in the heart and I wouldn't have even seen it coming."

I decide not to mention that I changed the trajectory at the last second. She doesn't need to know how close she was to getting impaled in the heart.

"How did that happen? You didn't even move," I say, staring at the dagger on the floor with a quizzical look as if it holds all the answers.

"I didn't see you move, let alone have time to react. My focus was on entering your mind to know what you planned, but somehow you blocked me. Before I knew what hit me, literally, I was bleeding," she says as the wound on her shoulder heals before my eyes. She looks from me to her shoulder. "Oh, that? Neat trick, huh? As a fae of the royal line, I heal fast."

"Good," slips from my lips. I let out a breath I had been holding, relieved she will be okay.

"As for how that happened, I would guess you have a very rare ability that allows you to actually stop time for a moment. I think they are called suspentionists," she says

"What does that mean for me?" I ask.

"You can suspend yourself in the veil between realms which allows you to stop time. So very rare." The corners of her lips pull up into a genuine smile.

"Rare?" My head is shaking in denial before my brain catches up to what she just said.

"I think the last suspentionist was a fae who lived two or three thousand years ago." Her lips pull to the side as do her eyes. "I have never heard of an elemental having that ability."

"Well, my mother has some witch in her blood, we think. Could that be why?" I ask.

My limbs vibrate with excitement at the idea that I have unique abilities, but my stomach clenches at that same thought. I have spent my life trying to blend in and all this new information is making me stand out.

"That doesn't seem feasible. The line would have to be extremely powerful for that ability to show up. Are you sure she wasn't fae?" Nat asks.

"I'm not sure of anything anymore," I tell her, dropping my head into my hands.

"Let me do some checking to see if I can find any information about your mother or where she came from," she says.

"I would appreciate that. Nat, can I ask you a favor?" I ask feebly, not knowing how she will respond.

"You can ask. Whether I will fulfill it is another story altogether." Her smile is dazzling.

"Can you find out how my brothers and friends are doing? I don't know what's happening there, and I'm worried about them." I'm sure she can see the hope in my eyes.

"I will do my best to get you information, but I will not make any promises. And just so you know, since you are a baby in this world, you must be careful with your words when speaking to demons and fae, especially. Well, witches too," she says.

After a deep breath, she continues, "Words can be binding. They are powerful. To promise something to one of us can bind you in our service until you fulfill the promise or one of us dies."

Her eyes glance at the floor and I see a glint of moister in them. She quickly uses the back of her hand to wipe it away. Not quick enough, though. I can see the pain. "And then you end up like me."

"Nat, how were you bound to John?" I ask.

"That is such a long story. I was young and in love." She takes a step towards me and asks, "Can I show you?"

"What do you mean, show me?" I tilt my head in question.

"I can show you my memories, but I need to touch your temple." Another step in my direction. "Do you mind?"

"I guess not," I answer, but my voice wobbles a little as I say it.

"It won't hurt. And I will not be accessing your mind, just projecting memories from mine. I promise not to invade your privacy," she explains.

She reaches out two fingers but stops just short of my temple, waiting for my permission.

I nod, and when the tips of her fingers connect with my temple, I close my eyes.

The image is gritty and takes a moment to adjust. At first, it's like sitting in a theater with the volume off. Darkness surrounds me, the only light coming from the picture far in front of me. The screen moves closer and, as it does, the picture becomes more clear. Sound reaches my ears, muffled at first and then distinct. It moves closer and closer until it connects with me. I'm no longer standing in my cell with Nat. I'm on a battlefield.

BOOM! The ground shakes under my feet as dirt flies up around me. I cover my head, but a tap on my shoulder has me peeking through my arms.

"Laya, there is no need to worry. You cannot sustain injury. Remember, you are only viewing my memories," Nat says in a smooth voice.

"So, why can I feel the ground shaking?" I ask.

Her eyes grow big as she says, "If you can feel the ground shake, then you must be very powerful indeed."

"Um, Nat, I can feel it, hear the explosions, and smell the dirt and smoke surrounding us. Is that supposed to happen?

I'm getting a little worried here," my voice shakes as I say the words.

"No need to worry. Most can only see the vision when I show them. But some can hear it and only a few can feel it. I have had no one smell it before, though." Her eyes pinch together in thought and her lips pucker. "No harm will come to you, but stay close to me, just in case."

"That doesn't boost my confidence!" I say as I scurry over to her side.

"Shhhh!" she says and points out in front of us.

My eyes follow the line of her arm and stop on a figure laying on the ground. He is dirty, sweaty, and bloody. The long spears of ice sticking out of his body make me wince. One through his stomach and another through his leg.

Though his eyes are closed, his hands wrap around the wound on his stomach and the moans escaping his lips reach my ears.

I flinch as an explosion rocks the ground. Green light radiates across the dirt not too far from us, causing vines to grow from the ground. Inching my way closer to Nat, I keep my head down. Arrows whizz past our heads and bursts of bright light flash closer and closer, but my focus is on the face of the girl who is curled around this mans head.

It's Nat.

Tears flow down her cheeks as she yells to the sky for someone to help her heal this man. I can tell by the uniform he *wears, he is a high-ranking officer. Why is no one trying to heal him? Why is he unable to heal himself?*

"Yes, a general in the fae guard." Nat's voice spooks me out of my thoughts.

"Did I say that out loud?" I ask.

"No, but we are in my head, therefore I can hear some of your thoughts. At least the ones you project to me," she says, her eyes still focused on the scene in front of us. "The witch responsible for the spears imbued them with a spell. Our healers could not heal him. I knew he would die if I didn't do something. So I called out, using my magic, to any being that could help save him."

I watch the scene as Nat talks. I can see the moment she sends out her magic. Like smoke swirling around her, it twists and twirls in the air before tendrils shoot off in all directions.

The memory fades. Like walking backwards through a tunnel, the light gets smaller and smaller until it is just darkness. I open my eyes. Nat is right beside me. Once again stone walls surround me and my heart sinks.

"John was the one to answer your call," I state, catching on to where this is going.

"Yes, the love I had for Mattenhue blinded me; adolescent love can be so intense. John, as you call him, said that he would keep Mattenhue alive. In return, I was to help him fulfill his mission. In the dire situation, I didn't ask questions. There was no explanation of what the mission was. He said it wouldn't take long, but that I had to stay until he accomplished what he set out to do or died trying," she says.

She fidgets with the hem of her shirt.

"I've since learned that 'long' is a relative term and when you live to be hundreds of years old, twenty years can pass and not be considered long." The heartache shows on her face, the way her lips form a slight grimace and how tears well in her eyes.

My heart clenches and I reach out to touch her arm. Her skin is cooler than mine, and a shiver runs down my spine. "I'm so sorry, Nat."

"As soon as I agreed, he bound me to him and sent me through a portal. I know he had to keep Mattenhue alive, but I now realize that didn't mean he would be well. I fear he is only a shell of himself at this point and I haven't seen him or heard anything about him since that moment. This became my home and my prison." As she turns her head away, I watch a tear roll down her cheek.

"Why are you helping me, then? Why not do everything you can to help John complete his mission?" I ask in a gentle voice.

Nat's face turns hard again. "Because, Laya, what he is doing is evil, and I would rather die than be an accomplice to his plans. He wants to enslave and kill off entire races. That is not something I can willingly contribute to." She lifts a brow at me and her voice drops to a whisper, "Plus, I think the alternative would be much more satisfying. Don't you?"

"Not to sound brutal, but I have been dreaming of the day that he is no longer alive, no longer able to cause any more pain, since my mother died." The words come out with venom and I realize how true they are.

"And that is why I will help you in any way I can. Our hate for him brings us together and makes us allies, but I can also see that you are a lot like me. You care for others to a fault. You will put yourself in harm's way to help someone in need, just because you think it is the right thing to do." A genuine smile spreads across her face. "Whether that is a blessing or a curse, only time will tell."

Nat's head whips to the side just as an awful crash comes from somewhere far away.

"I must go. Demar is back, and he is less than happy." She steps out the door and pushes a cart full of books, a battery operated radio, a flashlight and what looks to be lunch, snacks and a pitcher of water into the room.

"Here, I think this will help you pass the time," she says as she grabs one more thing from outside the door. A large, colorful beach towel is visible through the opening. The bright colors are a stark contrast to the dingy gray stones. "Use this to cover the cart."

As she tosses the towel over the cart, everything disappears and my mouth drops open.

"It's a cloak and will hide all I have given you from Demar. If he finds out you have this, I fear I may not live to see the sun rise again." I can hear another crash, closer this time. And with that Nat shuts the door, the lock clicking into place.

I sigh to myself, "Alone again."

Can she get the information we discussed? I hope so.

Mikal's face forces its way into my thoughts, and my chest tightens. I miss him. A fleeting thought that may not be so fleeting anymore consumes me as I grab a bite to eat. I scan the titles on the old metal shelf, stopping on a book called "Auras." *This might be helpful.* I cozy up to read, crossing my fingers that John doesn't make it down here in the mood he is in.

Unfortunately, it seems luck isn't with me today.

Chapter Fifteen

GOING TO HELL

~Mikal~

Cade storms into the office, where I am currently sitting in amongst piles upon piles of discarded books. Eddie is hot on his heels. My fingers hook the top of my laptop, closing the screen while I strain to hear through the phone pressed to my ear. The fact that I am busy doesn't stop Cade from interrupting.

Seething, Cade demands, "Mikal, terminate that call this instant! We have more pressing matters to attend."

I'm not sure what could be more pressing than finding Alayah, considering that has consumed our every waking moment for the last couple of days, but I comply.

Yes, Sir, I think to myself as I press a button ending communication to the current lead I have been questioning. I smile to myself, thinking about saluting Cade, but realize he might not find that as amusing as I do. So, I keep my hands by my side and my mouth closed.

Eddie must have returned with Alayah's belongings. He spent some extra time scouring the area and looking for information in her hometown. My heart speeds up, hoping that he found something useful. I can't help but picture her face and her full pink lips. I miss her more than I should, but that smiling face always turns into the look of horror as the portal sucks her in. My insides churn, and fur pokes through the skin on my knuckles; a low growl rumbles through my chest.

I quickly shut it down, knowing from experience my anger will not go over well with Cade. He has been a complete bastard since Demar took Alayah and I have become his favorite punching bag.

"Eddie, now that we are in the presence of your commander, I am eager to discern if you discovered anything relevant?" Cade says, getting right to the point.

"We sniffed out every lead that might bring us some information on Alayah, but have come up empty-handed. It doesn't seem like she had many friends other than Tara, and the people in that area knew even less about the stepdad." My heart sinks a little at that statement. He must have kept her isolated.

Eddie continues, "I called in a local witch to look at the scene at the farmhouse. Once she confirmed what we expected, that the demon was Demar, she got jumpy and fled," wiping one hand quickly past the other in a gesture to emphasize how quickly she left.

"So little to no information on John, then?" I ask, more to myself than to Eddie, but he answers anyway.

"Correct. We packed up all of Alayah's belongings. There was a hidden space below a floorboard in her bedroom that contained an old ratted teddy bear, a journal, some pieces of old jewelry, and close to twenty thousand in cash."

My eyebrows lift to my hairline. *Why would she have that much cash lying around?*

Eddie doesn't seem concerned about the contents of Alayah's stash, and his relaxed demeanor eases my anxiety as he gives us the details. His voice is smooth as he talks. You can't help but feel good when you are with him.

"Where are those things now?" I ask with interest. "If she had them hidden, there must have been some value to them."

"They're in the room we set up for her. Would you like me to bring them to you?" Eddie replies.

"No, I will look for myself when I'm done here. You can return to training. I think we are going to need our skills sooner rather than later." His lip pulls up in the corner. With Eddie, there's no need to push the importance of training. He's the one that instilled a work ethic in me.

"Get up, boy. You're not done until you accomplish your goal for today." Eddie's stern voice has me pushing myself up out of the mud on shaky arms.

"I can't do it, Eddie. Why do we have to fight with weapons? We have teeth and claws," I whine.

"There will be times when you cannot shift. It is best to know how to protect yourself and those they charge you with in every form." The mud splattered across his face doesn't detract from the genuine smile he gives me as his hand reaches out to help me up.

"AGAIN!" He shouts just after giving my shoulder a reassuring squeeze.

My small hand wraps around the large wooden broadsword, and I struggle to pick it up. At nine years old, I haven't built the muscles needed to wield the metal version, but if we keep working like this, it won't be long.

I swing and Eddie blocks my advance. All I have to do is touch him with the sword once and we're done training for the day. The sun is setting behind the trees and a beautiful glow of orange and pink covers the western sky.

I swing once more, feeling the energy drain from my body. He blocks me again.

"Boy, you can do this. I know you have it in you." His voice fuels me back up. Not all the way, but enough. He always supports me, believes in me, and encourages me. Unlike my father, who berates, belittles, or, when that doesn't work, ignores.

I lift my sword, taking the stance Eddie taught me. I make sure I've lined my feet up just how he said. My arms are in position out in front of me. I move forward, following the strike path he showed me and just as he's about to block, I duck under *his arm. Spinning around, I swing the sword and it connects with his back.*

I let the sword fall from my fingers onto the muddy ground beneath my feet and shoot my arms into the air in triumph.

"Woo-hoo!!" My heart is beating fast and my breath rattles from all the hard work. Excitement fills me. It fuels me. I am on top of the world.

Jumping up and down, I turn my attention to Eddie and his eyes beam with pride. I didn't realize it, but that is exactly what I needed. A role model to look up to. Someone to see my worth and encourage me to challenge myself. Someone to push me with love, not an iron fist.

Eddie's fingertips just brush the door handle when I ask, "Hey Eddie, how are the boys doing?"

His eyes light up as he turns around.

"They are a handful for sure," he laughs, a deep belly laugh that fills the room with joy, "Tad just shifted for the first time. He is having trouble controlling it, so whenever he gets angry with his brother, poof, he's a wolf."

"I remember those days," I say. The first couple years of shifting are the hardest. It takes time to find control.

"Yes, and Oli loves to rile him up just to see how long it takes Tad to lose control. Brothers!" You can see the love he has for his boys shining in his eyes. The same look he gave me when I was a boy.

"And how is Sarah doing?" I ask.

"She's good, but she definitely has her hands full," he says. The laugh lines at the corner of his eyes crinkle as his smile grows wider. "She's an excellent mother and a noble wife, though. We are lucky to have her."

"I agree, and they are lucky to have you too, Eddie." My heart pulls at that. I am lucky to have him in my life as well. But I don't say the words. Maybe it's because Cade is in the room, or maybe I have spent so much time hiding behind my ego and my position that I don't know how to say them.

"Thank you, Mikal. That means a lot," he replies.

"I better not keep you. Give them a hug for me. It seems like ages since I've seen them." I have been so busy with everything that is going on, I haven't spent time with the pack.

"Will do. Let me know if you need anything else," Eddie says, closing the door behind him.

I turn to Cade, whose fingers are tapping an angry beat against the desk in front of him. With his jaw clenched and the death stare he's shooting my way, I would say he's a bit agitated. *Hmmm...*

"That can't be what was so important that I had to hang up on a new lead?" I ask, a little disdain clouding my voice.

"Certainly not. I expect our fathers to arrive within the hour. They received information about Alayah's disappearance and have requested our presence for a meeting."

Cade's eyes are hard, and I can see a twitch of irritation as he stares at me.

He has been less than friendly and I can feel the irritation radiating off of him. Disappointed too, I suppose, that Demar took Alayah. He's pissed off that he took her on my watch. Even his anger at me cannot rival my own, though.

I have been pulling my hair out, leaving no rock unturned to find her. Hell, I even enlisted Cassie. She left to follow her own leads the day after we talked and hasn't checked in or returned.

What if she washed her hands of us and moved on? My chest clenches with remorse at the thought. I hope she's safe.

Those thoughts make me uneasy, like I am betraying Alayah even though I don't feel for Cassie what I do for Alayah. Something sparked in me during my conversation with Cassie and I think I care about her. It's an odd feeling and I'm not sure what to do with it.

Whether it's more like the way you care for a bratty little sister versus the way you care for a challenging significant other has yet to be determined. I hope for the former because if not, my life just got a lot messier.

"MIKAL!" Cade shouts to get my attention. "Can you even acknowledge that I am conversing with you? This will be disastrous for the lot of us. We need to formulate a solid plan and be forthcoming with pertinent information upon their arrival or they are going to have our heads." He makes a slicing motion with his thumb across his neck to emphasize his point, and I shiver a little. While Cade is exaggerating regarding his father, he is not when it comes to mine.

Seventeen minutes later...

I sigh as I hear boots pounding against the tiled hall-way floor. The clomp, clomp, clomp gets louder as they get closer and I shudder.

This is going to be bad.

The few minutes Cade and I had to chat did not touch on anything our fathers would see as pertinent information.

I stand at attention as my father enters the room followed by Cade's father, King Rorak. Both men have their shoulders back and heads held high, demanding respect. I give it to them even though only one of them deserves it, in my opinion.

"Son," my father nods at me as Cade's father glances his way, "Please give us the full report on this situation."

"Have you located my daughter?" The king asks.

"Regrettably, father, Alayah remains unaccounted for," Cade steps in, which is quite the relief to me. I have a hard time talking under the scrutiny of my father's gaze.

186

"We have diligently followed the established protocol and pursued many leads. It appears we are still some distance away from finding her."

I can see the veins bulge in the King's neck as he tries to rein in his temper. My father, on the other hand, does not control his emotions.

BAM! He slams his fist down on the desk and I see a crack form in the mahogany top. As shifters, we have immense strength when our emotions are high and I recoil at his ferocity.

Just as he is about to continue, the air beside us shimmers. I can feel electricity prickling my skin. I take a second to realize that what I am seeing and feeling is a portal. My father has moved in front of Rorak and I notice I have done the same with Cade. Years of tactical training at its finest.

On guard and ready for a fight, my eyes widen as Cassie waltzes through the portal, followed by none other than Dante.

My heart sinks a little, but I try to school my features into a hard mask. Dante and I just barely tolerate each other at our best. No one wants to be in a room with us at our worst. People think I'm arrogant, but he takes the cake in that department.

As children, we were friends. Playing hide and seek during diplomatic functions, climbing trees and chasing creatures through the woods when we were supposed to be on our best behavior. That friendship faded as we became teenagers and our races ended up on opposite sides of some pretty important issues.

Now that Dante is the fae king, his arrogance has reached unbelievable heights and anytime I'm in the same room as him, I feel like I don't quite measure up.

I always knew he was going to be a King; it just wasn't supposed to happen for years. And while, soon enough, I will be the alfa leader of the Northern Territory in the United States, it doesn't quite seem good enough. Plus, I don't want the role and the extra responsibility that comes with it.

Just as I think the portal will close, another figure shuffles through it. He is short but if I had to place him, I would say he's a troll. It's funny how the myths of trolls depict large murderous beings, and there are those too, but the reality is most trolls are a few feet tall, at best. Don't tell them that though, they kill mercilessly. It gives me the shivers just thinking about it.

Dante's smooth voice pulls me from my thoughts as he says, "Rorak, I understand your daughter's situation is of the utmost importance. When Cassie petitioned me for help, I couldn't resist getting involved. Especially since it sounds like your son and the general's son could not produce results over the last few days."

That bastard, I can't believe he just threw us under the bus like that... well, actually I can. I glance at Cassie and she squirms a little under my scrutiny, but it is fleeting as she squares her shoulders and meets my stare, chin held high.

My gaze slides back to Dante.

"Dante, please enlighten us with any discoveries or progress you have made thus far?" Rorak demands. I'm sure he isn't too fond of the slight against his son.

"I know where Alayah is being held. Gruff here has been an immense help as he has talked with Alayah in the dungeons below Demar's residence." My ears perk up at that, but I know better than to interrupt the king or his General. "I can make a portal that will get us close, though it will not be easy to extract her. There will be a fight and it will be brutal. Demar has an army of demons at his beck and call," he says as King Rorak nods.

"We will assemble a team of our most skilled fighters. May I inquire when you will be prepared to initiate the portal?" Rorak asks.

"Four days from now," Dante replies.

Cade's father looks from Cade to me and says, "Boys, begin your preparations immediately. You have four days to assemble a team"

"One last thing, your highness," Dante adds, "It seems, my cousin is also under Demar's control and I want her back. Demar tricked her into a blood oath which, as you know, is not a simple thing to break. I know *the boys* should be able to find a way, though, as repayment for my help."

My face grows hot as I stare at Dante, and I can tell Cade isn't pleased either with the way he clenches his fists. I choose to keep my bearings for the moment, though, because I know Dante is goading me. In front of the king and my father is not the place to work this out.

"Cade and Mikal will make sure they return your cousin to you." My father's stern voice makes me tense a little more.

"Yes, General," Cade and I say at the same time in similar tight voices. I notice he doesn't add in what condition she would return or when, which Dante seems to miss. Being a fae and the king, I would have thought he would correct my father, knowing that making a deal with a fae is binding.

Chapter Sixteen

MONSTERS

~ALAYAH~

The door to my cell slams against the stone wall, breaking the hinges and cracking the stone it hits. The boom it makes as it hits the floor, inches from where I am sitting, is deafening and I shake my head to clear it.

I sneeze as dust plumes around the room and I cover my face with the fabric of my clothes. Who knows what diseases I could get from inhaling the dust stirred up in that mess?

Demar is seething in the now completely open doorway as I struggle to get up.

"You!" He points at me with a red scaly hand. I prefer when he looks human to the disgusting face full of teeth that's aimed at me right now. I mean, I'm not trying to be needy or anything, but it's hard not to shit my pants when I look at him, which makes it even harder for my brain to function.

Not knowing what to do, I stay quiet. I don't know what he might blame me for this time around and, most likely, it actually has nothing to do with me. I learned at a young age no matter what the circumstance, he would push the blame off to the person or thing that was least likely to defend itself. In my current situation, I would say that's me.

"Because of you I have lost the warlock I was looking for and you will pay the price every day until I find him again." I'm pretty sure I can see steam wafting from his ears. To be honest, this doesn't look good for me. I back away, sliding my fingers against the wall to keep myself grounded.

What color do you turn when you're angry if your skin is already red? I can't tell if he is darker than before, but I would guess that could be the case.

"Natash!" He demands and I see her face in the space between his shoulder and the doorframe. The look she shoots my way tells me this is going to be worse than I thought. That scares me because I already thought this would be pretty darn bad.

Damn us all to Hell! Oh, I guess we are already here. I snicker. And then I realize it was a mistake when Demar turns to Natash and says, "Throw it."

Quicker than I can follow, a dagger sinks into the muscle of my left arm. A scream rips from my throat and a tear trails down my cheek.

I wasn't expecting that. Nor was I expecting that rogue tear to land on my boob about where my nipple sits nestled in my bra. It looks like I'm leaking. Dang it!

Demar says, "Again!" Another dagger sinks into my skin, right above the knee on my left thigh.

The pain shoots up my leg and my stomach churns. Bile rises up my throat, but I hold my ground.

The third time he gives the order, I am ready and a shield of white flickering light erects in front of me, causing the dagger to ricochet. It clanks to the floor, spinning once, then twice before it stops with the blade pointing towards Demar.

The fury of his roar has my brain rattling around in my head, and the fourth dagger finds its way to the flesh of my stomach. I look up to see surprise in Nat's eyes. She isn't the one that sent the last dagger flying in my direction.

My eyes drift to my stomach, where blood is pouring from the wound. I drop to my knees, trying to cover the wound and stop the flow of blood. My left arm is practically useless at this point. When my knees hit the floor, the dagger in my left thigh gets jostled, sending excruciating waves of pain through my body.

I grimace, clenching my teeth tight, and I see the look of satisfaction on Demar's face right before blackness clouds my vision. As I completely lose consciousness,

I hear myself whisper, "Well, this day just got fucking worse."

I can feel the thunder as it rattles the windows and shakes the house. Lightning cuts through the sky outside my bedroom and I pull the covers over my head, curling into a ball. If I can just get small enough, maybe he won't find me.

My door creaks open, sending shivers down my spine. I'm afraid to look. I don't want to see his face in the doorway.

The light from the hallway sneaks into my room and I hear a soft voice say, "Ali, baby, we need to go. Do you think you can be as quiet as a mouse, kind of like a game? Let's see who can make the least amount of noise."

It's my mom and when I carefully pull the covers away from my face, I see the marks that mar hers. She is bleeding from her lip and her eye is swollen shut. Bruises are forming on her neck in the shape of fingers. I notice she is limping a little as she moves closer to my bed.

"Hurry, sweetheart, we need to move fast. We still need to get Jake." She grabs a backpack from the floor and shoves clothes in it as I climb out of bed on shaky legs.

She takes my hand and as we turn to leave my room, a silhouette in the doorway blocks the light from the hall. Fear grips my soul and I take a step back, releasing my mom's hand.

John looks at me, and I cringe. The veins in his forehead are popping out. I know this isn't good. I try to step in front of my mother, but she quickly pushes me behind her, whispering, "Go back to bed, Ali, I love you more than the world itself."

I gain consciousness and I fear that when I get out of bed, Officer Mahoney and Doctor Smith will knock at the door. Standing there in trench coats with grim looks on their faces, to tell us that my mother died in a car accident. A heart attack, they said.

I can still remember how the doctor's voice was so disconnected as he talked about my mother's death. His eyes were glossy, and he stared over my head out the large bay window behind me.

Officer Mahoney was quite the opposite, animated even. His demeanor went from grim to almost giddy as he talked with John. He tried to hide the smile that was creeping across his face when he noticed I was looking at him. It seemed odd, but I was so in shock from the words falling from the doctor's lips that I paid little attention to the officer at the time.

I knew the truth; my mom didn't die from a heart attack. John had killed her for trying to leave. Jake had been sleeping, and I never spoke of that night or what I had witnessed.

As my eyes open, I can tell I'm no longer in my childhood bedroom. Blinking once, twice, three times to clear the blur, I realize I'm not in the dungeon, either. The bright white of my current accommodations is a stark contrast to the dingy rock walls I've grown accustom to during my imprisonment. The room I'm in looks rather similar to a room you would see in a movie. Probably one where they're dissecting people.

I try to roll to the side and my shoulder blade grinds into the hard surface below me. I feel a pull on my wrist but my mind is groggy, so I pull harder. My wrist chafes and I wince. When I move my head, not only do I notice the throbbing of a horrible migraine setting in, but I see I'm not on a bed at all. I am strapped to a stainless-steel table.

Ah! Shit! This can't be good. Thoughts swirl through my mind and I forget to breathe.

I hear footsteps somewhere far away, but they're moving closer. Seconds pass and with each one, the clack, clack, clacking on the tile floor grows louder. When the doorknob rattles, I close my eyes, pretending I am still unconscious.

"Is she healed?" I hear Demar's harsh tone cut through the room as he enters.

"Yes, Master, the wounds have closed up, but she may be sore for quite some time. We did almost lose her, you know." I peek through slitted eyelids and suppress a gasp when I see who Demar is talking to.

It's Doctor Smith, but as I continue to look at him, his form flits between that of the Doctor Smith I knew as a child and a slimy gray-brown salamander. The gills on the side of his neck flutter as he breathes, drawing my attention. The bright red color contrasts with the tone of his skin. It reminds me of slicing into the center of a rare steak.

He may be the reason I never liked salamanders as a child. Ew! His beady eyes shift in my direction and mine slam shut. I slow my breathing, making sure it's even.

"I need her up and ready to train by tomorrow morning. She has been out for two days. I lost the warlock, and she is now my only hope for completing this mission. I cannot wait to see their faces as I enslave their puppy dogs and slaughter their families in front of them!" His laugh is pure evil as he walks out of the room, leaving me with the creepy doctor.

"Alayah, I know you're awake," he says as he loosens the restraints connecting me to the table. I try to scoot away from him. It's really weird that so far, the beings I've met in Hell are trying to help me. I have to remember I cannot trust anyone, even if they seem nice. *They are demons, for Christ's sakes! Or at least this one is.*

"Don't fear me, child, for Demar does not know, but I have done my best to watch over and protect you through the years. I may be a demon, but just as there are good and bad humans, we are not all evil." He takes my hand and looks me in the eye. I realize that with my eyes open, I don't see the flicker of his different forms, but when I close them slightly, I can.

"Why can I only see your demon form when I squint, but when I look directly at you, I see your human form?" I ask, perplexed.

His eyes go wide. "Aren't you full of surprises, my dear? You should not be able to see through the glamour I wear."

"So that's what it's called? A glamour? Are demons the only ones that can do that?" I ask, while thinking in the back of my mind that maybe that is what I saw with Dante.

"Most demons cannot use glamour to hide themselves or change their appearance. A powerful demon can do it and convince only the weakest minded humans." I puff up a little at that, like, wait a second.

"Wait and you will understand. The fae are the most powerful users of the magic that makes a glamour possible along with witches and warlocks. Certain elementals can produce a powerful glamour, but not all." He pauses for a second while I take in the information.

"Natash is the one that creates the glamour that Demar and I wear, along with a few others, but it takes a lot of energy. It is one reason Demar ensnared Natash to begin with." Just as he finishes his sentence, the door creaks open.

"Did I hear my name?" Nat peaks her head in. "I am so relieved you're awake." I can see the shame in her eyes as she apologizes, but I hold up a hand to stop her.

"If anyone knows the toils of being around Demar, it's me. I forgive you," I say with sincerity.

"Thank you, Laya." I can see her shoulders relax. "That means a lot to me."

She turns to the doctor, "So, what were you discussing?"

"Just glamours and who can create them. Alayah mentioned that if she squints, she can see my true form," he says matter of fact.

"Ah, I see. Well Laya, that shouldn't be possible, but from what I have seen, you make the impossible possible." The pride is clear in her tone and I notice she has discarded the jumpsuit for a floral spring dress. It flows beautifully over her slender body.

"I love your dress, Nat. Boy, do I miss getting dressed up with my best friend back home." I also miss our late-night conversations that kept us awake until the wee hours of the morning.

My thoughts flit back to Jake, Tara, Mikal, and Cade. *Are they are safe?* I want to ask Nat if she found anything, but I feel I shouldn't bring it up in front of the doctor. I've decided that you just can't be too careful.

"Thank you, I am going to show you to your new room and maybe later I can find some time to visit you," she says as she opens the door. "I think we have a great deal to talk about."

My spirits raise a little. As I get off the table, I can feel the aftermath of being stabbed multiple times. I flex and lift my shirt to look at my stomach. "A new room? I won't be in the dungeon anymore?"

"No, you won't, since you will train now. I talked Demar into giving you a room on the third floor. It is still secure and you won't be able to escape, but it has a full bathroom attached so you can shower." She pauses and looks at my stomach where I am still holding my shirt up. "We cleaned you up some, but I am sure a shower will help make you feel more whole, along with some rest in an actual bed."

"Anything would be better than the piss covered floor." I grimace, remembering the smell. "And I can't wait to use the shower. Is the water warm?"

"Well, this is Hell," she states with a smile, "Pretty much everything is warm or, in most cases, very, very hot."

"My aching muscles will appreciate that, I'm sure," I sigh and follow her down a long, well-lit hallway.

Once we reach the end, I look up to see a mountain of stairs in my path. My muscles tighten and I groan in pain. This is going to be miserable. We climb for what feels like hours to my aching body. I'm guessing we are in a hidden back stairway because it's dingy and I haven't seen a single soul or, should I say a soulless creature, anywhere.

Slowly, I make it to the top of the stairs and into another long hallway. This hallway is dim, the only light coming from a few brass sconces on the wall. The candlelight flickers and shadows seem to scurry along the edges where the walls meet the floor. More than once I see something move and I don't know for sure what it is.

"Nat, did you see that?" I ask in a squeaky voice.

"Don't worry about that. You are probably just seeing pixies moving about, or possibly some lesser demons. The little things are like rats and mice around here," she shrugs.

"Wait! What? Rats and mice!" I stop in my tracks, shaking my head.

"Oh, you'll be fine. They can't get into your room. I warded it to keep them out. And they aren't actual rats and mice, just demons and pixies that act similar." She stops in front of a huge wooden door that looks exactly like the twenty other huge wooden doors we passed on the way. "This is where we part ways for now. I'll try to come back later."

My head is still moving back and forth as she opens the door and shows me to my room. Little demon rats and pixie mice. Nope, not for me. The click of the door behind me echoes through the space. Turning towards the noise, I find Nat is gone. My hand reaches out for the door handle, but it's also gone; vanished just like that. Well, I guess I'm stuck here until someone comes for me.

CHAPTER SEVENTEEN

WHAT'S THE SOUND

~ALAYAH~

The steam cascades around me as I open the glass shower door and step out. The soft navy blue rug is squishy between my toes, further relaxing me as I wiggle them for a moment.

I reach for the fluffy red towel I placed on the stone countertop, wrapping it around my weary body. I don't care that water is dripping down my legs and making a puddle on the marble floors.

This bathroom is nicer than any bathroom I have ever seen, with a beautiful walk-in shower and a wooden soaker tub. They made the tub from an actual stump. A huge one, hollowed out, and big enough to fit two adults. The banding in the wood is gorgeous greens, yellows and browns. I would love to take a bath, but today the shower was a more efficient way to get the blood and grime off me. I promise myself a soak in that tub soon, though.

A squeaking sound draws my attention to the door.

E-er, E-er.

What is that? I hope it's not demon rats or fairy mice. Nat assured me they couldn't get in here.

I tiptoe, trying not to make a noise, and strain my ears, placing one against the wooden door. Holding my breath, I work to decipher who or what might be in my newly acquired room. There isn't much in this bathroom to use for a weapon unless I want to try my luck at knocking the intruder out with a bar of soap.

I grab the golden handle and turn, opening the door just enough to peek through the crack. What I see on the other side brings a smile to my face and I laugh out loud as I swing the door wide open.

Who's on the other side? None other than Gruff still cloaked in a yellowish hue and he is bouncing on my bed like a child on a sugar high.

E-er, E-er.

I watch for a minute, waiting for him to notice me. When he does, he says, "Well, lucky little Laya, I do so prefer these accommodations to your last ones."

I raise a brow at him, remembering how disappointed he seemed as he exited the cell the last time we interacted. "You seem to be in a much better mood this time. I see you are calling me Laya now, too."

"Laya," he says it again, "It's fitting isn't it? Like Princess Laya and all that." His head tilts in contemplation.

"Oh my gosh, Gruff, this is not a Star Wars movie," I huff, putting a hand on my hip, making sure the other one is securing the towel that I have wrapped around me. Which reminds me I need to get dressed and at the thought, my cheeks flush with embarrassment.

"I don't suppose you know if there are clothes here I can wear?" I ask Gruff, pulling his attention to my state of undress. *Oops*, I think as his eyes roll over my body like he has just realized I'm standing here in a towel. And honestly, he probably has.

"When Nat snuck me in here, she put some things in the walk-in closet over there." He points to a door beside the bathroom that I hadn't noticed until now.

As I enter the closet, I realize it's full of clothes. Flipping through the pieces, I also notice they are all in my size. I grab a pair of purple yoga pants and a gray tank top with the word FIT on it.

Turning to the left, I spy a built-in dresser that I hope contains undergarments. I have gone far too long without underwear and I just can't bring myself to put on my nasty blood and sweat soaked bra. To my relief, the top drawer is full and I pull out a sports bra and some panties that match.

Gruff peeks his head in and I jump, "Gruff, privacy please."

"Privacy, smivacy! I just wanted to let you know to put on something comfortable, but I see you have that covered," he says with a flick of his wrist as he turns to leave. "We will work on your mind and body."

"Wait, working? I'm tired! Why can't I crawl into that cozy bed and rest?" A sigh leaves my lips and I can hear a whiny tinge to my voice. "I thought I didn't have to train until the morning."

"You worn, weary lass. You don't have to train for Demar until tomorrow. Tonight we work on training your mind and magic so that you can choose what to show him and what to keep hidden," he says as he swings himself back atop my bed with his long arms.

"My brain is mush and I can barely move. This is not a good time to focus on whatever magic I might have inside me," I retort with exasperation.

"On the contrary, child, this is the perfect time," and his lips curl up into a smile that sends a shiver through my body.

After about three hours of what Gruff considered training, which to set the record straight seemed more like torture to me, I flop down on the bed, ready to pass out. I sink into the comfort of the covers and pull what seems like a thousand pillows around me. Tucking a few underneath my head, a couple under my back and one under each knee, getting myself into the most comfortable position possible.

I relax, thinking about the progress I made tonight puts a smile on my face. But I can't keep my eyes open, and blankets and pillows are two of my favorite things at the moment. I close my eyes and throw an arm over my face to block out the light from the room. As I do, a slight knock sounds on the door.

"Gruff, get that, please. I can't move anymore." Pulling the blankets tighter around me, I wait for him to see who is at the door. When I peek at him, he gives me a look, eyes narrowed that reminds me he isn't supposed to be here.

"Who is it?" I shout, my voice wavering with exhaustion.

I hear Nat's soft voice as the door swings open, the door knob reappearing. *That is so weird,* but I realize that isn't even in the top one hundred weirdest things I have seen. I giggle at myself, the overwhelming exhaustion making that thought seem funnier than it should be.

Gruff scoffs at me like I'm crazy and moves into the shadows, I assume, just in case Nat isn't alone. But when Nat enters and closes the door behind her, Gruff moves back into view.

I look at her as I pull myself up from my pillow fortress and sigh, missing the comfort of the fluffy pillows already. I wait for her to fill me in on what she's found. There are wrinkles marring her previously flawless skin. Dark circles line her eyes and her complexion is pale.

"How do you like the room?" she asks, waving a hand in the air.

"It's nicer than the last one," I say and give the best weak smile I can muster at the moment. My body feels like mush along with my mind.

She walks closer to the bed and I pat the spot beside me, letting her know she can sit if she wants.

Nat hesitates, looking at my hand. Almost like the idea is too intimate. Her eyes dart across the room to the chair sitting in the corner but Gruff moves to sit in it, leaving my invitation or the floor as the only options.

I can see her mind working. She rarely seems indecisive, and it's almost like the decision is painful for her. At last, she moves toward the bed and takes a seat at the foot of it.

She turns to Gruff, "You better get outta Hell before you're noticed. I feel you have been here too long as it is."

Gruff nods, turns to me with a smirk that says he thinks tonight went well, and vanishes before my eyes. I blink twice in rapid succession before shaking my head and turning my attention back to Nat.

"Have you learned anything from the books, Laya?" Nat asks.

"Well, the one Demar gave me was a lot of illustrations and not enough information. It gave me some idea of the different beings and monsters out there," I say, thinking back to some of the most hideous creatures you could imagine. The illustrations were very colorful, to say the least.

"Don't let it fool you, Laya. Even the prettiest creatures can be the monsters in a story," she says, turning her head away from me. "How about the books I gave you?"

"I haven't had as much time to look at them as I would like, considering the circumstances here, but most of what I have read while I was in the dungeon seemed to be the stuff of fairytales and myths." I am still having a hard time believing any of this is real.

"You can find grains of reality in myths and fairytales," Nat replies.

"Right. Some things I knew, such as vampires have an aversion to the sun because it weakens them and that a stake or beheading will kill them. Also, shifters are allergic to silver and that silver bullets can kill them." I take a breath, contemplating whether I should bring up the book on Auras.

I decide against it and ask, "Were you able to find out about my friends and family?"

"About that," she says with a nervous twitch I haven't seen from her before. "I was able to get a message out to your elemental brother, but I have yet to receive anything back. The messenger said that he and the wolf seemed well. I'm sure they're taking care of the rest of the people you love."

She sucks in a shallow breath, "Everyone who has lived in this world for any amount of time knows that you have to take precautions. I'm sure they have made safety a priority for anyone close to you."

Her mood is off and I can tell something is wrong. There is a bit of a bite that underlies the words she just said, but I'm not sure what it means.

"I hope so. I worry about my brother Jake and my best friend Tara now that I know about what's actually lurking in our world. Jake is too trusting and Tara is too sweet."

I miss them dearly. What I wouldn't give to have Jake ruffle my hair again, or for Tara to give me one of her amazing hugs. I feel a pinch and my eyes fall to my hands sitting atop the covers on my lap. When I get worried, I have a tendency to pick at my nails and right now they are not fairing well. A little bead of blood wells up and I press the tip to my lips, sucking the blood from it.

I am counting again, too. Something I haven't done in so long. I know it's nine steps to the window from the bed and twelve from the bed to the bathroom door. It's another seven to the door that exits the room.

There aren't a lot of things for me to have counted out since I am locked in one room, but it's a habit I have suffered with since I was a child. It's a way to regulate my trauma so it doesn't consume other areas of my life. Old habits die hard when your world keeps getting flipped upside down.

Nat looks uneasy, and I wonder if she has ever had a friend to just hang out with and do girl things. Usually she is so stoic in our interactions, but she's fidgeting just as much as me at the moment. I want to ask her, but I don't want to make her more uncomfortable than she seems to be already.

She stands up, startling me, and my hand flies to my chest. Nat takes a step towards me and her mouth opens, but no words come out. She shuts her mouth with a click and spins towards the door, her gaze glued to the old wood, and I can see her shoulders tense.

"Nat, is something wrong?" I ask, not wanting to pry too deep.

"Demar knows something is up, I'm afraid. I feel like I'm being followed, and I'm sure that's not a good sign," her eyes roaming from me to the door and back again. I watch as her hand goes to the hilt of her dagger and I tense as well. She doesn't pull it out though, just rubs her thumb over the handle and as she does, the tension seems to release the slightest bit from her body.

Meeting my eyes again, she asks, "What have you and Gruff been working on?"

"Now that he knows I'm a Suspentionist, he's coaching me on that and how to focus my mind. Elaborating on what you taught me," I say as a smile lifts across my face. Just thinking about how far I have come in a short period fills me with pride.

"I can now focus that energy in just a few seconds and suspend myself in the veil." Her lips lift into a smile as well. "I can only hold it for a minute."

"Keep practicing," she encourages.

"We also worked on my shield and what Gruff calls my pulse, which is..." I say as Nat's gaze clouds over.

Her head turns towards the door again, and she finishes my sentence for me, "The power you emitted that knocked us off our feet."

"Yes, that and we tried some different things that other elementals can do. We found I have an affinity for air and water. My previous abilities probably come from a connection to spirit." I let out a long breath with a smile because I am proud of what I have learned about myself in the last few hours.

"Very good, Laya," she says and stands as her hand returns to the hilt of her dagger once more. She seems to be deep in thought as her face falls. She spins on her heel 180 degrees, releasing the dagger I hadn't even seen her pull from her pocket.

It stops in midair as a being shimmers into view, the dagger dead center of the creature's throat. It hid in the shadows. I wonder how long it has been there listening.

The creature's skin is black as coal, with no defining features other than its very large red eyes. As the body collapses to the floor, I feel a vibration in my head, a very strong painful vibration that has me pressing my palms to my temples. My eyes close tight, a moan escaping my lips as the pressure builds, but just as quickly as it started, it stops.

I open my eyes, looking to the spot where that thing fell to the floor, but it is no longer there. My gaze drifts to where Nat was standing, but she is no longer there either.

What in the ever-loving fuck just happened? I ask myself, searching the room for any sign of where they went.

Chapter Eighteen

RISE UP

~Alayah~

My eyes spring open and I sit straight up in bed, the events of last night racing through my mind. I sense a panic attack coming on and I grasp my chest to stop my racing heart.

My brain automatically starts counting things in the room to calm my nerves. One chair in the corner, two floral and very gaudy curtains hanging beside the windows, three fluffy pillows on the floor. I search for things to count while my heartbeat slows down. Sixteen tiles in front of the fireplace, five pictures on the wall, the beats finally returning to a normal level.

I take a deep breath.

Bringing a hand up to my face, I wipe away tears I didn't realize were falling. I take another glance around the room. Nothing seems amiss, but somehow, someone was in my room while I slept because there's an array of food on the table by the window. Steam rises from the platter, implying they were recently here.

I slowly get up and walk to the table, picking up a white note sitting by the food.

Alayah,

Eat and dress. I will send someone up to get you shortly. Training starts now. With some recent discoveries, I have decided I will not be going easy on you. Lessons need to be learned. You will come clothed or naked, starving or fed. It is up to you and how fast you can get ready.

-John

"Well, shit," I say out loud, grabbing what looks to be a croissant dipped in chocolate and shoving it in my mouth as I head to the closet.

What does someone wear for training with an evil high demon who loves for them to suffer?

To my surprise, I find an outfit laid out in the closet. Not my style, but I'm guessing Nat picked it out for me, knowing what I would be up against.

I pick up the black leather pants and I pull them on. They fit like a dream. The leather is strong enough to resist tearing, at least for a little while. The shirt is also black and long-sleeved but it breathes, so that's a plus, since we are in Hell and all. I slip on a pair of socks and pull on the leather boots to finish the ensemble.

Turning to the full-length mirror in the closet, I realize I'm pretty badass. I bet Mikal would throw a few sexy or sarcastic comments my way if he could see me in this Cat Woman outfit.

Yep, not anything I would wear on the regular, but I have to admit it's growing on me. The blood stains will blend into the material. So there's that!

I walk back out to the table, grabbing a glass of fairy nectar, and I chug it down. The instant it hits my stomach, my body tingles. My eyesight gets sharper and my attention to detail goes into hyper drive.

It's disorienting at first and I take a few seconds to adjust. I'm unwilling to sacrifice more time before moving again. Today, I need all the help I can get. My eye catches on eggs and bacon. At least, I think it is eggs and bacon? Okay, now I really want to know, are there chickens in Hell? Before today ends, I need to ask someone about that.

My thoughts turn to what I think will happen in this so-called training Demar wants me to do. If he's behind it, I know it won't be fun, but I hope I can learn some more about myself. While mysteries can intrigue, when it's you that is the mystery to yourself, it isn't so exciting.

What am I capable of? I want to understand. Can I get myself out of this mess?

I've never been one to rely on others, since there was no one to rely on. I trust Cade and Mikal, but I can't rely on them to rescue me.

Plus, I want to find my strength and end that miserable demon who posed as a step-dad to my brother and me, the piece of donkey dung that killed my mother.

A loud knock on the door has me jumping out of my seat. I peek at the door, hoping to see Nat, but I see a man's face instead. It's one I have seen before but just can't place.

He has black eyes and creamy white skin. His hair hangs in his eyes in an emo sort of cut, and it's just as dark as the black holes that are staring daggers in my direction.

My eyes narrow, trying to figure out where I have seen this guy before, and I realize I don't see another form to him when I squint.

Interesting!

Even more interesting, he doesn't have an aura. Not one that I can see, anyway.

His muscular arm reaches towards me as he holds out his hand like I'm supposed to take it or something. The veins in his arm are also black and while that is one attribute I find sexy in a man, I'm a little taken aback. As I study him, I realize I do indeed find him attractive.

Stockholm Syndrome?

"Alayah, if you would please come with me, Demar is waiting for you," he says, his face remaining stoic.

I don't move.

"Alayah, I don't think it is wise to keep him waiting." His eyebrow twitches with impatience.

"After you," I say, pointing at the door. There is no way I am going to have him at my back.

He looks at me for a second before he turns and walks into the hall.

That's when I realize where I have seen him before. He's the one who got away unharmed at the club.

The walk to the arena takes forever. I wonder if this place is that big or if this guy is walking me in circles to confuse me. Maybe it's both. The stone walls have changed from a dark gray to a pristine white. I have to admit, with all the red and black accents, this place is gorgeous. It's like an old castle made modern. Statues of snakes and demons are everywhere, but it isn't gaudy. It's mystical.

The arena doors are huge and my mouth hangs down as I gape at them. I can barely hear the last few words to "Eye of the Tiger" over the roar of the crowd beyond those doors. It takes three large muscular demons to push them open, clearing the way so my escort and I can enter what can only be described as the room of death.

Bloodstains plaster the walls and floor. I draw my eyes up and realize blood plasters the ceiling as well. There are chunks hanging there. Hairy, bloody chunks. *Ew!*

Weapons of every size and shape imaginable cover one entire wall. The ceiling has to be at least four stories high, so that's a shit-ton of weapons. It's impressive and a little terrifying. Daggers, swords, maces, bows and arrows, crossbows, and axes of all shapes and sizes line that one wall. There are so many weapons, most of which I've never seen before.

I fidget, rubbing my hands over my clothes. I slip my fingers into the leather pockets of my pants to hide the shaking. The only weapon I have used is a dagger. It doesn't seem like that weapon will measure up in this situation.

I turn to the right, and my heart drops to my stomach. Nat stands, chained to the wall with more of those black beings surrounding her. She's in terrible shape. Her head is hanging low, face swollen with blood dripping down her body. Her floor length dress is torn and my heart sinks for her.

Before I can come to terms with Nat's condition, Demar is standing inches away. *Yikes!* I roll my shoulders and take an involuntary step back.

"Natash has been a terrible fae, and I can't have my people disobeying my orders in my absence." He looks over at her with a huge smile on his face. Then he turns back to me, "That would cause chaos in a place where control is key. Wouldn't you agree, Alayah?"

I swallow down the lump in my throat and dare to ask, "What have you done to her?"

"Well, when I found out she was aiding you and offering you luxuries you didn't deserve, I decided a little tough love was in order," Demar states, and I don't think I'm the only one within hearing distance who knows tough love is possibly the only love that Demar is capable of.

"Why isn't she healing?" I know she heals quickly; I have seen it with my own eyes.

"Those chains you see are pure iron," he laughs to himself, "Very harmful to the fae. She will be fine once I release her from them, as long as she doesn't die before that happens."

I suck in a little breath. I don't want her to die for helping me. She has kept me sane in this crazy place and for that, I'm very thankful.

"What shall we do to get this show on the road, then?" I ask, turning my attention back to Demar.

"In a hurry to wither in your own pain, Alayah? Just so you can ease that of somebody else. Very noble of you." He looks me up and down as he continues, "You always were too soft, but today's events should toughen you up a little, or kill you."

I narrow my eyes at him.

"Don't worry, Alayah, I am hoping for the former, since I still need you," he says as he walks to the center of the arena, red scales shimmering in the light like rubies in the sun.

I try to move towards Nat, but Demar's lackey grabs me by the arm, holding me in place as he whispers in my ear, "I wouldn't do that if I were you."

"Fuck you," I hiss as I pull my arm from his grasp.

His lips twitch up in a smile as he whispers again, "Maybe later, but for now, I am here to help keep you alive. Not everyone in this place wants Demar to succeed." His eyes move to Demar, who is looking in the opposite direction for the moment, talking to a green slimy slug shaped demon.

"So it seems," I say.

"Like Natash, I am not from here. I would love to be free again. Three hundred years is too long to serve an evil bastard and I'm over it."

Interesting. I remember my conversation with Mikal and Cade telling me that the beings at the club were minor demons. I'll have to revisit that later, when my life isn't in danger; if that time ever comes.

"So, Alayah, are you going to help free all the poor souls under Demar's control?" He asks as he runs the backs of his fingers down my arm, sending shivers through me and causing heat to pulse low in my center.

Did he do something to me or is it just my reaction to him? I enjoy the bad boy type, but does he have a power that can make me feel this way? I step away to clear my mind and I turn back to Demar without saying a word.

As I sweep my eyes around the arena, I notice more and more demons; tall and short, scaled and smooth skin, many of them have heinous scars crisscrossing their bodies. I can tell those are the warriors. Those are the ones I should fear, but at this moment, I'm not afraid. I feel a need to protect Nat and loathing for the bastard that thinks he can enslave and torture other beings for his sick amusement.

Heat rises in my belly as I look at the wall of weapons again. I am so out of my league right now, but I can't bring myself to care.

As I stand here with emo dude, I decide that I'm not afraid to kill if that means keeping myself and the people I care about safe. So, I will do what I have to do to get through this.

That determination dies when a door opens and two guards bring in a man. I don't know who he is until Nat's chains rattle and her soft voice says, "No, Mattenhue." When I look at her, she barely has her head lifted, but I can see the tears trailing down her cheeks.

My attention shifts back to Mattenhue. I see nothing on his face that says he cares or even recognizes her. His eyes are clouded over with a nothingness behind them that scares me a little. It's like he isn't there at all, his mind completely gone. Demar looks at Nat and scoffs, then he looks at me and says, "Natash didn't realize that I've had her love here the whole time. I promised he would be alive, but I promised nothing past that. I have turned him into a weapon. He has no feelings and does what I command."

Nat cries harder and my heart breaks a little more for her. The tears running down her cheeks smear the dust on her skin, leaving tracks. It adds to her addled state.

There are murmurs around us, and I see the displeasure on Demar's face as he tries to get the audience's attention.

"Quiet, you heathens," his voice booms and as the room quiets, there are still two demons talking in the far corner. I watch as Demar's left eye twitches and his face falls into an all too familiar look. He lifts his hand, still staring at the two disruptive demons and as he snaps his fingers, they both fall to the floor, lifeless.

I gasp, and Demar looks my way.

"They're disrespectful," he shrugs as if taking their life was nothing more than a small slap on the wrist.

Emo dude whispers in my ear, "When demons die in Hell, they are reborn to a far worse torment, but they do not die in the way you are thinking. They will work their way back here or they will suffer for all eternity in the abyss. They will not cease to exist."

Well, that isn't as comforting as he meant it to be, but now is not the time for distractions.

My eyes focus back on the room.

"Today we are going to test Alayah. There are no rules. I just want you to cause her the most pain possible without killing her. Rumors are circulating. She has friends from the mortal realm searching for her. I am displeased. Cause as much pain as possible. She needs to be punished. But remember," he pauses dramatically, making eye contact with everyone in the arena before he continues, "If you kill her I will torture you and dispose of you myself!"

Well, at least that supports the idea Cade and Mikal are looking for me.

"We will start with one on one, hand to hand combat. Rachel, if you would enter the center of the arena now. As our youngest warrior in training, we will start with you and work our way up to Mattenhue." He turns to me and swipes his hand towards the center of the arena where a young demon girl is bouncing back and forth on her feet.

She has her long red hair pulled away from her face. It's tied in a high ponytail and braided. She looks human except for her face, which resembles a pig type creature. She has a snout and beady, black eyes.

I watch her intensely, using my enhanced sight to take in every little nuance she has. She is favoring her left shoulder. I realize I never would have spotted this partic-ular weakness without the fairy nectar. She looks small and meek, but I will not be taking her size for granted.

She wouldn't be here if Demar didn't think she would cause me some pain. He is a sadist if nothing else.

A hand brushes my arm, and I hear emo dude in my ear, "She's quick and stronger than she looks. If you can land a punch or a kick in her left armpit, that will put her out of commission and you can move onto your next opponent. Your greatest asset will be your ability to slow time, but you cannot make that obvious. It would be in your best interest to keep that a secret from Demar."

I turn slightly and lift an eyebrow at him.

He gives me a half smile then continues, "I also added some herbs to the fairy nectar that should help you, enhance your senses, speed, and also help you heal faster."

With a wink, he steps away from me. I glide to the center of the arena. I hide my emotions behind a wall in my mind.

Rachel doesn't give me time to get situated. A right hook comes out of nowhere and my head whips to the side. I taste blood and the anger builds in the pit of my stomach. That cheating bitch. I suppress it. No sense in losing my head in the first two minutes.

As she comes in for another blow, this time a kick to my side, I wait until her foot is a couple of inches from my body. I block it and drop to the ground, sweeping her other leg out from under her. She hits the ground hard and her head bounces off the dirt.

I move back, allowing her to get herself back together and giving me time to analyze her a little more. I've heard patience is a virtue and I hope it works for me in this fight.

When she charges me again with an earsplitting shriek, I see my opening and I take it. I move as though I am going to swing at her left side; as she brings her arm up to block, I switch my stance and kick her in the armpit like I was told.

She drops to the ground instantly and her eyes roll back in her head. I wipe my mouth where she got me with the right hook. The back of my hand turns red with blood which brings awareness to the throbbing pain in my lip.

My eyes follow her limp body as she is drug away. I almost feel sorry for the girl. Not only does she have the face of a pig, but I could take her down in less than five minutes. I know that isn't the entertainment Demar was looking for.

He enters the ring and I take a few steps back, bumping into a solid mass. I gasp and whirl my head around to look over my shoulder, only to see emo dude standing behind me. I should ask his name, but I can't bring myself to care at the moment, even though he gave me the tip that ended the fight so quickly.

Demar's voice booms and I can hear the anger in his tone, "Bring her to the dungeons, I will take care of her punishment later."

Then he turns his head to me and I watch a smile spread across his face, the one that terrifies me more than his angry tone, "Well, that was anticlimactic! I think we will have to ramp up this training if I want to see what you are capable of. You barely broke a sweat, and I didn't see a single ability surface."

His frown is almost comical, but I hold in my smirk because I know he has it out for me. I don't want to add any more fuel to his fire.

"Valcan, grab a weapon and get your ass in the ring." When Demar's eyes shift to the other side of the arena, I almost drop to my knees.

Valcan must be at least 16 feet tall, his skin shifting and flowing over his body like molten lava. He is huge and his red eyes scare the shit out of me when he looks in my direction. There is not a sliver of humanity in them and if the hiss behind me is anything to go by, this will not be an easy fight.

Again, I hear a velvety voice in my ear, "He will ask you to pick a weapon. I know the only one you have used is a dagger, but that should do as long as your aim is true. A dagger to the eye will take him out, but it will not be easy, and you will need to stay away from him and his weapon. His skin will burn you, and he is the strongest in this arena. He isn't the quickest, though, so at least you have that on your side."

"Alayah, you may pick a weapon," Demar says watching Valcan chose his, which is a mace the size of a beach ball. That is going to be hard to avoid. I notice he twirls it through the air with ease and my stomach drops to my knees, knowing I wouldn't even be able to pick it up.

That thing is going to crush me.

There's a brief squeeze on my hand and a whisper in my ear, "Just stay away from it and you'll be fine."

Ha, easier said than done.

I walk to the wall slowly, trying to get my bearings and take my time looking over the weapons, even though I have already spotted the daggers I'm going to choose. I can feel a vibration from them, like a warm summer breeze across your bare skin or the caress of a silk sheet. It feels like home and I am drawn to them.

I make a show of looking at and touching other weapons, a small axe and a heavier sword, continuing to move toward the daggers. The hilts are black, made of onyx or some other black stone that gleams in the light, reminding me of the night sky and the Milky Way. There is a dark blue stone imbedded in the black of each of the hilts and the blades are white like bone but brighter.

As I run my finger across the sharp edge, I know these daggers will cut through the toughest substance, like a hot knife through butter. Holding one in my hand brings a familiarity, filling a void in my soul. When I pick up the second one, I feel a rush of power through my body and a series of images flash before my eyes. Images of me using these blades in a battle with my people at my side. Demar and the demons who follow him threaten to destroy our world and enslave all those who oppose him. We fight for freedom. Hundreds of bodies are left on the battle field. With these images comes a feeling of victory, but also a significant loss.

When the images stop, I take a deep breath, gathering myself and my thoughts for a moment. This is intense! I need to get myself back in the game or I am going to lose my head. One thing is for sure, though, I will not be leaving without these daggers.

CHAPTER NINETEEN

READY, JUMP

~MIKAL~

That smell! It's faint, but smells like lightning with a pine undertone. Not the lemon and honeysuckle scent of Alayah that has me panting every time I'm around her. No, this is fainter. It's old, almost lost in years of use and just barely holding on to the teddy bear I have gripped in my hands.

I can't put my finger on who the scent belongs to, and it's bothered me since I came to Alayah's room to peek at her belongings.

There's no time to dwell on it now. We have a rescue mission to get to and I'm sure it won't just be a quick in and out. It's going to get bloody. I need my head in the game.

Ding!

Another message from Tara. Flipping my phone open, I glance at the words.

When are we rescuing Ali?

This is the eighth message this morning from her, not to mention the five from Jake and the rest of the messages since Demar took Alayah.

I've told them what I can and more than I should have, I suppose. Keeping them placated has proven to be a hopeless endeavor. Just another day and then they will see her again. Only a few more hours for me. The wait is tearing me apart, but to know that she is alive and safe, that keeps me going.

I shut my phone off and watch the screen fade to black. The life slowly leaving the device brings a flood of emotion to the forefront of my mind and I work hard to contain it.

A knock at the door startles me, and I turn to the brief whisper of the door opening. I rub my eyes, composing myself. The stubble on my chin prickles my shoulder as I peer towards the noise. Laying the teddy bear on the bed, I turn to address Cassie, who is staring at me with a quirked eyebrow.

"Can I help you with something?" My tone comes out sharper than I mean it to, but Cassie doesn't react negatively.

"I came to inform you, we're ready to review the final plans before we step through the portal to Hell." The corner of her lip lifts in a smirk.

"Okay, thanks for the heads up. I'll be down in a minute." I run my fingers through my hair, pulling a little before I drop my hands down to my side.

"You really like this girl, don't you?" she asks, not taking my cue to leave.

"I do, and I feel responsible for her being taken. Not only that, but I have Tara and Jake asking questions I just can't answer. Cade is at my throat because he trusted me with Alayah's safety. Honestly, I failed him and I just want her back here. I have no idea what's happening to her down there, but it can't be good." I sigh and rub my hand over my face, feeling defeated.

Something passes over her face for only a split-second before she schools her features again, and I wonder if it was a hint of jealousy.

"Well, stop moping because today is the day we get her back. You'll be even less useful in a fight if you don't get your head in the game." Yep, there's the snarky Cassie we all know, but it works. I get to my feet, ready to face all the demons of Hell.

With one last glance at the teddy bear, I head down the hall to the main living area where voices are muffled by the swinging door. As I turn the corner, pushing the door aside, I can feel the tension radiating off of Cade. His face and shoulders are tight. The glare he directs at Dante could make the strongest men piss themselves. Wow, I'm glad he isn't shooting those daggers at me.

Dante's hands ball into fists at his side. And the scowl on his face tells me he isn't too happy either.

Cade turns to me and says, "We received information from Dante's informant indicating Alayah will be undergoing training in the the arena today, where she will face Valcan. Demar intends to raise the stakes and select a new opponent if she is victorious."

"Valcan, shit! That will not be an easy fight. I've heard stories about that ugly bastard and he's not someone you want to fuck with. If she can best him, she'll make another enemy, even if she's being forced to fight. And if she doesn't, he'll make sure she ends up as ugly as he is." I pull a face because I can imagine her screams as he burns the flesh on her body, causing scarring until she is still alive but unrecognizable.

I've seen it happen before when I used to frequent the underground fighting ring. My dad would bring me to witness the fights; said it would make me tougher, which it probably did. It scarred the little boy I was, though. No child should witness the shit that goes on underground.

"She has already fought one fight and won. Do not underestimate our girl," Dante says with some bravado.

"She's not yours, in any way, shape, or form," I say, glaring at the pompous asshole.

"We'll see," is all he says in return, but it is enough to ruffle my feathers and I really want to hit him square in the jaw. Unfortunately, we need him and the fifty fae that he has brought to help in this fight.

I have about twenty of my best trained wolves ready to go and Cade has ten elementals. Elementals are the strongest in abilities, but they are few, due to wars. We can't afford to lose anymore. We will assign one wolf to each elemental to protect them as they wield their magic.

Cassie has recruited a few witches. Plus, a handful from other races are here to help, probably just looking for a fight with the demons, but we'll take what we can get.

And then there's Gruff. His size is deceiving, but he's fierce. Gruff never loses a fight and his enemies seldom survive. He's helped to set up this plan, and it seems he has a soft spot for Alayah, which I'm thankful for.

Gruff has informed us that Alayah is coming into her abilities and that he has been helping to train her the best he can. I fear for her, but at least I know she isn't helpless.

Cade draws my attention back to him as he speaks, "We are well aware of our plans and individual assignments. It is crucial to acknowledge that the upcoming battle in the arena will not be an easy one, as Demar's most formidable demons will be present. However, our primary objective remains the safe retrieval of Alayah. We will enter through the portal created by Dante and proceed to the arena accordingly. Each group has been assigned specific tasks. Does anyone have any further inquiries or concerns?"

Dante scoffs and asks, "Aren't you forgetting something?"

If looks could kill, Dante would be dead. "We have a dedicated group assigned to the task of rescuing your cousin. However, it is important to note that their mission can only be accomplished if Demar is eliminated. Your cousin has made a binding oath that will only be released upon the completion of Demar's mission or his demise."

"You will kill Demar. My cousin's return is nonnegotiable." I can see the anger flare in his eyes.

"The intelligence provided by Gruff gives us valuable knowledge of the castle and the demons in the Arena. We have organized groups based on their strengths against specific demons. Our immediate priority is to secure the safety of Alayah. However, we must remain vigilant in our pursuit of Demar, as his actions could lead to the enslavement of all races and the destruction of realms. Our mission to prevent this outcome is of utmost importance. Rest assured, we will exert every effort to bring Natash back. Nevertheless, if there arises a situation where ensuring Alayah's safety is compromised, I trust that you will make the necessary decision to safeguard the well-being of all races." By the end of that, Cade is breathing hard, fists clenched at his sides, as if willing them not to reach out and punch Dante.

I, for one, would love to see Cade's fist connect with Dante's face. This thought makes me smile and I get a sideways glance from Cade. The smile drops from my face.

"Wouldn't it be easier just to kill Alayah then? Problem solved!" Dante is baiting Cade, getting jabs in with an audience. It's a political move. Putting doubt in the minds of the members of this crowd will help him in the future.

I see the switch in Cade instantly as he realizes Dante's motive. The tension eases out of him, not the reaction Dante was looking for, and he knows he lost his advantage.

"Alayah's role as the next queen and her potential rulership over all races, including the Fae, makes her life of utmost importance. We will prioritize her safety above all else. Any discussion or suggestion of harm towards her is considered treasonous and will not be tolerated." The crowd shifts uneasily, realizing just how grave this situation really is, and I feel a pride in my friend.

Alayah isn't just Cade's sister, she is their next leader and while most of them do not know her, have never met her, protecting the future queen is important to them.

Rorak is a good leader. He's respected by everyone in this room, including Dante, but he's just holding a place for the future queen. We've awaited the next woman to take the throne for years. As children, they taught us the power of the female line of elemental royalty and everyone has just remembered how important Alayah is to our survival.

Until a few weeks ago, no one knew there was a female heir to the throne, but in that short amount of time, hope and excitement have grown.

My family and the wolves have done our duty. We've protected the elementals, but we understand our numbers are diminishing. Both humans and demons can take credit. We have lost countless family members and friends. Yet we protect and coexist with humans to the best of our ability, but there are always rotten apples. Our destiny to protect the good from the evil is noble, but when wars happen, it's hard to remember that.

Rorak could not get the demons under control and their lack of morals have been spreading throughout the realms, causing chaos. With a female leader, a strong queen, there is hope that so many wrongs in this world will be righted. Hope there will be peace and we can live our lives without worrying about the next senseless casualty.

"Well, let's get this show on the road, then," Dante recovers, and adds, "I will only be able to hold the portal for a few groups at a time, and the return portal will move to the courtyard to the west of the castle. Everyone should have received a map of the castle to study. It is important that you memorize your routes."

The crowd nods in unison.

Dante looks around the room and then stares Cade in the eye, "Once I open the return portal, you will have twenty minutes to make it through. I have two groups of my strongest fae protecting me and the portal. Once they exit Hell, you will have mere minutes before the portal will close and I will not be opening another one."

Cade inclines his head and replies, "If you find yourself unable to reach the portal in time, it would be wise to make yourself scarce. There is a transport area located two miles south of the castle that serves as your only alternative for returning home. This area is designated as a safe zone and, once you reach it, powerful wards will provide protection. It will then transport you back to your realm. However, I must caution you that reaching this area will not be easy. Demar is both cunning and merciless, and he does not leave his castle vulnerable or unguarded."

"The forest between the castle and the safe zone is full of unimaginable and gruesome creatures. The plants eat flesh and the layout changes. I suggest you do not miss the portal, because I have little faith you will make it out alive if you do," Dante adds in a condescending tone.

The crowd shifts uneasily. I can see who is full of fear and I catalogue those faces. I cannot count on them as allies when the time is short. Their top priority will be to save themselves and damn the rest of us.

Fortunately, they are few. Our army generals trained most of the supernaturals we chose for this mission. They will give their lives to save the future queen. I also catalogue those faces. My gaze roams from Gruff to Cade to Cassie and even Dante. I see the determination. They are all in, ready to complete this mission, and I am at peace with what will happen in the next few hours.

A warrior and a protector is what I am; it's how my family raised me and what I was born to do. I'm ready to die protecting the people I care about. Obviously, I don't want to die. I hope this mission goes smoothly, but I will put myself in harm's way to save these people...to save Alayah. With that thought, my heartbeat slows, and the warrior in me buzzes with anticipation.

Dante's hands whirl through the air as he creates the portal. I look on with apprehension. Wolves do not fare well in portals. At least not ones made this way. We have safe zones and transport areas in every realm, but they make the portals in those areas with unique magic. Permanent magic.

I don't know what happens with these impromptu ones, but the magic conflicts with the magic of our wolf and it makes for a nauseous ride. Most likely I will enter it a man and exit it a wolf, and that's if I'm lucky.

Multiple shifts in the portal can be excruciatingly painful. The worst is when you get stuck in a half shift. It's painful and takes time to recover before you can complete or reverse the shift. I haven't experienced it, but I've heard tales.

I feel a shoulder bump against my arm and look over to find Cassie smirking at me, "Not a fan, are you, wolf?"

"I liked the eggs and bacon I had for breakfast, but I don't want to taste them a second time," I reply with disgust.

She laughs at my unease, and I smirk back at her, "At least the discomfort only lasts a few minutes. I can deal."

"It's Dante. I'm sure he will have some way of making it extra uncomfortable for you and Cade," she says in a matter-of-fact way and I wince.

"Of course he will. Can he do that?" My face dropping in thought.

"I'm not sure. If he can, he will. You better prepare yourself," she shrugs and walks away.

"Fuck!" I say under my breath. Looks like the probability of a partial shift just increased. The people closest to me hear, and glance my way. I give a slight shake of my head and try to focus on the plans we have set in place. Maybe someday I can drop that asshat down a notch. Right off the pedestal he seems to think he stands on.

The portal starts about the size of a dime. He's putting a lot of power into this, but reserving most of his power for the return portal. No one wants to be left in Hell. He's a jackass, but even he doesn't want the mission to fail.

As the portal reaches the size of a softball, car tires crunch on the gravel behind me and I can hear the faint sound of Van Halen's "Jump" through the glass. I give Dante a little respect because the sound doesn't pull his concentration in the same way that it seems to pull everyone else's.

"Shit," I recognize the car and groan, swearing louder than I mean to. Again, I get looks from the people standing closest to me, but I ignore them heading over to intercept Tara and Jake.

"Are you going to get Ali? Where is she? We are coming with you!" Tara spouts off as she exits the car while it's still moving.

My exceptional hearing picks up Jake's reprimand as he curses his new girlfriend out for not waiting for the car to stop. It's kinda cute the way the care shows in his voice even though he is swearing; not at her, of course. Jake is too good of a guy for that.

"Tara, this is important! I need you to get back in the car and head home." I try to look stern, but she looks like a hissing cat right now, and it's all I can do to hold myself together.

"Mikal, we are coming with you wherever you are going," Tara says with a hand on her hip.

I take a few more steps so our noses are inches apart, blocking the view so the others won't be able to hear or see our exchange. Other than the wolves, of course. Our senses are exceptional.

"Tara, the best thing you can do for Alayah is to go home. You don't know how to fight. Not only will you and Jake be in danger, but your presence will make it more dangerous for everyone involved." I'm not trying to be a dick, but the truth is the truth and we need to focus on retrieving Alayah, not babysitting her brother and best friend.

"She is my best friend, Mikal, my only real friend and I need to help, to find her, and see that she is okay," she deflates a bit.

"I get it, Tara, but we're going to Hell, literally. It's not the place for a human to be traipsing around. I will alert you as soon as we get back with Alayah." I'm trying to placate her, but I can see in her eyes that she isn't on board.

Looking past my shoulder, she seems to light up. "What is Dante doing? I just want to see. That's magic, isn't it?"

"He's creating a portal to Hell so we can enter Demar's castle undetected."

She arches an eyebrow, "Who's Demar?"

"I mean John." I updated her and Jake on certain details, but I may have missed that.

"So, John is a demon from Hell whose real name is Demar, and you guys are taking a portal into his castle to rescue Alayah from the step-monster?" She catches on quick.

"Yes." She has walked towards Dante and I am matching her step for step, trying to persuade her to get back in the car. I can hear Jake following.

By the time we reach the portal, the size has grown to that of a front door; the colors swirling in a circle. Vibrant blues, greens, and purples all mix together to make a million different shades. When the portal is done, it will reach the size of an overhead garage door; big enough for an entire team to cross through at once.

"You just jump through that and you end up in Hell?" she asks innocently.

Jake gives me a "what the fuck" look. He was a few steps behind us and must have missed the rest of our conversation.

"Yep, that's the gist of it," I say, nodding.

Before I can react, Tara jumps through the portal, grabbing Jake and pulling him with her. The collective gasp from the group doesn't begin to describe my feelings right now.

"Fucking b..." Cade puts a hand on my shoulder, cutting me off. I'm glad, too, because that's Alayah's best friend and a woman. I have no right to call her derogatory names. My mother raised me better than that. I won't treat any woman the way my father treats my mother. She worked very hard to teach me to respect women and I will not disgrace her.

"We better get in there," he says to me.

Then he turns to the crowd, "Alpha Group, we go now. Beta, you will wait for the portal to finish forming before you enter. Each consecutive group after that on Dante's go ahead." He turns to the portal and I only see a slight hesitation as he steps through, the rest of the Alpha Group following his lead.

Chapter Twenty

CALM DOWN

~Tara~

*I*n hindsight, probably not the most elegant move jump-ing through the Portal. My eyes won't focus, blurry with tears from the tossing and turning. When I caught glimpses through the tears, I was in awe. The rainbow of colors swirling around us almost made the the journey worth the churning in my stomach. It was beautiful.

Jake doesn't seem thrilled that I drug him with me. *Ooops!* The fact that he is throwing up behind a house plant right now makes me feel even worse. I doubt he would agree the beautiful colors were worth the ride. I also doubt he is happy to be in Hell. Most people spend their lives trying to avoid this place. Most people, but obviously not me. I jumped in head first without a second thought. I probably should have had a second thought.

It's HOT here. I remove the hoodie I'm wearing and hand it to Jake to wipe his face off. I'm not going to need that in Hell, which is great because the streaks of saliva on the black material have my stomach churning.

"What? Was? That?" Jake asks me, still breathing hard from losing his breakfast.

"I'm so sorry. All I could think about was finding Ali and I just couldn't stand back and do nothing." I try to defend my actions, "I obviously didn't run through the ramifications of that decision."

"Well, I agree with you there. What are we going to do now? I love you, Tara, but Mikal is going to be pissed and I'm not really a fighter." He throws his hands up in the air.

"Don't worry about Mikal. I'll deal with him. He is going to be mad, isn't he?" I scrunch up my nose. I'm usually the reserved one who runs through every scenario. I can't believe I just acted.

"Yes, and have you seen his muscles? He could wipe the floor with me without even breaking a sweat." Jake is still shaking a little. I'm not sure if it is because of me or if it has more to do with the twisting, turning ride we were just on before getting spit out in Hell.

I turn my attention to the stone walls surrounding us. When they say castle, they really mean like an old authentic castle. My admiration of the architecture is cut short when Mikal, Cade, and a few other people drop from the portal in a heap. Now my hands are shaking, and my knees, and pretty much my whole body. Cade and Mikal both glare at me with an intensity that has my knees buckling.

I reach down to help them up, but they ignore the offer. I think I'm in trouble.

"Alpha Group spread out and secure the area," Mikal commands and I can see the army general coming out in him. It isn't the goofy, cocky Mikal I know, but a stern, authoritative version. I wish Ali was here to share this moment because he is pretty sexy when he takes charge like this.

I glance at Jake to make sure he doesn't notice me staring, to find that he is staring as well. That's hilarious, and I burst out laughing. We're made for each other.

My outburst draws the attention back to me. *Shoot!*

"Tara, that was the most irresponsible, outlandish, dreadful thing you could have possibly done, considering what we are dealing with at the moment," Cade chastises me and I shrink into myself.

"Cade," I try to apologize when Mikal cuts me off.

"It doesn't matter. She's here now, and we are in enemy territory. Time to get our heads in the game and rescue Alayah." He turns and looks at me and Jake.

"Escorts will accompany the two of you to the extraction point, and you will stay hidden with your own personal guard until we retrieve Alayah and meet you." His face stays stern, "You will not argue about this or disobey. Alayah cannot be in more danger because you were too foolish to think before you acted. Plus, she would skin us all if either of you were to get hurt."

He's so intense. I notice the crinkles around his down-turned mouth and the tension in his face, neck and shoulders. I'm guessing that the ride through the portal wasn't a breeze for him and I am also impressed that he can hold it together when I am sure he wants to pull a Jake and puke.

"Bosco and Raff, please escort these two to the return transport area. Make sure they stay put, and if anything should try to hurt them, protect them with your life." He waits until both Bosco, in human form, and Raff, in his wolf form, nod in understanding before he nods back, turns to us and says, "Go now and do not pull anymore shit."

I look at the ground like a reprimanded child. Raff comes up behind me and nudges me gently in the back with his snout. Jake, who is standing behind me, grabs my hand and gives Raff an accessing look. I can't tell if he's being protective of me or if he's just taking this all in. My intuition tells me it's a little of both, and I lightly squeeze his hand to give him some reassurance.

It truly is a lot to take in. I mean, we just found out about this world a few weeks ago and I have always believed that there is more out there than just humans. But to believe something could be is one thing. To have it so drastically thrown in your face is a completely different, life-changing event.

I take a deep breath and follow Bosco. We have instructions to be silent. We need to make it out of the castle to the courtyard without alerting anyone to our presence.

I concentrate on being quiet and keeping the group quiet. I can sense the tension, but more than that, Jake's fear for me and for himself is wafting off of him in waves.

Bosco's tension is more about being ready for a fight. The harder I concentrate, the more I detect his anticipation, the adrenaline rush he gets from hand-to-hand combat. He likes the fight.

Raff is in wolf form, so it's harder to pinpoint what he is feeling. His feelings are more animal like and sporadic, but his tension comes from being on alert. He doesn't seem to be worried about himself or even us, but is cautious and doesn't want to walk into an ambush.

I haven't told anyone how intuitive I am. Not even Ali. I fear people would tease me, or worse yet, think I'm crazy. Ali has always known that I am more intuitive than most, and she has mentioned the calming effect I have on her. She doesn't know the depth of it, though.

Now that I know more about the world we live in, I'm so excited to tell Ali how attuned I am to the people and animals around me. About my ability. I'm finally comfortable enough to tell her. And what happens? She gets taken and I can't reach her.

My eyes are scanning the area, and I send out a wave. That's what I call it when I try to detect the emotions of things around me. I don't sense anyone besides the four of us. I don't know how far away I can feel emotions, but I would guess it's only a couple hundred feet. Maybe a few rooms away. I never tried to expand or focus my ability until I learned I wasn't an outcast a couple of weeks ago.

For now, we are alone in this section of the castle, and I am glad about that. Unlike Bosco, I am not looking for a fight. I just want my friend back.

"Once we reach the bottom of the stairs up ahead, there will be a door that exits to the courtyard. We need to be cautious not to alert anyone, but most of the demons should be in the arena right now watching Alayah fight," Bosco says in a whisper.

Both Jake and I jolt at his words. "A fight? Ali can't fight demons. We need to go help her."

Jake's words don't really resonate with me because at that moment, I detect someone coming up the stairwell. I throw a hand over Jake's mouth and put a finger to my mouth to shush the other two.

Bosco and Raff both glance at the stairwell, and Raff nudges us into a little alcove just ahead. It's well hidden, but the three of us barely fit. I know there is no way Bosco will squeeze in here, and his excitement intensifies when he realizes it, too.

He's ready for a fight and he stands in the hallway, waiting. His hand reaches for the sword strapped under his coat. The glint of the metal is a bright flash in this dingy hallway. I'm a little taken aback that he doesn't shift. I figured he would prefer to fight as a wolf, but he stands his ground as a man. My interest piques. I would love to see what he can do.

The footsteps move closer and the sound of shoes sliding against the stone floor reaches my ears. They are light and I have to wonder if they're from a woman or a child? Surely a man would make more noise.

I send out another wave. There's no malice coming from the intruder. I can, however, sense the shock when the small girl sees Bosco. Her eyes grow big and her mouth opens. Before she can scream, his hand wraps around her small face, covering her mouth so she can't make a sound.

I step into the hall before he can do anything drastic. My knees bend and I lower myself until I am looking straight into her big brown eyes. I scan her face. Those brown eyes glisten with flecks of caramel. Her rosy cheeks and pink lips remind me of a porcelain doll I had as a child. The way her curly blond hair falls around her shoulders and the puffy blue dress she wears just add to the effect. She's adorable, and she is human. At least, I am pretty sure she is. Why on Earth, or in Hell, is she here?

She thrashes against the man holding her in place. The scowl on Bosco's face tells me he's uncomfortable. And maybe a little disappointed that he didn't get to swing a sword.

I push feelings of safety and calm her way. She stops struggling against Bosco's hold and her eyes meet mine for a second time. I watch as the tension and fear leave her body, and she relaxes in Bosco's arms.

I nod at Bosco and he whispers in her ear. She moves her head up and down in reply to his words, and he removes his big burly hand from her mouth. I didn't realize how big he was until this moment. The girl looks so small wrapped in his arms.

"What is your name?" I ask.

"Elise," the girl answers, timidly.

"Is this your home, Elise?" I ask softer. Her eyes are wide like a deer trapped in headlights and her fingers tremble against Bosco's arm.

She shakes her head, thinks better of it , and nods.

"Did you have a home before this?" I'm probing, I know, but something is nagging at the back of my mind. She doesn't belong here. She shouldn't be here.

"I did. I lived with my mommy in Seattle." Her voice is so soft, like a melody.

"How did you get here?" I ask.

"My mommy lost a bet with the devil." Her eyes grow wide and she slaps a hand over her mouth like she wasn't supposed to say that.

"It's okay," I coax. "We won't tell anyone. You are safe with us."

Her eyes start to tear up a little, "The Devil, he's big and red and scary. He stabbed my mommy and brought me here. Now I help the maids clean the castle."

My heart sinks a little, "Do you have any other family? Where is your daddy?"

"I don't know my daddy. His name was Tim, but he never came to see me." Her lips pull together like she is thinking.

"Do you want to be here, or would you like to come to Minnesota with us?" I ask, hoping she agrees just as Bosco shakes his head.

"I would like to go back to Earth. Hell is scary and hot. May I touch your face?" She asks, seeming a little unsure of herself.

I step up to her, knowing it's a risk. We don't know this child, but I can sense her intentions are pure, so I let her place a small hand on my cheek. When she does, I get the weirdest tingling through my face and head. It doesn't hurt, but it feels like someone is tickling my brain.

Bosco looks at the girl in surprise and says, "You can read minds?"

She nods tightly, "I would like to go with you, Tara. I can help you stay safe."

"Bosco, we can't leave her. She doesn't belong here," I urge.

"Fine, the girl comes with us, but we cannot pick up any more strays along the way." He sets Elise down and starts walking.

She scurries after him and grabs his hand, pulling him in another direction, towards the alcove. She startles a little when she sees Jake and Raff, and then she shakes it off. Her fingers tangle in Raff's fur as she pets him like he's a dog. Patting his head, she squeezes her way to the back of the alcove, where she pulls on a sconce. A section of the door slides inward, revealing a secret passageway. I notice Raff's tail wags at the girl's attention and I giggle at the exchange.

That's awesome!

I love castles and adorable little girls and even big hairy wolves that act like dogs.

"There are scary things the other way, but if we go this way, we can hide in the courtyard where they won't see us," she says in the most serious voice.

Bosco nods and we all follow her in to the dark opening. I hope this isn't a trap.

CHAPTER TWENTY-ONE
NEED A FAVOR

~MIKAL~

Honestly, Tara caught me so off guard by what she did that the ride through the portal didn't faze me the way it should have. Sure, my stomach is rolling, but it isn't so bad that I can't keep it together. I thank the stars for that, but I will not let Tara get away with being so reckless, not when Alayah's life is on the line.

After assessing my situation, I pull myself from the heap we landed in. Raff lets out a groan as I use his shoulder for leverage to heave myself up. A wave of guilt washes over me when I glance at him. He didn't fare so well in the portal.

He is now stuck in his wolf form. The gray fur around his muzzle and neck has matted from saliva. A low whine escapes as he stands on four shaky legs. Another pang of guilt tries to work its way into my mind, but I stomp it down. They train us to withstand times like these and he will be a better soldier for it.

Raff's loyalty to the pack exceeds most others and I trust him completely, even in the state he's in. I've decided he and Bosco are going to be in charge of keeping Jake and Tara safe until we can leave this godforsaken place.

Bosco is a fighter. In his wolf form, he is huge, just like his human form. His fur is tan with white patches. As a human, he has vitiligo, which causes his skin to lose pigment in some areas.

This doesn't hinder his ability to fight. He lives for the fight and can be a little on the wild side. His loyalty to me and the pack keeps him in good standing. It also keeps him in my inner circle.

My gaze shifts to Cade. He looks proper as usual, not a hair out of place. I don't know how he does it, but I'm sure the strenuous royal training has a lot to do with it.

My eyes scan the room, looking for danger. Luckily, our group is alone in the room, for now. Then my eyes fall on Jake and I can see he didn't take to the portal too well. It shows in the way his fingers shake and that greenish tone to his skin. Oh, and the disgusting smell of vomit in the air. It's times like these that I wish I didn't have a heightened sense of smell. *Gross!*

Tara didn't have that problem. I kind of wish she would have. A ramification for her actions, at least.

"Alpha Group, spread out and secure the area," I say in my most commanding tone. I may be a fun-loving guy when I am not on a mission or in training, but this is war and there is no room for mistakes.

Tara laughs and I want to strangle her. She isn't taking this seriously at all. I'm about to reprimand her when Cade beats me to it and I am thankful because I probably wouldn't have been as nice, if you could call it that.

"Tara, that was the most irresponsible, outlandish, dreadful thing you could have possibly done, considering what we are dealing with at the moment," Cade whisper yells and I can see Tara visibly shrink.

Good! She needs to realize the severity of this situation. This isn't a party open to the public, it's invitation only.

"Cade," Tara starts.

I cut her off instantly, looking at Cade. There is no time for this. We need to find Alayah. "It doesn't matter. She's here now, and we are in enemy territory. Time to get our heads in the game and rescue Alayah."

I give Tara and Jake a stare along with a dramatic pause before I continue talking. At least that's what I'm aiming for.

"Escorts will accompany the two of you to the extraction point, and you will stay hidden with your own personal guard until we retrieve Alayah and meet you." My eyebrows pull down in an *I mean business* sort of way, "You will not argue about this or disobey. Alayah cannot be in more danger because you were too foolish to think before you acted. Plus, she would skin us all if either of you were to get hurt."

I'm ready to get a move on. I can feel the sickness from the portal leeching into me. Just because I didn't shift doesn't mean it wasn't nasty. The sooner I get moving, the better I'll feel.

"Bosco and Raff, please escort these two to the return transport area. Make sure they stay put, and if anything should try to hurt them, protect them with your life.." They both nod in understanding and I get calm, knowing that they are the right two pack members for the job. Then I turn back to Tara and Jake, "Go now and do not pull anymore shit."

They jump into action and I watch their backs get further away, giving myself a moment to collect my thoughts.

Turning to my men, "Fan out and get into position. We need to keep the area secure for the rest of groups to come through the portal."

Then to Cade, I say with a smile, "Work your magic, friend."

I am always enthralled when Cade works his elemental magic. I watch as his face grows even more serious. As a male elemental, it takes more concentration for him than it would for a female, but his power is immense. Maybe even more so than his father.

I can't wait to see what Alayah can do once her training is complete. With her different bloodlines, she may be the most powerful elemental the world has seen in thousands of years. It brings a smile to my face knowing that she doesn't care about power. Unlike other leaders, she cares about people.

Even Rorak, who is an outstanding leader, revels in the power that comes with the position. He hides it well, but I have some special abilities of my own. I know he isn't one hundred percent on board with having Alayah take over. My guess is that he will make sure we draw her training out so he can hold on to power as long as possible.

Power won't affect Alayah in the same way, though. She would give up her comfort to help someone in need. She cares about her family, her friends, people she doesn't even know, and what endears me to her the most is that she cares about me.

Most people care about what I can do for them. Not Alayah. She would jump in front of a bullet to save me, which would be stupid unless it was a silver bullet, of course. But she would do it to save me just because she protects the people she cares about.

As the white light from Cade grows, I have to look away. Like welding, this light can blind you if you look at it for too long and right now, he is putting a little extra power into it. Cade needs an enormous amount of energy when creating a shield to protect a group this large. Keeping our allies safe as they step through the portal takes precedence over Cade's reserving power.

His strongest affinity is to air. As a royal, he can access more than one element, but he is currently using air to create a soundproof barrier to keep us concealed and protected. It's a nifty little trick, if I say so myself, and it comes in handy as hell. Not only is his shield soundproof, it's impenetrable and makes us invisible.

The only catch is his hold on the magic only lasts for about fifteen minutes and moving with it cuts that time down to a third. Still a very cool ability.

As the groups file through the portal, some of them not faring so well, I direct them into position. The majority will head to the arena with us, but some smaller groups will immobilize any threat outside of the arena and clear our path to the pickup point.

When Cassie exits the portal, she heads straight towards me. The scowl on her face lets me know she's beyond pissed. That, accompanied with the black tactical uniform we all wear and all the weapons that adorn her body, makes her downright scary. Really, I just hope I look as good in the uniform as she does.

"What the hell was that? Are they trying to get us all killed?" She reminds me of a pissed off baby leopard, hissing and scratching but still kinda cute.

Her hand strikes my shoulder and I narrow my eyes at her. She gets away with a lot, but striking me is not something I take lightly. The way she withdraws her hand and steps away tells me she realizes hitting me was a dangerous move.

"I've taken care of the situation. They care about Alayah and, though misguided, they want to help," I say in a calm tone. No use in riling Cassie up anymore. She needs to have her head in the game.

"Well, it was stupid and reckless," she huffs and walks towards her group to go over some final details.

I nod and continue taking inventory of the groups entering. As the last group steps out of the portal, I take a deep breath and settle myself for what's coming.

Best-case scenario, we are in and out with no casualties. Worst case, we all die horrible excruciating deaths and we fail our mission, leaving Demar to use Alayah.

Eddie walks up to me and puts a hand on my shoulder. Other than Cade, there is no one I would want by my side more in a fight. A warmth radiates through my chest when his eyes meet mine. I can see the pride in them.

I wrap an arm around his shoulder, patting his back, and he pulls me in for a quick hug.

"You are going to be the best leader our packs have ever seen." Stepping back, he puts a hand on my chest and pats the area over my heart, "Don't lose this. Let it guide you and you will never become your worst fear."

I understand he's talking about my father, and my stomach clenches. Going through life only caring about power and control is one of my biggest fears. It has been since I was a child. Losing the people in my life that I care deeply for, Cade, Alayah, Eddie and the pack, that is my worst fear.

Eddie is an amazing father and mentor. I mean, he took Pablo in and treats him and the boys equally. That's a feat in itself.

The way Pablo averted his eyes when we told him he couldn't be here tore at my soul. This isn't a place for a kid, though. Eddie gave him the important task of taking care of Eddie's wife, Sarah, and his two boys while we were away. Pablo knows how important family is to Eddie and takes the job seriously, but I'm sure he's still sulking a little.

"So, boss, we ready to do this?" he asks, a grin spreading across his face.

"As ready as we will ever be, I presume." I run a hand through my hair, breathing in deep and centering myself.

"Don't worry, boss, we will get your girl back," he says with a wink.

"She's not my girl, but I have no doubt we will get her back. If not, Cade will probably dismember me with his glowing light," I shudder and Eddie smiles.

This guy. The uncle that isn't my uncle. He's the one I look up to and joke around with, the one that I had my first beer with and we kept the shared secret from my father. This man has never let me down. I don't know what I would do without him as a constant in my life.

I look around at the others, some I know and some I don't, but what I understand is they all have family and friends. I hope everyone makes it out of this battle alive. Because I will not fool myself. This will be a bloody battle, not a pretty one. Not that any battles are pretty; well, maybe a dance battle or something.

Demons of Hell do not fight fair. They will rip your heart out and eat it while simultaneously dismembering your body. They will not care that these people have loved ones at home because demons lack empathy. It's what makes the rest of us toe the line. Demons do not toe the line, they ravage it.

The portal shrinks and blinks out of existence. "Cade, it's time to drop the shield and head out."

As soon as the shield drops, everyone moves. With this many beings, you would think it would be chaotic, but everyone stays synchronized and the ball of dread in my stomach loosens a bit.

Cade and I take the lead. We follow the route we mapped out in our planning sessions. This castle is a labyrinth of hallways and stairs. It wouldn't surprise me if the passageways move like in the movie *The Maze Runner*.

As we move along though, everything seems to match the schematics we studied leading up to this mission and again, the dread eases a little.

As we turn the corner before we hit the stairs, we come face to face with the first obstacle. Two vampire guards, which surprises me. Demar uses the vampires in the Earth Realm, but I didn't realize he employs them in Hell.

I take less than a minute to disarm them by removing both their heads in one fell swoop. Cade uses air to catch the heads before they hit the ground and make a sound. Eddie and I grab the bodies just as quickly.

We move the bodies to an alcove as Cade floats the heads over. Do you know how unnerving it is to see heads floating around detached from their bodies? Well, it kinda churns my stomach.

It just isn't right and that's when it hits me.

Turning to Cade, I ask, "Those were vampires, right? Why didn't they turn to dust?"

"That is an extremely intriguing question for which I do not have an answer," he shrugs and continues walking.

I store that away in my mind to work out at a later time, knowing something is off. Why would the laws of physics which govern a vampire's death change from one realm to another?

The rest of the trek to the arena is quiet. This seems too easy, but I push that down as we approach the last corner before the arena. The doors come into view and I take a deep breath, stepping back behind the wall again. This is it.

I use hand signals to motion for the group to stop and use a mirror to look around the corner. Thankfully, the three guards there are talking and peeking through a crack in the door, trying to get a look at what is happening in the arena.

I whisper to the group to stay put and ask Cade to use his ability to make him, Eddie, and myself invisible. It will be the easiest way to take out the guards undetected before we storm into the arena.

Cade moves back into the hallway a little because he can't control the white light that emanates from him when he uses his magic. As soon and the shield is complete, it will mask the light, but until then the light is like a beacon in the dark night sky.

Unfortunately, he doesn't move far enough away, and the guards notice the glow. I hear them talking as footsteps move in our direction.

Fortunately, Cade finishes the shield before the guards reach the corner and he has the insight to make it big enough to cover the entire group.

As they peer around the corner, they see nothing. One of the guard's shrugs and turns back to the arena, but the other guard squints down the hall. It's something you can't miss, considering the one gigantic eye he has in the middle of his forehead. And it's times like these I'm glad I was born a shifter. He's hideous.

Dodged a bullet there.

Just when he's about to turn around, Cade's shield flickers. At least I think it's a he. It's hard to tell with Cyclops demons.

The gasp the guard lets out is comical, and before his brain catches up to what is happening, I jump into action.

CHAPTER TWENTY-TWO
SURVIVORS

~ALAYAH~

As I enter the ring with my daggers, all I can think is *I don't want to die!*

I'm not ready for that shit yet. At eighteen, I have barely lived. I have so many new people in my life that I want to get to know better. One name comes to mind and my heart skips a beat.

Mikal.

What I wouldn't give to see his face again. To run my fingers down his muscular abs and for his arms to wrap around me. *Yum!*

And then you have Cade, Jake and Tara, too. I need to find out how Jake and Tara's relationship is going, and I desperately want to check on Pablo. Plus, there's Eddie. Such a kind man, who always has a warm smile on his face.

The list goes on and on, including the beings I have met here in Hell. I have more friends than I've had in all the years I've been alive combined, and I'm not ready to give that up yet.

My boots kick up dust as I walk to the center of the arena. The crowd is roaring, but it doesn't bother me. I have found my resolve. I will beat Valcan any way I can. Demar will be next, and I will figure out a way back to my friends and family.

As I come face to, well, that's unnerving. I guess I'll just say it. As I come face to crotch with Valcan, he lets out a deep laugh that makes me want to cover my ears.

He looks down at me, presumably sizing up his competition and he scoffs, turning to the crowd and then to Demar, "You want me to fight this puny little girl?"

"Um, RUDE!" I retort just as Demar nods and I hear the bell ring announcing the beginning of the match.

I don't waste any time and I aim a punch at the area closest to my face. Yep, that's right. I hit him in the dick. Thank goodness he's wearing pants because I'm not interested in finding out if his skin really will burn me.

He lets out a bellow and bends over in pain. Good to know that works as well on male demons as it does on disrespectful humans.

Quickly moving away from him, I assess the situation in the few seconds he takes to get his bearings back, or should I say, get his balls out of his throat.

I snicker to myself and Valcan looks at me like I'm a disgusting rodent that he wants to stomp on. Lucky for me, emo dude was right, and he doesn't move fast at all.

I shimmy a little further away and watch as his knuckles turn white around the handle of the mace. Well, actually more of a yellow-orange, considering the color of his skin, but you get the picture.

As he swings the mace around in the air, following my movement with those creepy red eyes of his, I prepare myself to dodge the attack.

He walks closer to me, his foot falls shaking the dirt beneath me. I inch back. He looks pissed, teeth bared in a sneer, and I'm second guessing my decision to begin this match with a low blow.

I can sense the crowd to my back and the irritation wafting off of them. They want more excitement and they are going to get it. The demon directly behind me pushes me forward just as Valcan swings his mace towards me. I fall right into the path of that giant ball of spikes.

The surprise of the movement stuns me and I lose precious seconds that I would have had to get out of the way, leaving me scrambling for balance.

Time slows and just as the mace is about to connect with my body, I twist away. Instead of getting a gut full of enormous spikes, I end up with two horribly nasty gashes to my biceps.

I lose the grip on the dagger in that hand as my muscles struggle to hold on. The blood flowing down my arm isn't helping my grip any. Tears well up in my eyes, making it hard to focus. The whirling of the mace through the air as Valcan readies himself to take another swing accosts me. I need to move.

"This is going to be fun, little girl. I think I will make this extra painful as payback for the cheap shot at my groin," Valcan says as I use the sleeve on my good arm to wipe my eyes.

Our eyes meet. He lets the mace swing in my direction and I know for a fact that I do not want to get hit with it again. My arm is pulsating, and the blood dripping from my fingertips stains the sandy arena floor.

My stomach rolls and bile inches its way up my throat. I swallow it down, wincing at the burn in my chest. I can't be sure that Demar would stop this match if I was to pass out. Luckily for me, my legs still work, as do my instincts. Jumping back out of the way of the swinging ball of spikes, I throw out my good arm, sending a shield of blue light out in front of me.

As the mace hits the shield it ricochets, sending Valcan off balance. Demons in the crowd scatter, but one isn't lucky enough to get away. This particular demon is furry with horns protruding from the sides of his head. His body and horns remind me of a bull but as his tongue whips out, I see it's forked like a snake. I truly hope this is the asshole that pushed me, but I'm probably not that fortunate.

As he focuses on the long spikes embedded in his stomach, he lets out a roar that ends in a drawn out hiss. Valcan rips the mace out of the guys' body. Another roar, another hiss, and a death glare accompany that move. Valcan isn't the one who receives the glare though, I am.

Great! Another crazy ass demon to look out for.

I hear gasps and a few snickers from the onlookers, but the sound that rings out louder than a church bell on a silent night is that of Demar clapping.

"Perfect, Alayah, let's see what else you've got," he says with a dubious smile spreading across his face.

Not good!

Valcan regains his balance quicker than I had hoped and starts towards me again. I need to get out of his reach and reassess this situation. Running full force, I fake a frontal assault with my daggers raised. At the last moment, before I'm in striking distance, I veer to the right, sprinting to the other side of the arena.

Valcan turns slowly, following my movement, and lets the mace connect with the ground by his feet. The powerful blow shakes the floor of the arena and I can feel the vibrations from my feet to the top of my head. My teeth even chatter a bit.

"Little girl, are you scared?" he asks in a voice that I'm sure will give me nightmares.

If I can keep him talking, it might give me a minute to catch my breath.

"Scared? Of what? An ogre that has more brawn than brains?" I taunt, breathing hard.

"I am going to smash you into dust, you puny child." He spits at the floor in an overdramatic attempt to make me tremble where I stand. All it really does is fill me with disgust as a string of spit hangs off his chin.

How am I going to put a dagger in his eye? I wonder to myself.

I can't get close to him. He'll either smash me or I'll get burned, and I'm still not interested in seeing how that feels.

I suppose I could throw it. I'm just not sure I have that much faith in my aim, and I really do not want to lose one of these daggers.

He beckons me with his index finger, "Come here and play, little girl. Let's have some fun."

"Yeah, I don't think we have the same idea of what fun means," I retort.

The crowd is getting antsy again and I can tell by the look on Demar's face that if we don't get back to fighting soon, there is going to be hell to pay, literally.

I have to get closer to him, preferably at eye level, but stay out of reach.

I know I can't climb with a tattered arm, and I choose to fasten the dagger in that hand to the belt loop on my leather pants. Looking around the arena as my opponent gets closer, I remember I've been working on using my elemental abilities.

What I've learned to do with water probably won't help me because I don't sense an ounce of water in this place. I suppose I could work with bodily fluids but... *GROSS!* Let's table that idea for later, or maybe never.

Air, now that might be helpful. I should be able to use air to my advantage.

As Valcan gets closer, I stir up a gust of air to push him back. His face falls into a frown. His head tilts, and he stares at my outstretched hand.

I glance at Demar. He has moved back to where Nat hangs from the wall. She lifts her head until her swollen eyes meet mine and her hands raise from her sides, palms up. I'm not sure what she's trying to tell me, but if I don't do something soon, Demar is going to get bored.

I do not want Demar to get bored.

What could she be trying to tell me? I send another gust of wind towards Valcan, trying to keep him at a distance. He leans into it but isn't able to break through.

I wonder if I could use air to lift myself off the ground? That would give me a better angle to throw the dagger and still keep me at a distance. I bring my hands up, mimicking Nat's motion, and focus on my intention. My body lifts a couple of inches into the air.

That's it, but just as I'm internally congratulating myself, I realize Valcan has thrown the mace at me and is charging this way like a mad bull facing a matador.

I dodge to the right, hitting the sandy floor with a hard thud, sending currents of pain through my body from the mangled arm I just landed on.

The mace misses my head by less than an inch and I can feel the breeze as it passes. I barely have time to move before Valcan is almost on me and as I try to roll away from him, his hand grasps my ankle, burning the flesh. I try to hold back a scream, locking my jaw, but as the pain intensifies, I can't help but let the sound escape. Pulling with all my might, I work to get my ankle out of his grip.

When that doesn't work, I hit him with a gale force wind that loosens his grip enough for me to pull away. Without even thinking, my body lifts into the air and I move myself backwards multiple feet.

Valcan rights himself and I can't help feeling a little nauseous at the energy my body and mind are using. Thank goodness the blood has stopped dripping down my arm and the burn isn't bleeding at all.

As he charges toward me, I raise my dagger and throw it. Time seems to slow even though I am not tapping into my suspensionist powers. The dagger flies end over end just as Nat taught me and, to my surprise, my aim is true. It hits Valcan right in the center of his left eye and drops him to the ground.

I also drop to the ground, not able to hold myself up any longer. The struggle not to puke is real, between the pain and the yellowish gray puss pouring from Valcan's eye. I gag but manage to hold back the flow.

I don't get time to revel in my victory as Demar walks towards me and calls to the next competitor. As he reaches the center of the ring, there's a massive explosion. The giant doors fly from their hinges, landing on a group of observers on the other side of the arena.

I stumble to my feet, readying myself for an attack. It's no simple task, and a pulsing pain shoots through my body while I work to gain my balance. When I see the first face walking through the huge opening, my heart skips a beat. My eyes glisten with joy and a smile works its way to my lips.

But there's no time for relief because just as Mikal makes his way into the room, a hoard of demons attack and I lose sight of him.

A horrible wail leaves my throat when I try to take a step towards Mikal. Whether that be from the pain pulsing through my leg or the worry that Mikal will die, I'm uncertain.

I am about to try another step, breathing through my teeth at the pain, when a hand wraps around my good arm. I turn, ready to fight, but hold back just in time.

Emo dude pulls me into his chest and whispers, "We need to get you out of here."

"No! I need to help my friends," I say.

My mouth drops as I watch the arena flood with allies, including Cade and Eddie. My head tilts up to the heavens and I send out a silent thank you, hoping that God will hear me even though I'm in Hell.

I mean, it isn't my fault I'm down here. I did nothing to justify this visit. You can't count my bad luck of having a demon as a stepfather against me. Not under my control, not at all.

I take another step towards my people, wincing at the pain.

"You can't even walk. How are you going to help?" His black eyes boar into mine and I lick my lips. I feel like I can see his soul in those eyes.

Wait, does he have a soul?

Another question for later, I suppose as I pull my attention back to the fight. The bodies are stacking up.

Cade's white light grows from the palm of his hand and he directs it like a laser at the demons surrounding Mikal. Eddie shifts in midair, taking out two dark green reptile demons with his giant claws.

More and more allies flood the room, including wolves, fae and a few elementals, from what I can tell. There are demons attacking with claws, teeth, swords and some that even spit venom that dissolves the skin like acid.

I see the vile bull demon with razor sharp horns sneaking up on Cade and notice his skin is decaying, falling off in clumps. That's nasty. Why can't demons be cute and fluffy?

I send a gust of wind in Cade's direction. I don't know if it will work from this distance, but I have to try.

The gust is strong enough to knock some of the closer enemies down and just enough to get Cade's attention. He turns in time to block an attack from the bull with a sword I didn't realize he was holding. In mere seconds, the bull's head disconnects from his body, hitting the floor.

I get a sense of relief. That bull was a complete asshole and now I don't have to worry about him coming after me. Or do I? What did emo dude say about demons dying in Hell?

Cade's eyes meet mine and he nods a thank you before turning back to the encroaching demons.

"Alayah, it isn't safe here. As soon as Demar focuses back on you, he will grab you and disappear," he sighs, making it seem like I'm an unruly child that won't listen to reason. "If he gets you out of here, this is all for nothing. Please come with me."

My gaze shoots to Demar, who is still standing by Nat. Mattenhue is on his left, staring straight ahead like a statue. Demar has Nat's face gripped tightly, and I would assume painfully, in his hand. He's yelling in her face. She tries to shake her head no, but with his grip so tight, she can't move. I can see the fear in her eyes as Demar lets go of her face, turns to Mattenhue, and stabs him in the stomach.

Nat screams a gut-wrenching scream and her eyes drop as she nods. I can see the strain in her features as she builds a portal that she is too weak to build. If it wasn't for the chains holding her up, she would be on her knees.

Demar's eyes seek me out and he takes a step towards me. I flinch at the hatred in those eyes, but as he goes to move closer, his brows furrow together, and he looks around, searching the arena.

Cade steps up beside me, and my shoulders relax a little.

"I have masked our forms with invisibility for now," he says in a stoic tone. "We need to protect you or this will all be for not."

Emo dude looks at me with a lifted eyebrow as if to say, *what did I just tell you?*

I narrow my eyes at him and stick out my tongue. Childish, true, but seriously!

As I look around the arena again, I am relieved to see that most of the demons are dead or gone. My gaze flicks back to Demar. He must have realized this, too, since he is working his way towards the forming portal.

My heart leaps into my chest when I see two wolves moving towards Demar. They are low to the ground, moving with stealth.

Mikal and Eddie.

Demar's head jerks to the side, and his eyes land on the wolves. My wolves! He bends over, wrapping his fingers around two very large axes on the ground by his feet. I didn't even see them there until now.

The wolves circle around him for a minute before Mikal makes his move. He rushes Demar straight on, veering to the right at the last second. I watch as a piece of fur falls to the ground; the axe coming close enough to give him a shave.

Eddie darts in from the back, nipping at Demar's arm. From where I'm standing, I can see a faint line of blood trailing down his arm. I hope with all my heart that the cut hurts like a bitch.

The way Demar wields the axes would have me impressed if I didn't loath him the way I do. They glide through the air, slashing and twisting, keeping Mikal and Eddie at bay for a few minutes.

Mikal finds an opening and pounces towards Demar, coming at him from the side, as Eddie does the same from the back. Before either of them can get close enough to deliver a blow, Demar has the axes out, stopping their advance.

They try again, missing another hair cut by mere centimeters, and I gasp. My muscles tense watching this dangerous dance. I'm frozen, even though I want to help. I understand Eddie and Mikal have trained together for years, and my help just may be a hinderance.

I pull my gaze from the fight to glance at Cade. His jaw is tight like mine. His hands fisted at his side. It seems he is holding back the same as me and my earlier thought that I should stay out of the fight cements in my mind.

I take a deep breath and focus on Mikal. He jumps at Demar again and this time the axe connects with Mikal's shoulder, causing blood to pool on his fur. The momentum forces Mikal's body away, but not before Mikal's claws scrape down Demar's chest. Four bright red gashes cover Demar from collar bone to belly button.

I cheer! I can't possibly express the utter enjoyment that moment brings me.

Demar rubs his fingers down one gash. When he pulls them away, blood coats his hand and his long black tongue darts out, licking his fingers clean.

I gag. He is so disgusting.

Out of the corner of my eye, I watch Eddie get low, ready to attack. Mikal is gathering his senses a few yards away, and I know he will be down for a few minutes.

I try to move towards them, but Cade and emo dude both move to stop me. Two hands grab my shoulders from opposite sides, and all I can do is watch the scene before me.

Eddie makes his move. He leaps into the air while Demar has his back turned, his razor-sharp teeth opening and aimed for Demar's neck.

At the last second, right before Eddie's teeth meet with the flesh of Demar's neck, he turns. The axe heads clenched in his scaly fingers and jams them both into Eddie's chest. Spinning, he throws Eddie to the ground.

Demar, still bending over Eddie, roars as he pulls the axe heads apart, ripping Eddie's chest wide open. He twirls one axe around. One, two, three times before swinging it over his head and bringing it down across Eddie's throat. His head separates from his body with a loud crunch.

My knees give out and I fall. Tears stream down my face. I'm gasping for breath and I don't know how to control it. Tremors wrack my body, and I dig my fingers into the dirt below me.

Cade hits the ground beside me, and I see a tear glisten in the corner of his eye. He stares at me and his lips move, but I don't hear any words.

I didn't know Eddie that well, but he was a good man, probably one of the best, most caring men I have ever met.

His wife and his children are going to be crushed. Oh, Pablo. Poor Pablo, Eddie meant the world to that boy.

My attention shifts as a gut-wrenching howl breaks through the trauma and I see Mikal throw himself towards Demar again. Demar doesn't evade this attack as well as he did the others. Mikal's teeth sink into the flesh of Demar's shoulder and he shakes his head with a ferocity I have never seen before. Demar sinks his claws into Mikal's back, pulling him off and sending him flying into the arena wall over twenty yards away.

I glance around the arena and realize our allies have disposed of the demons. They're closing in on Demar. He must realize the same because he grabs Mattenhue and says something under his breath. The chains around Nat disintegrate and he walks through the portal, dragging her with him.

"Cade, drop the invisibility thing," I say urgently.

He does and I yell to Nat just as she is about to walk through the portal, "Nat, wait."

Her eyes meet mine and I can see the sadness in them. She shakes her head and mouths the words, "I can't stay. He has Mattenhue," before walking through the portal and letting it close.

My heart sinks. Nat is my friend, and I need to get her back. I take in the destruction around me and I can't help but let the tears fall. We lost quite a few allies, from what I can tell, but the demons lost more.

When my gaze moves back to Eddie, a sob leaves my chest and I feel hands pulling me to my feet. Mikal stands in front of me with tears in his eyes.

He doesn't say a thing, just pulls me in for a tight hug, his strength crushing me to his chest. I don't pull away from him. I'm so happy that he's here, and that he's alive.

Even as my heart breaks for Eddie and all those who love him, I can't help but be relieved Mikal is okay.

Mikal loosens his grip on me, just enough for me to pull back and stare into his eyes. They seem to bore into me with more love and admiration than I have ever felt from anyone before in my life.

Mikal inches his face towards mine and just as I think he is about to kiss me, someone clears their throat from behind us.

"Ahem, I'm so glad you guys have had this moment, but I think it's time we find a way out of here before Demar sends reinforcements."

My heart sinks a little, but emo dude is right. Though the smug look on his face says he timed that perfectly to interrupt. *Bastard!*

Then again, I probably shouldn't be thinking about that in the middle of a battlefield.

Mikal lets me go and stalks towards emo dude, "Who the hell are you?"

Just as he says, "My name is Jude," Mikal punches him in the face and cuts off the rest of what he was going to say. I put my hand on Mikal's arm before he can punch Jude again. Jude, at least I can stop calling him emo dude, I guess.

Jude looks at Mikal with blood dripping from a now crooked nose and says, "We need to get moving before Demar sends reinforcements."

"What do you mean, we?" Mikal spits out. I can see him shaking with rage.

"Mikal," I say in a soothing voice, "Jude has been helping me. If it wasn't for him, I don't think I would have been able to survive the fights I've faced in the arena."

His gaze slides to me, and his features soften. "I don't trust him."

"Neither do I, but we can deal with that once we are home and everyone is safe," I say and he nods.

With one more disgusted glance at Jude, Mikal moves to his fallen friend and kneels. As he places a hand on Eddie's shredded body, he lowers his head. I can see his lips moving and watch as a single tear falls from his eye. He takes a deep breath and exhales slowly. When he lifts his head, I can see the resolve on his face.

He is all business again as he addresses our people, "It's time to go. Those of you who can carry the dead, bring them. I won't have their souls left here to be tormented by that sick piece of shit."

Blood drips down Mikal's arms from Eddie's broken body as he leads the way out of the arena.

He turns to Cade, "Burn the rest of the bodies. I want nothing left of this battle."

Cade nods and motions to a couple people off to the side. Whether they are elementals or witches, I'm not sure. We usher our remaining allies and our dead out the door. A blinding white light engulfs the entire arena as the last of our group exits. I wait in the doorway for Cade to finish. Jude remains by my side, helping me to stand.

When Cade and the others are done, the arena is bare, no bodies left, and it looks as if the torture of this place was all a figment of my imagination.

I turn to follow the others, but before I can take a step, I crumple to the ground and everything goes black.

CHAPTER TWENTY-THREE

BLOODSUCKERS

~ALAYAH~

*I*mages of Mikal flash through my mind. His smile, his muscles and his soul catching eyes. I feel a peace settle in my soul. He is gorgeous, a protector. He's someone I want in my life.

In an instant, those images turn to another boy, one I had a crush on when I was younger. A boy that would make me origami flowers in school and would walk me almost all the way home from school every day in seventh grade. Kyle was such a sweet friend. An innocent boy.

"Today, I am walking you all the way home," he says in a confident tone.

"Kyle, you can't! We've talked about this. If the step-monster is there, we'll both be in trouble." I try to hide the fear in my voice, but I'm not sure that I accomplish it.

"Ali, you don't have to worry. It'll be fine," he says as he continues walking towards my house.

Five houses away, four, three. My palms are damp and my hands are shaky. He stares at me with determination and I realize I cannot change his mind today.

As we reach my house, the door flies open, crashing against the siding. You can see multiple rips in the tattered old screen, its edges frayed. Flakes of paint fall from the door and swirl on the breeze before they land on the rotten wood of the porch. John doesn't take care of this place. My cheeks flush red. My stepdad isn't the only reason I don't invite people to our house.

John stands in the doorway, leaning against the frame. His shoulders seem relaxed, but the set of his jaw tells me he's anything but.

"Alayah, haven't I told you that boys are bad news?" he asks, staring daggers at Kyle.

Kyle doesn't even flinch, and I'm a little amazed. "Sir, I just wanted to ensure Ali made it home from school safely."

"Well, thank you for that, I suppose, but Ali cannot have friends. It's time for you to leave." His grin spreads and I get a nauseating feeling in my stomach.

I find it odd that he didn't say I'm not allowed to have friends over but that I cannot have friends.

Kyle, being a little bolder than he should, asks me if I'll be okay and when I nod back, he leans in and lightly kisses my cheek before turning and walking away.

John's face turns red, veins popping out on his neck and forehead. He's upset.

"Get in the house, Alayah," he yells.

Worry churns my gut and it takes a long time for me to fall into a fitful sleep. It seems like only minutes before my alarm is blaring. I shoot out of bed with an awful feeling that something is wrong. I rush to get ready and run to school. My tattered sneakers don't offer a lick of support and by the time I reach the front doors my toes ache.

Once inside, I frantically search for my friend, but Kyle is no where to be found. He isn't at his desk, or in the hallway by his locker, and the other boys assure me his isn't in the bathroom. I bite my lip and head to the office.

"Mrs. Peterson, have you seen Kyle today?" I ask, through deep inhales.

"I'm sorry dear, he's not here today," she says.

"Where is he?" I ask, my voice verging on hysterical.

Mrs. Peterson's warm hand covers mine and she says, "I'm sorry dear, he had a family emergency in Florida. He won't be coming back to school here."

My legs grow weak and I have to grab onto the counter to steady myself. John did this.

"Never should have brought him home," I whisper to myself.

"What was that dear? These old ears can't hear very well," Mrs. Peterson asks.

Without answering I walk back into the hallway, shaking my head in a daze. In that moment, I know I can never bring a boy home, ever again.

Something cold hits my lips and I sputter on the liquid trying to make its way down my throat. A hand is slapping my face and as I open my eyes, I realize I am still in the doorway to the arena.

I take a minute to get the memory out of my head and focus on what's going on around me. I try to bat the hand away; the face staring back at me is Gruff's and a smile breaks on my lips.

"Ah, there's my brave, beguiling beauty. We lost you for a minute." Gruff's beady eyes stare back at me, and I can't help but smile bigger. I didn't know he was here.

Taking in my surroundings, I notice there are three other men leaning over me. Mikal, Cade, and Jude seem to deflate a little with relief. The tension in the air deflating with them.

"Oh, Gruff, I missed you," I say as I try to push myself up from the ground.

"Careful there, Alayah," Jude says, which gets him a sharp glare from Mikal.

"Now that you are awake, time is of the essence. The effects of dehydration and exhaustion caused a brief period of unconsciousness. Are you able to continue our journey?" Cade says as he hands me a bottle of water. I will never get used to his formal speech, but I grab the water and stand.

"Do I have a choice?" I ask.

I feel like shit. Like a train hit me, but that wasn't enough, so it backed over me a few times.

"There is always a choice, Alayah, but the consequences of that choice may devastate you or those around you," Cade replies.

"I can do it. Let's get going before Demar sends more minions." At the thought of him, I shiver. I can't wait for the day that he dies. It can't come soon enough.

A tinge of guilt nags at me. How can I think so little of the death of another being? But the evil that is Demar needs to be extinguished.

Hopefully, his death will come sooner rather than later though, because not only do I want to be done with him, I want to get Nat back.

Everyone agrees, and we move through the castle. I notice our group has gotten smaller and I worry, looking around the hallways.

"What happened to the rest?" I ask, stopping to glance behind us.

"We sent them ahead. Only so many can go through the portal at once, and we want to get out of here as soon as possible," Mikal fills me in.

Our much smaller group includes Cade, Mikal, Gruff, Jude, myself, two wolves I do not know, and a girl strapped to the nines with weapons. Her short hair bounces when she walks and as she looks back at me, I notice she has a resting bitch face that could scare the strongest of men.

Eddie's body is nowhere to be seen. I assume Mikal sent it to the portal with one of our other allies. Thinking of him makes my heart break all over again. His poor family, poor Pablo.

The girl with us grabs Mikal's arm and gives him a stern look. "We need to move our asses, so get your little princess girlfriend to stop slowing us down or carry her. I don't care which, but I will not get trapped in Hell again."

When her eyes slide to me, the glare she shoots my way is stone cold. I'm pretty certain whoever she is, we will not be friends in the future.

I'm not too sure I like the way she's touching Mikal either, or that he is allowing her hand to linger on his arm.

"Cassie, watch your tone," is all he says before he turns to me and asks if I need to be carried.

"I can make it on my own, thanks," I shoot him a dazzling smile and then glare at the dark-haired vixen who is really rubbing on my last nerve.

We move again, Cassie and Mikal having a hushed conversation in the front, with the rest of us trailing behind. Jude moves to my side and slides a hand around my elbow to help support me.

Cade glances at us but says nothing. I can tell he doesn't approve of Jude, but no one else seems to want to help me and, honestly, I probably won't make it without some help.

The wounds on my ankle are probably festering by now, but I grit my teeth and bear the pain.

As we reach a door that will take us outside, the wolves move to the front. Mikal slowly opens the door and they stick their massive heads out to peer around. The coast must be clear because he opens it the rest of the way and we venture into a courtyard the size of a football field.

Black and red roses surround the perimeter. They have also planted them in planters throughout the space. Fires shoot straight up out of holes in the pavers. The flames must go at least ten feet into the air, maybe more. With all the granite benches and ornate statues, you would think you were in Europe, not in the depths of Hell. It's gorgeous.

At the far end of the courtyard, I see something that brings tears to my eyes, not the sad kind, but the cheerful kind for sure. Jake is standing by the portal with an arm around Tara, who is holding a small child.

Jake and Tara seem so happy, but I know I haven't been gone long enough to become an aunt, so who is the little girl? And while I'm happy to see them alive, why are they here in Hell?

"Why are Jake and Tara here?" My gaze shifts from Cade to Mikal, "And who is the little girl?"

A low growl comes from Mikal as he informs me, "It's a long story and as for the girl, I don't know, but they seem like the people who would bring home strays."

He storms forward, Cade and the two wolves on his heals, leaving Cassie, Gruff, Jude and myself behind.

Cassie moves to my other side, sneers at me, and says, "You don't seem so amazing. Not sure why they care so much."

"What are you even doing here?" I ask in a tone that would make most people cringe. I don't like to be rude, but this girl has a chip on her shoulder the size of Texas.

Before she can answer me with another snide comment, there is a loud crash not too far away. Boots smack the pavement in a synchronized march, and an army comes into view. Hundreds of vampires stream out of the castle doors and into the woods. They surround the courtyard and the portal, which incidentally puts them between our group and Cade's group. Not good!

Their cold sunken eyes and pale bald heads give me the shivers. These are not the glamorous vampires you see in the movies or read about in books. No, these vampires are deranged killers who lack any form of humanity.

"Fuck!" Cassie says under her breath and she tries to make her way to the portal. She doesn't get far before the courtyard is full of vampires and she has to turn around to avoid being seen.

"Oh what a..." Jude says so low I barely hear him speak. I can't quite make out the words, but I think it may be a line from a song by Olivia Rodrigo, "Vampire." If so, it seems to fit our current situation.

I see Mikal take steps in my direction as Cade pushes Jake, Tara and the girl through the portal. Tara's eyes widen at the realization of what is going on, which is the last thing I see before the swirling mass engulfs her. I lose sight of her and my brother, but I am relieved that they are on their way back to Earth.

Two more wolves hidden by the roses step up beside Mikal and Cade, teeth barred and ready for a fight.

The vampires form a wall between us and the portal, cutting off my line of sight to Cade and Mikal. My heart sinks into my stomach. They cannot rip me away from my friends again, but there are too many vampires standing in the portal's way for us to make it. I send a silent prayer to whoever will listen that Cade and Mikal exit through the portal before vampires overtake them.

The vampires haven't noticed our little group yet, with all their focus on the portal. I back up slowly, putting more distance between myself and the attackers.

Gruff, Jude, and even Cassie follow my lead and we conceal ourselves behind a statue just as Officer Mahoney enters the courtyard.

Cassie gasps at the sight of Officer Mahoney and all the bitchy bravado she had earlier fades away. Her face pales and goes slack, and I notice a slight tremble in her hands. This is the face of trauma and I wonder to myself how they know each other.

Jude breaks the silence in a whisper, "We need to get to the woods. There is another gateway to earth about two miles away."

I take a deep breath, "Two miles doesn't seem that far. We got this."

Jude's face falls a little, but it is Gruff that speaks, "My open, offbeat little optimist. It will take days to make it to the gateway from here. And that's if you don't run into any of the beasts. You would have to be very lucky."

"He's right, and we will have to find a healer first. There is no way to make it with you in such deplorable shape." Jude looks at me with concern.

"I'll find Doctor Smith and have him meet you at the Red Rock in two hours. Do you think you can make it that far?" Gruff asks, and both Jude and I reply with a yes. Even though I don't know where the Red Rock is, it's our only option at the moment.

We won't make it to the portal across the courtyard, that's for sure. Just as that thought crosses my mind, I watch the edges flicker. With Officer Mahoney's appearance, the vampires have shifted, ready to attack Cade, Mikal and the four wolves, giving me a better view of them.

"Best of luck, Alayah!" Those are Gruff's last words before he disappears into thin air. I wish I knew how he does that. It seems like a pretty useful trick. If we have time to have another training session, I am going to ask him to show me and hopefully I have the ability.

Officer Mahoney's voice pulls me from my thoughts, "Where is the girl?"

I can see Mikal's face but thankfully he doesn't look in my direction when he answers, "She has left and you won't be able to get your grubby paws on her."

"Grubby paws," he scoffs, "that's interesting coming from a mangy mutt."

Mikal's hands ball into fists as anger takes over. Before he can retaliate, Officer Mahoney gives the order for the vampires to attack and, as one, they close in on Cade and Mikal's group.

Cade's gaze meets my eyes, and he mouths the word "sorry" before grabbing Mikal's arm, which has sprouted chestnut hairs. I'm worried he won't get Mikal into the portal before Mikal turns into a full-blown wolf, but as the portal flickers, Cade pulls hard. They both fall backwards into the closing portal.

The four wolves take down a few of the closest vampires with teeth and claws before jumping into the portal themselves. The last one almost doesn't make it through before the portal closes on his tail, but luckily, he is the smallest of the group and seems to be pretty quick.

I wonder what would happen if part of you didn't make it through? Another question for another time, I suppose.

A sigh passes through my lips, maybe a little too soon because just as relief soaks into my bones, the vampires turn as one and stare straight at us. Their bald heads and cold eyes send shivers down my spine.

"It's time to go," I say as I grab Jude's arm and pull to get his attention.

Without me asking, he scoops me up in his arms and I gotta say I'm not disappointed to be cradled against his firm muscles. Another plus, he's fast. It isn't long before Cassie is trailing behind.

When I look to see where she's at, possibly to tell Jude to wait for her, I see what looks like little sparks coming off her fingers. Her lips are moving silently, and I wonder what she's doing.

I few moments later she's keeping pace with a cynical smile on her face. She seems to take pleasure in the astonished look on my face.

"Don't worry about me, Peach, I have tricks up my sleeve you couldn't even imagine." Her condescending tone doesn't go unnoticed by me, but it's just not the time for a catfight. Even though I'm wearing the clothes for it.

I'm still a little disappointed that the leather pants didn't do a better job of protecting me from Valcan's touch, but I'm alive, so there's that!

I watch as Cassie does her thing again and am amazed when she turns, running backwards and throws her arms into the air. The vampires that were almost on our heels slam into an invisible wall, dropping in a pile on top of each other.

That had to hurt. Yikes. *Do vampires even feel pain?*

That was a sweet move on Cassie's part, but I won't tell her that. Her ego already seems too big for that petite body. Whatever she did, she gave us the advantage. It's wonderful to put some distance between us and our attackers. Thank God!

Jude slows slightly and nods at Cassie.

"Thank you. My speed is like that of a cheetah. It only lasts for short bursts, and vampires have the speed and stamina to run for hours." He pulls his eyes from Cassie and looks down at me. "Do you think you can walk for a bit?"

I nod, not being able to speak because of those lashes! Seriously, the man has beautiful black lashes that any woman would die for.

"No problem, you carry her. I carry the team." The snark behind her words is getting old.

Jude ignores it, but I don't know how I am going to get through the next few days.

"We need to get to Red Rock, and soon," Jude says as he frowns at my limp.

"I hope you know where it is because I spent my time here on the other side of Hell," she says, looking around.

The pain is taking its toll on me, so I decide to try the air thing and I lift myself off the ground. Moving forward is a little trickier, but after a couple of tries, I get it.

"Wow, isn't that helpful? You think you could give us a ride to so we can relax in luxury?" Cassie says with a decent helping of sarcasm.

"Enough!" Jude says in a loud voice before he thinks better of it and whispers, "What's your problem?"

"My problem is I came here so I could get revenge by killing a few demons and some bloodsuckers. That was it. Now I'm stuck babysitting the helpless princess in the last place I want to be," Cassie retorts.

I suck it up. She risked herself for this mission, even if it was for reasons that had nothing to do with me.

"Thank you, Cassie. I appreciate your help," I say in a tone that I hope conveys my sincerity.

Some of the tension disappears from her shoulders and she says, "You're welcome," before she storms ahead.

"That girl has issues," Jude says in a hushed voice.

"I know, but there's no telling what she's been through in her life, so let's try to be nice. Make the best of it and all that," I say patting him on the arm.

"It won't be easy, that's for sure," Jude adds.

I know, right! Is all I can think, but I keep it to myself as we walk in silence.

Chapter Twenty-Four

SO FAR AWAY

~Alayah~

My mind and body are vibrating, and my head swivels constantly back over my shoulder. Each glance proves we are alone on our journey, though. And as the minutes tick by, I relax a little more.

We don't encounter anymore obstacles on the way to Red Rock, but by the time we reach the landmark I can barely walk. Puss drips from the burn on my ankle and it's swollen to the size of a softball.

I've lost most of the feeling in my arm. Only a dull tingle remains. I hold it against my chest. The cuts have healed over, stopping the blood flow, but the pain has not receded. I'll have to ask Doctor Smith about that when he arrives.

Jude, ever the gentleman, does his best to help me, but I don't feel comfortable having him carry me. I've done my best to suffer in silence without letting on how much pain I'm truly in.

As we approach the magnificent formation, it takes my breath away. The rocks tower above us, and water cascades from the top to a pool at the base. The deep blue of the water is a vivid contrast to the red of the rocks.

The formation stands in the middle of a clearing on the edge of the woods. Wildflowers surround it in varied colors, from pinks and purples to whites and yellows. Tall grasses frame the pool and wave in the light breeze blowing past us.

The breeze tickles my skin and adds to the wonder. I take a deep breath, centering myself and bask in the floral scent surrounding me. It's hypnotizing, memorizing, relaxing. I never want to leave.

"Beautiful," the word escapes my lips in a sigh of relief, which is soon squelched.

"Don't let the beauty fool you. This is not a safe place," Jude says in a whisper. Both he and Cassie have gone on alert, looking around the clearing and out into the woods.

Other than the beautiful rock formation, these woods don't look all that different from the ones behind my old farmhouse.

"Should we call out to Doctor Smith? See if he's close?" I ask.

"Are you stupid? That would alert the beasts nearby to our presence," Cassie says in an extremely derogatory tone.

I blanch a little. I can only take so much. As hard as I try to be nice and understanding, Cassie makes it pretty difficult not to go into full bitch mode on her ass.

"This is one of the primary water supplies for the beasts of this realm, so we need to be quiet and cautious. We haven't begun the journey through the woods yet, but if I know anything, it's that the real danger starts here and doesn't end until we enter the safe zone," Jude interjects, drawing my attention away from the one girl that I really want to stab with my daggers.

I hear a scuffle coming from behind a tree back towards the castle and turn, hands reaching for my weapons. I realize it's the first noise I've heard since we entered the forest, aside from Cassie and Jude. Not even the waterfall is making a sound.

Doctor Smith shuffles out from behind a tree, looks around, and then walks toward me with a satchel slung over his shoulder.

"Alayah, I am so glad to see you alive. I feared for what might happen in the arena, and then when I heard Mahoney brought the whole nest of vampires in to find you, I almost had a heart attack," he says in a quiet voice, his hand going to his chest.

I see Cassie shiver out of the corner of my eye. *What might that be about?*

Doctor Smith looks over at the others. "Cassie, Jude, good to see you are well."

They nod in acknowledgement as the doctor turns his attention back to me, "Alayah, please take a seat on the ground so I can look at that ankle."

I do as he says, lowering myself to the ground with my good arm and only wincing a little. The grass is soft beneath me and I wish I could lie down and take a nap.

"Valcan really did a number on you, it seems. Most of the flesh is gone from your ankle and I can see the bones showing through. I'm going to have to wrap this. The salve I have should block the pain and help you heal faster." He rubs the salve, which looks like mud and green slime, on a long strip of gauze before wrapping it tightly around my ankle. It stings for a minute before the pain completely eases away.

"Wow, that is amazing. I don't feel a lick of pain from my ankle anymore," I say, looking at the gauze like it's magical.

"Let me wrap your arm up, too," he says, pulling at the sleeve, "It seems your ability to heal yourself is growing. The gashes to your arm are mere red marks now."

Astonished, I look at my arm to see that he's telling the truth. I knew they had closed up, but I didn't realize they were gone completely.

"That's wonderful, but why have I lost the feeling in it?" I ask, perplexed.

"Many nerve endings were severed, and it's possible he dipped the mace in poison. Valcan has done that in the past." His fingers move to my arm, gently pressing around the area. "The salve should help speed up healing. A couple hours at most and you should have feeling back."

Well, that's a relief. The corner of my lip pulls up in a smile as my eyes meet the doctor's. I watch him pack the gauze and salve into another bag with a strap on it. He adds a few more items to help us with our journey and hands the pack to Jude.

"Can't you come with us, Doc?" I ask, hoping he will say yes.

His eyes soften, "Please call me Greg, my dear, and no, I cannot leave this realm with you. I have work to do here and until I've finished helping all the lost souls that don't belong, like you, I need to stay."

"That seems like a lot to have on your shoulders." The words are sincere and I give his hand a little squeeze. The skin feels slick beneath my fingers and I remember his appearance is a facade. It must only change what you can see, not what you can feel.

"That it is, but it also gives my life a purpose," he smiles.

"Do you know what happened to Natash?" I remember I need to find my friend.

"She escaped with Demar. I'm sorry, Alayah, I don't think she was being honest with you," his eyes glance away and the muscles in my stomach tighten like a vise.

"What do you mean?" I wonder. "Demar took her, beaten and chained."

"I don't want to be the bearer of bad news, but I believe that was an act to hurt you, to test you further and see what you would do, to find your weaknesses." He won't quite meet my eyes.

I squint at him, trying to read if there is truth in his words. His aura is light green, the color of a healer, but also, weaving through the green is a lemon yellow. If I remember correctly, the book on auras related lemon yellow to a fear of loss.

What is the doctor afraid to lose?

"Are you saying I shouldn't trust that Nat is my friend?" I narrow my eyes at him, not really sure what to believe at the moment.

That was not an act. I truly think she went with Demar because he had Mattenhue. I know she didn't fight him, but maybe she couldn't. She couldn't really have been pretending to be my friend all this time, could she? The thoughts swirl quickly through my head.

"I'm saying that you shouldn't trust anyone that's been in Hell for any extended period." He looks pointedly at my two companions and then back at me.

"Like you?" I ask hesitantly.

"Trust no one, not even me. Betrayal attaches to your soul down here and becomes a part of who you are. Everyone has their own reasons for helping you and as soon as those reasons change, as soon as it no longer benefits them, they will turn on you." At his words, the hairs on the back of my neck stand up and a chill runs down my arms.

"Maybe I can't trust others to do right by me, but I can trust in myself that I will deal with whatever comes my way and persevere." I lift my head just slightly, knowing that these words are true. And then I continue.

"I am strong and becoming stronger by the moment. I know I'm trustworthy and my intentions to protect the people that cannot protect themselves are honorable. That's my purpose in life, one I'm happy to fulfill."

"Spoken like a true queen. I believe you are just what the realms need, but do not forget what I told you and don't let your guard down, especially while you're still in Hell." I can see the admiration in his eyes and I hope with all my heart that he's wrong about the people I care about, including himself.

I honestly do not trust Cassie. She cares about herself and only herself. I suppose, if Mikal felt she was worth bringing to Hell to save me, then I must have faith she will at least help until we get back to Earth. Plus, from what I can tell, she's a witch, so she has to have some valuable tricks up her sleeve, right?

As for Jude, I am not sure what his motives are other than what he told me in the arena. So far he has given me valuable information, carried me when I would have perished at the hands, or should I say teeth, of the vampires and treated me with respect. I will be cautious, but my intuition tells me he is on my side. At least I hope it is intuition and not hormones.

Greg's hand grasps mine again as he helps me to my feet. For someone who appears to be old, he lifts me with ease.

"As you both know, the forest is full of unimaginable creatures, but the hell hounds are the worst of the lot. They are smart and will track you. I have packed a spray that will take away your scent, but use it sparingly. It only works for a short period. I'm sure you will need it more than once. They cannot climb trees, so if they are after you, get yourself into a tree," he advises, peering into each of our eyes.

His chest puffs out as he takes a deep breath, taking a few seconds before he exhales and continues, "Also, the terrain changes during the night. You could go to sleep in the mountains and wake up in a meadow. It can be disorienting. It's best that you take shifts, so one of you is always awake at night."

"Is there anything else you can tell us? I've never actually ventured into the forest," Jude says with hesitance. This is the first time I've seen him rattled and I don't think I like it.

"I have," Cassie says under her breath, but when she says nothing else, Greg continues.

"Stay away from spider vines. If you get caught in them, they will drain your body of blood and you will perish, but not before their acid causes you excruciating pain." I grimace and he looks at me.

"Is that it?" I ask, hoping he has no more to tell us. I don't think any of us actually want to hear any more bad news.

"Nothing in this forest is safe, especially for your kind," he says looking at me. "The vampires will look for you. I'll do what I can to get them off your trail, but it will not deter them for long."

"Thank you!" I say as I wrap my arms around him. Even though he told me I couldn't trust him, I do. Maybe it is naïve of me, but he has done nothing but help me since I have known him. As far as I can tell, at least.

The doctor gives us all one last look before turning and walking back towards the castle. We watch until he's out of sight and then I turn to the others.

Cassie has a solemn expression. Her eyes focused on the forest. I've gathered that she has had terrible experiences in Hell, but I'm not close enough to her to ask. I doubt she would open up to me even if I did ask, no matter how sincere I am.

As much as I dislike the way she acts, there has to be something good inside of her and I have a hard time holding someone's past against them. Look at me and what I went through. I'm in no position to judge.

"Let the shit show begin," I say, trying to lighten the mood a little, but before anyone else can reply, I hear clucking coming from the direction of the waterfall.

I take off jogging, ignoring the harsh whispers from my companions. It's nice to move again without the excruciating pain.

Jude, who is on my heels, grabs my arm and pulls me to a stop when I am about ten feet away from my destination.

"Alayah, what are you doing?" he whispers, the sound harsh in the silence that surrounds us.

"I heard something that I need to check out," I say, pulling my arm out of his grasp. It isn't hard since his touch is gentle.

"You can't just go running off, you're going to get yourself killed," he says, eyes narrowed.

I give him a quizzical look and then crouch down, edging myself towards the rock formation once more. I hold my finger up to my lips to tell him to be quiet and he gives me a look back that says, *No Shit!*

As I make my way around the rock, the grass tickling the skin on my arms, I burst into laughter. Jude wraps a hand around my mouth, presumably to shut me up and stop me from moving, but he won't deter me that easily.

I pry his fingers one at a time from my face and meet his eyes, mouthing "sorry." I inch forward a bit more, letting Jude move with me.

The rock beside me brushes my sleeve, its uneven edge catching the fabric. I have to pull harder than I intended to detach, causing me to fall into Jude's lap.

My lips pucker, trying to hold back another laugh, and Jude shakes his head. He encircles me with his muscular arms. The firm hold and our proximity do funny things to my stomach. His eyes twinkle with mischief, like stars in the night sky, and he pulls me closer, focusing on my lips. His gaze is intense, drawing me in, and I'm interested to see if he will kiss me.

Will it be as good as the kiss I shared with Mikal?

That thought is a wake up call and my mood changes. What am I doing? I break eye contact, pushing myself out of his grasp. The corners of his mouth turn down and the disappointment written all over his face hurts my heart. It's gone in a flash, though.

I turn back around, remembering the mission I was on. Slowly, I peek around the corner one more time to see the scene I had been expecting and I bust out laughing again.

Cassie sneaks up behind us, slapping me in the back of the head to shut me up. She peeks around the corner and says, "Are you absolutely fucking dumb? What could you possibly be laughing at right now?"

I look at her with my most serious expression and say, "There really are chickens in Hell!"